DIAMOND MASQUERADE

M. E. COOPER

Copyright © 2026 by M. E. Cooper

This is a work of fiction. Names, characters, business, events and incidents are the products of the author's imagination. Any resemblance to actual persons, living or dead, or actual events is purely coincidental.

All rights reserved.

No part of this book may be reproduced in any form or by any electronic or mechanical means, including information storage and retrieval systems, without written permission from the author, except for the use of brief quotations in a book review.

*To all of us who lived through the 1980s
and survived
Oh, the tales we could tell*

Chapter One

Throwing the papers across the room, Remy growled in exasperation. "Why am I wasting my time on this again? It's a fool's errand. It's not like I'm going to find anything new. I've been through this a hundred times before."

Sitting back, gazing out the window and thinking over how she wound up in this depressing situation, Remy shook her head. She never thought she'd find herself serving drinks to rowdy drunks in a bar close to the university. Despite the regulars, who she considered her friends, it was certainly not a place the tourists would frequent. But it definitely was the kind of place the underbelly of New Orleans was more than familiar with.

Trying to earn enough to stay ahead of the payments for her mom's medical treatment, she relied heavily on the tips in addition to her regular pay. While it was better than some places, it still wasn't enough to allow her to save for anything more.

Gathering the papers she had thrown on the floor, she started shoving them haphazardly back in the box when an envelope fluttered to the ground. Picking it up, she saw it was a letter addressed to her deceased dad from someone named Neil Evans. The postmark was from Los Angeles in the late 1960s. How had it remained unopened and undiscovered after all these years?

She tried thinking back on the stories her mother had told her of her father's time living and working in Las Vegas, and the memory of a cousin named Neil resurfaced. He inadvertently wound up there when he was trying to run away to Los Angeles. Her dad had somehow helped him out of the jam he found himself in and got him a record deal, which helped to launch his musical career.

As another old memory surfaced, she remembered a time when she was younger and her dad was still around. He had snuck her into a local bar in the French Quarter where Neil was playing, taking her backstage in between sets to meet him and the rest of the band. She had been in such awe meeting who she thought was a real rock star. Of course, she wasn't old enough to know any better, and in hindsight; he wasn't actually a rock star, at least not yet. Oh, he would become one later on, but there had been little more contact between her and him since that one night.

Turning the envelope over in her hands, she wondered, what is this letter and how did it get in with these other papers? How is it I've never seen it before now since I've been through these papers hundreds of times, it seems?

Not giving herself a second chance to change her mind, she opened the envelope, revealing a handwritten note and yet another sealed envelope inside. The note was in handwriting she could only surmise was Neil's. But the other envelope was definitely in her dad's handwriting. Do not open, written on the outside. So why write something and then tell the recipient not to open it? This was becoming more of a mystery than she knew she had time to deal with. Glancing over the note from Neil, she saw he was returning this letter back to Frank, since it was no longer necessary. 'No longer necessary? For what? Pretty vague if you ask me,' she mused.

Deciding there couldn't be any harm in opening the letter after all these years, she read the contents of the second letter twice, only to discover the truth behind what she thought had been a family myth all those years. Finding out her dad really had been involved in the theft of Marilyn Monroe's necklace all those years ago practically took her breath away. If she remembered the story right, the necklace had been reported stolen by the jeweler in New York after it had been worn by Marilyn for some event at a casino back in Las Vegas. But how that connected to her dad, she had no idea. Was that the one where he had worked those years when he was gone from New Orleans? Her mom had told her it was just a story. Coincidental timing, she had said. The necklace went missing, and the rumor was that it had been the courier who had made off with it. Of course, back then, the mob had been running the casinos, so if they were involved in the theft, it shouldn't be a surprise to anyone. Surely the diamonds that had been in the necklace were long gone by now too.

But now, reading over this letter, seeing her dad's handwriting and explanation that yes, he had been involved, and the diamonds had been left in hiding for his family, including her and Neil, only led her to more questions with no idea where to start looking for answers.

Chapter Two

After putting away the box containing the rest of the old papers, she tucked this newfound letter along with a few of the old ones she was keeping into another envelope. She stuck those in her purse before she went back downstairs to check on her mom. Finding her dozing on the couch, she covered her with a light blanket and left a note to let her know she was going out for a while, but would come back later to check on her before she had to go to work.

Walking the streets of the neighborhood, she tried to sort through all the thoughts running through her head. The letter stated the diamonds were safely hidden away, but gave no indication of where. If only she could somehow get her hands on them, that would solve so many of her problems. She could pay for Vanessa's medical treatments, quit her job, and stop having to run the cons she had been perpetuating on the men she picked up at the hotel bars. Those had been lucrative in that she had been able to either talk them into lavishing her with gifts that she turned around and pawned, or at a minimum, she would take money from their wallets. But she knew her luck would run out on her at some point. The last thing she wanted to do was wind up in jail. Then who would take care of her mother?

Maybe it was time to change where she found these men. The bartenders at the Hotel Monteleone had gotten to know her, and while they weren't aware of what she was up to, she knew she had to be careful not to get overzealous.

There were certainly enough opportunities in the city at any given time. Conventions, balls associated with all the Mardi Gras events that attracted the society of the city, the Jazz Heritage festival that drew in people from all over the country, even the world. These were a few of the places she should start exploring.

As she walked into a local boutique with nothing in mind aside from browsing to take her mind off everything else, she overhead the sales associates talking about an upcoming black-tie event. Clients had been in all week in search of just the right thing to wear. Knowing that would be prime hunting grounds, she turned her attention to any more details she could gather.

She knew that if she were going to get into the party, she would need a new dress. Something more elegant than anything she currently had hanging in her closet. Since none of that would even come close enough to resemble what she'd have to wear to an event like this. Hearing that it was to be held the next night, she was going to have to find something fast.

Considering her finances being what they were, she couldn't very well go all out buying a dress either. Even if she left the tags attached and returned it the next day. The funds weren't available to make that purchase possible. And if she had any sort of mishap that would damage the dress, then she wouldn't be able to return it, and being out that money wasn't an option she wanted to face. Dismayed, she frowned at the thought of how she was going to get in?

Browsing the racks, she tried to make it appear as though she was looking for something specific, while not finding anything to try on yet. Hopefully, she would be able to find something on the clearance rack. Or maybe she would find someone's purse lying around and she'd lift the wallet to pay for what she needed. She didn't enjoy having to resort back to pick-pocketing and this sort of theft, even though she had done it in the past and had been good at it. Now she much preferred it when the person she was conning was a willing participant in the relationship and they were separated from their money. She had no remorse in those situations. After all, they allowed it to happen to themselves, quickly getting so emotionally involved with her. But when she had to resort to taking without that interaction, it caused her moments of self-doubt, guilt, and fear this might be the time she actually gets caught.

She avoided most of the sales staff, even in this small of a shop. The fewer people involved, the better and the easier it would be to get what she needed. When she found a couple of options to try on, she made her way back to the dressing room. Finding that both dresses were too big to fit in her purse or wear out under her street clothes, she would have to think on her feet and smooth-talk her way through this one.

As she stepped out of the dressing room, she saw a well dressed gentleman walk into the store. In addition to the expensive looking watch on his wrist, and the air he was giving off of someone sure of himself, she thought he could be a potential mark. Standing in front of the trifold mirror gave her the advantage, allowing her to keep an eye on him before he saw her. Turning her head to the side, she watched as he made his way through the store. The salesgirl asked if he was looking for anything in particular.

"No, just browsing for a gift for my little lady," he drawled as his eyes scanned the entire store before she saw them stopping on her back.

'Oh, one of those guys,' she thought to herself. 'Too much money on his hands, and some little thing on the side that he's trying to keep mollified. Perfect.'

Grinning to herself, she saw him watching her as she sashayed back into the dressing room. Taking off the first dress, she came back out in the second one she had picked up. Knowing she would have to execute this perfectly in order for him not to detect that he was being conned, she ran through her plan to get him to pay for items that would not wind up in his bag.

Stepping back in front of the mirror, she said just loud enough for him to hear, "I can't decide which dress I should get. I have a black-tie event to attend, and well, I've never gone to one before. I mean, what do people usually wear to something like that?"

Sensing she had caught his attention, she continued to

Diamond Masquerade

consider herself in the mirror, as though she was trying to decide. When he sauntered over and offered his opinion, saying, "the black one," she knew her plan was working.

"I'm sorry?" She said as she turned to face him.

"The black one you had on before this one. I heard you say it's a black-tie party. You can never go wrong with a little black dress. Add to it a necklace like this one," he indicated to one of the four that he had picked up on his walk towards her. "And no one will be able to take their eyes off of you."

"I couldn't possibly afford the dress and one of those as well. But I do thank you for your kind advice," she demurred.

"Please, humor me. Would you try on the dress again?"

"Um, well, I suppose..." she replied as she started walking back to the dressing room, wondering if he could tell she didn't have the funds for either of the purchases he was suggesting. Maybe he was just being nice and trying to flatter her, hoping to get her number. Little did he realize, she was also trying to use him.

Changing back into the black dress for the second time, she was fiddling with the zipper as she came out, walking over to where he had taken a seat. Turning her back to him and moving her hair aside, she said, "Do you mind helping here? I can't quite seem to get it the rest of the way. And I'm sorry, I don't think I got your name?"

"Jordan, Jordan Dubois. Nice to meet you?"

"Oh, thank you, Jordan. I'm Daphne," she replied.

"Well, Daphne, I was right. That dress looks stunning on you. And I guarantee you will turn every head at the party if you walk in wearing that. If you add this to your ensemble, you'll have them falling at your feet." He said as he stood and placed a necklace around her neck, the likes of which she had never worn before.

A large ruby, surrounded by diamonds, suspended from a chain of white gold, the exact perfect length, as though it had been custom made for her. Looking in the mirror, she couldn't take her eyes off the piece. Never before had she even dared to try something on as expensive as this piece.

"Jordan, while I appreciate your suggestion, there really is no way I can afford this. I barely have enough to pay for the dress. I probably should be looking at the clearance rack, or not even bother with a dress and skip the party altogether."

"Nonsense! Every woman should have at least one dress in her wardrobe that makes her feel spectacular. Tell you what, let me buy them for you, no strings attached."

"No, I couldn't. You don't even know me. I can't accept such an offer."

"Yes, you can and you will." Turning to the salesgirl, "Please charge both the dress and the necklace to my card. I won't take no for an answer."

"But -"

"No, it's a done deal. Trust me, Daphne, you have brought a smile to my face today, and I'm just pleased to do something like this for someone. I expect nothing in return. Go to the party tomorrow night and have a wonderful time."

Before she could say anything more, she saw Jordan at the register, signing the credit card slip and making his way back out the door.

The salesgirl stood watching in disbelief. "I've never seen anything quite like that before. It was as though I was watching a scene from My Fair Lady or something."

"Yes, me neither." Remy said, a slight smile curving at the corners of her lips.

AFTER MAKING his way out of the store, Jordan quickly turned into the cafe next door where he could watch as Daphne, as she called herself, came out with her gifted purchase. He had almost slipped and called her by her actual name, Remy, and not the false one she had given him. Why she had used a different name, he wasn't sure. She had no way of knowing who he was, or that he had any connection to her, even as tentative as it was. No, that information would definitely be his secret to hold on to for now.

Picking up a discarded newspaper from the table, he sat down and hid his face behind it, watching as she made her way down the street before turning out of his line of sight. Now that she was gone, it was time for him to put his next step of the plan into play. Making his way to a pay phone in the back of the cafe, he dropped in a dime and placed a call. As soon as the person he was calling answered, he began the conversation without preamble.

"Hey, Theo. I want you and Lily to get into George's party tomorrow night. And yes, it's last minute, but I'm sure you can swing it," he said as he hung up the phone, cutting off any debate before it started. Walking back to the table, he threw the paper back down and left, making his was back out into the city he now called home.

The next stop he had planned on his outing today was a house in the Garden District. He had a vague idea of where it was, but since he didn't have an actual address, he was going to have to be careful in his search. While the neighborhood wasn't huge by his standards, having lived in New York and Las Vegas for years prior to coming here, he had already ruled out some of the smaller houses on the edges of the neighborhood. Knowing the house he was looking for had been a large family estate at one time, he knew it would encompass more land than most. Not wanting to draw any unnecessary attention to himself, he didn't ask around, knowing it would be best if he found it on his own.

He was, after all, a patient man. It had been years now that he had been planning this quest to find what he felt he was owed. And while a good part of his time had been spent in prison, he took advantage of everything that was offered to him and used it to his advantage. It had given him time to access resources, do research, and make the connections he now had in place. Mr. Costa was counting on him to find what had been taken from them, and he wouldn't rest until he completed his task.

Turning a corner, he came to an abrupt stop when he saw someone he thought he recognized. Watching as the gentleman walked up the driveway, towards an old carriage house in the back, Jordan continued on down the street a little further so he could see where the man went. Remaining back far enough not to be noticed, he saw the man enter the carriage house, closing the door behind him without a second glance.

'Well, I think I've found the house. And if I'm right, I've also found the person I'm looking for too. This might just be easier than I first expected,' he thought to himself as he turned, retracing the steps that brought him here. Once he felt as though he was far enough away, he stopped to give himself time to get his heart rate back under control and to hail a cab back to his club. He had a call to make and next steps to figure out.

Chapter Three

Struggling to steady her shaking hands, she barely got her key in the lock of her apartment door. On the third try, Remy managed to get the door open, and she stumbled inside. Had that really happened? Finding out about a party tomorrow night, then some random stranger buying her not only the perfect dress but a stunning necklace to complete the outfit? 'Heck, with just the necklace alone,' she thought, 'I could take to any of the local jewelers and sell it. I'm sure I could get more than enough for it.'

But no, not yet. Perhaps it was best to wear it to the party, and see who she could charm into plying her with more. Sometimes you have to look like you have money in order to get more handed to you, and this necklace certainly would help complete that look. Walking back into her bedroom, she hung up the dress and tucked the necklace into a dresser drawer.

The next night she had no trouble walking into the party, and as she did, just about every head turned, men and women alike. Only supporting the fact Jordan had been right. It wasn't long before the men who were without dates were lining up, attempting to ply her with drinks, appetizers, and, more importantly, propositions. Even a couple of women made suggestions of what they would like to do or had to offer, if she was so inclined. Never before had she commanded this much attention. It was like shooting fish in a barrel; she thought to herself. Now she just had to be sure to take her time, study her options, and then choose the right mark.

She tried to pace herself, declining more drinks than she accepted. Early on, she asked the bartender if he would kindly make her drinks weak if someone should order one for her. She couldn't allow herself to lose control; otherwise, the entire night would be blown. After the sixth watered down martini, she switched to club soda, tipping the staff as much as she could afford as her way of thanking them for their help in her subterfuge.

Her choice of who the next con would be run on was narrowed to three by then. Two gentlemen and one rather overzealous woman. She wasn't sure if it was the number of drinks the lady had consumed that was making her so brash, or if she was always this forthcoming. But after another fifteen minutes of conversation, Remy realized this lady would not be an easy one to fool. Excusing herself, she made her way across the room to her next subject.

He was a financial trader, slightly older than her by a few years, she guessed. A sharp dresser, who obviously had money to burn based on the Rolex on his wrist and the diamond tie tack, positioned ever so precisely in the exact middle of his tie. He was telling her about his boat, which he kept for cruising around on Lake Pontchartrain; and his winter ski cabin in the Grand Tetons. Had she ever been skiing in Wyoming?

"No, I'm afraid not. I've spent my entire life here in New Orleans. As much as I would like to travel, I really haven't had the opportunity to do so."

"Well, you must let me take you to Jackson Hole once it's ski season. You will absolutely love the place, the people, and of course, the company you will be keeping won't be bad either."

"Um, that's a bit presumptuous, don't you think? We've only just met and haven't even had one date yet. Don't you think we should get acquainted a bit more before you start planning vacations for the two of us?"

"What more do I need to learn? You're a beautiful woman, who has never been out of town before, and I have the means and opportunity. I see it as a win for both of us."

Remy took a moment to consider this. On one hand, she could take him up on the offer, string him along for a while and see where it leads. Or would it be best to cut ties right now and see where things could go with her other mark? She looked across the room to where he was and found him pawing at another young girl, who had obviously had too much to drink and would soon regret coming to the party tonight.

Her decision was obvious. "Alright. Say I do agree to join you on this trip. That's still a few months away at the earliest. What exactly do you suggest in the meantime?"

"For starters, how about a name? I'm Matt Hanson."

"Daphne. Nice to meet you, Matt," Remy replied.

"The pleasure is all mine, I'm sure. Now, how about we

get out of here and go somewhere we can get a bite and talk at a more conversational level instead of having to shout over all this noise?"

As they began walking toward the coat check, she spotted Jordan coming in the door. What on earth was he doing here? When she chided herself for being so foolish? Of course, he would be here. This was, after all, the crowd that he would associate with.

When she saw him approaching, she exclaimed, "Jordan, what a surprise to see you here!"

"Daphne, my goodness, you look even better than when I saw you yesterday. Was I right? Did the dress have the desired effect?"

Just then, Matt walked over, placing a hand protectively on the small of Remy's back. "Going to introduce me to your friend?"

"Oh, sure. Matt Hanson, this is Jordan. Jordan, this is Matt. I'm sorry, Jordan, you told me your last name, but I'm terrible when it comes to remembering those sorts of things."

Smiling at them both, Jordan replied, "It was rather a whirlwind meeting. The last name is Dubois. Nice to meet you, Matt. It looks as though you two were on your way out. Please don't let me hold you up."

"Of course, I should have recognized you. You're Jordan Dubois of Acme Consolidated. We've had some dealings in the past, but I think this is the first time we've ever met in person. I should have expected to see you here tonight. But I thought I heard you were out of the country. And what a surprise, you know, Daphne. But then again, I've only just met her, and she's been full of surprises."

"Yes, I imagine she is. We've actually only recently become acquainted as well. But I'm delaying you two further. Please, go. Enjoy the rest of your evening." Jordan said, raising an eyebrow at Remy.

Matt looked at Remy, then back at Jordan. "This might be presumptuous, but why don't you join us? We were going out for a late bite. I'm sure Daphne won't mind the company, would you, darling?"

"No, not at all," Remy said, looking at Matt with a quizzical expression, unsure at the turn of events and his use of the endearment darling.

"I have a better idea. Why don't you two join me at my table here? There's another couple who are supposed to be joining me, and I think they are someone you'd like to meet as well," Jordan replied.

Matt turned to Remy, nodding. "Is that okay with you? I'm sorry. I know we were going to try to go somewhere a little quieter."

"Of course. It's fine. Isn't that what these parties are all about, anyway? Making connections?" Remy laughed. After all, that was what she was here trying to do.

"Fantastic. Please this way," Jordan said, sweeping his hand toward one of the tables set next to the dance floor.

As they sat down, another couple walked up and joined them.

"Theo, Lily, I'd like you to meet Matt Hanson and his date, Daphne, and now I'm the one who isn't displaying proper manners. I don't believe I ever learned your last name," Jordan said as he made introductions around the table.

"Martine," Remy quickly replied. "Nice to meet you both."

"Likewise," Theo said, as he held out the chair for Lily.

"Daphne, what a lovely name," Lily drawled. "Is it a family name?"

"No, I think it was just something my momma had read in a book and it stuck with her." Remy laughed, smiling broadly at both Lily and Theo. "I'm guessing you aren't from around here, though."

Lily looked puzzled at first before replying, "How did you figure that out so quickly?"

"Ah, easy. No accent. At least not one from around these parts. Trust me, when you've lived in this area long enough, you get familiar with all the dialects from the area. And yours is definitely not from around here. So let me guess…" Remy paused, taking a sip of her drink. "Somewhere up north, I'm going to go with Chicago, perhaps."

"You're right. But if you tell me what part of Chicago, then I'm going to start to think you're a clairvoyant or something."

"No, I'm not that good. I had a friend who was from Chicago, and I recognized the way you said some of the same words he used to say."

Lily nodded, looking at Theo, then Jordan, trying to determine what they wanted her to do next.

"Well, I need to go powder my nose. Daphne, would you mind showing me where the ladies' room is? I seem to have gotten all turned around in here."

Rising from her seat, Remy extended her arm toward the doors. Glancing over her shoulder, she said, "Follow me. We'll be right back boys, so try to stay out of trouble until we return."

Matt rose slightly from his chair as Jordan laughed, and Theo sat stone faced. Remy was still attempting to get a read on him, but couldn't seem to get him to break at all. As they made their way out, she turned to Lily and asked directly.

"If you don't mind my asking, what's up with Theo? He seems a bit uptight."

"Oh, he's just quiet. Not one much for parties or meeting new people. But believe me, once he and Jordan get going, he'll loosen up in no time. But tell me about Matt. He seems like quite a catch. Have you two been dating long?"

"Honestly, I can't tell you much. We only met earlier this evening. I can tell you he has a place in Wyoming and a boat for days out on the lake. Aside from that, he's some sort of financial guy. But tell me, how do you know Jordan?"

Without trying to be obvious, Remy was trying to fish for information. She found it odd that Jordan had shown up at the party as she was making her way out, and how convenient Lily and Theo had been right there too. Something didn't sit right with her, and the thought crossed her mind that perhaps she was the one being conned.

"Oh, well, he's the reason we're in New Orleans. See, he and Theo have known each other for some time. When Jordan suggested we come for a visit, and with us having nothing better to do, we said sure. So here we are."

"Oh, so you're just visiting then? How much longer do you think you'll be in town?"

"Not sure. We really don't have any set plans. We've rented a small place temporarily instead of wasting money on a hotel. I'm really liking it here. And to be honest, wouldn't mind staying permanently. Chicago is nice and all, but this city has so much to offer."

As Lily continued talking, Remy washed her hands. When she looked up in the mirror to check her reflection, she realized the necklace she had been wearing was gone. Looking frantically around, Remy saw Lily hold up the necklace and say, "Looking for this?"

"How? What?" Remy sputtered.

"Simple. I distracted you long enough to slip my hand around, undo the clasp, and pocketed it without you noticing."

"But why?" Remy, now flustered that she had been taken in, by a stranger no less, was starting to get angry.

"Only to see how easy of a mark you were. I would have thought someone with your skills wouldn't have been duped so quickly."

Stepping back from the sink, Remy turned to Lily, coming within inches of her face. Grabbing the necklace out of her hand, she growled. "I should go out and turn you over to security right now."

"You could. But then you'd have to explain how you got the necklace, and, well, not to mention, the invite to this little party. And I suspect that none of the answers you'd have for those questions would be exactly above board, shall we say?"

"What do you want?" Remy demanded.

"Nothing at the moment. Jordan wanted me to check you out. See if you were as good as he thought. Though

I'm not sure yet," Lily replied with a shrug of her shoulders.

Taking a deep breath and time to consider what had just happened, Remy waited a beat before asking her next question.

"Okay. Maybe you should start at the beginning. What do you mean by Jordan wanted you to check me out and see if I was as good as what now?"

Looking around, Lily shook her head. "Not here. Not tonight. I'm sure the guys are wondering where we are. Let's get back out to the party and have a good time. I'm guessing you had something in store for Matt. So, you do what you have to do tonight. You want answers, meet me for coffee tomorrow. Cafe du Monde, eleven o'clock."

Chapter Four

It didn't matter what time of the day you went; Cafe du Monde was always busy. Remy arrived a few minutes before eleven, looking around at all the tables, trying to see who else might be there. She had a hunch based on her interaction with Lily last night that Jordan would have other spies around as well. Something about him didn't sit right from the first time she met him, and based on their interaction the night before, her suspicions continued to grow.

Finding an empty table far enough away from the foot traffic of the street in front of the cafe, she sat with her back to the kitchen, monitoring everything going on around her. After ordering a café au lait and beignets, she spotted Lily looking for her. Deciding not to make it easy, she sat until Lily noticed her. Only then did she give a little wave as if she had only just now recognized her.

"I took the liberty of ordering already. Figured it would save a little bit of time and interruption." Remy said in greeting.

"Wonderful. I'm starving. I barely had a chance to eat at the party last night, and we have nothing in the kitchen at home. I really need to make a run to the store, but with so many good places to eat around here, it makes that a challenge," Lily said as she settled into her seat.

"So, what exactly is going on?" Remy demanded, not giving Lily any time for niceties or small talk.

"Okay. So that's how you want to play this?" Lily asked. "Are you sure you're ready for the truth of the matter?"

Noting Lily's tone, Remy took a moment before answering.

"I have no idea who you are. I have no idea who Jordan is other than some guy who decided he needed to buy me a dress and necklace. I was perfectly capable of taking care of my purchase when he stepped in."

Interrupting, Lily questioned, "Are you sure about that? From what he told me, it was pretty obvious what you were attempting to do in that boutique. You were either going to somehow slip your purchase into his and have him pay without noticing, or you were going to buy the dress yourself, leave the tags on and return it today, hoping no one would be the wiser. Tell me I'm wrong, and I'll leave you alone right now."

Remy leaned back in her seat, scowling at Lily. "Alright. Say you are right. I was going to do one of those things. What gives him or you the right to accost me like that and check me out, as you so eloquently put it last night?"

Taking a large bite of beignet, chewing slowly, then following it with a large sip of the coffee, Lily sat and watched Remy, not saying anything. After she felt sufficient time had passed, she answered.

"You're right. I'm sorry. Let's start over, shall we? I feel like maybe we've gotten off on the wrong foot here. And I was under the impression you knew more about Jordan than you apparently do."

"You think?" Remy replied acerbically.

Holding up her hands in surrender, Lily sighed.

"Okay, I obviously assumed too much. So let me give you the rundown. Theo and I have known Jordan for a few years now. We met him on a trip we took to Las Vegas. Theo was losing terribly at blackjack, while Jordan seemed to be beating the house what seemed like every other game. Taking pity on Theo, Jordan suggested we take a break from the table and offered to buy us dinner. Dinner turned into drinks, a show, more drinks, but thankfully no more gaming that night. We wound up spending a couple more days there, hanging out with Jordan and a rotation of showgirls he had hanging off his arm. We left, agreeing to stay in touch, and returned to Chicago. During a call with him a few months later, Theo mentioned we were coming to New Orleans. When Jordan said he had a place here too. Long story shorter, he invited us to stay with him for a couple of weeks, we fell in love with the city and have been here pretty much ever since."

"Blah, blah, blah. You haven't given me any good reason to sit here and keep listening to you or any explanation as to why Jordan wanted you to 'check me out'. Either tell me something or I'm out of here," Remy demanded.

Lily shrugged. "I don't know a lot. Just that after you two met at that boutique, he called me up and told me you'd be at the party that night. He thought maybe you'd be interested in working with us. You had an intriguing set of skills is how he put it. He told me the salesgirl had no idea what you were up to and that most guys would have never noticed. He only noticed, because, well it's what he does."

"So what exactly is it that I would be doing? Working for him or with you, or whatever? I have standards after all. And before you suggest I prostitute myself - "

"Oh, god no. Nothing like that. No, Jordan has a few different businesses he's involved in. One is some manufacturing business or something. He also owns a few clubs, here and in Las Vegas. The one in Las Vegas is open to the public; the others are private clubs that cater to a more discreet class of clientele. Gambling mostly, sometimes private parties. The one here is called the Carrington. But no, definitely nothing along the lines of what you mentioned," Lily exclaimed. "I'd never do that. And I've never been asked to do that. If I were I'd be out in a heartbeat."

"So, eye candy then? Or are we actually working the gaming tables, serving drinks? I'm not familiar with much when it comes to gambling. My dad spent some time in Las Vegas when I was a kid, but I didn't really know him then and was never around any of that."

"Well, pretty much what you described. You'll go through some training on your first night. I or someone else will show you what to do in all the different areas. It's a decent salary; one of the benefits is you get to keep the clothes and tips, and sometimes those tips can include some pretty nice pieces of jewelry too. Anything more you choose to do is up to you."

"Why me?"

"Why not you? Like I said, Jordan called me, said he thought you might have some skills, and maybe you were looking for work, or at least needed money. If you're not interested, tell me now and I'll pass along the message to him. We'll go our separate ways, and you'll never hear from either of us again."

Remy sat back in her seat, brushing powdered sugar off of her blouse, contemplating everything Lily had described to her. If it were true, she wouldn't have to do anything she didn't want to, and god knows she was not going to sell herself like that, then maybe this was the answer to her current predicament.

"Give me a day to think about it."

"Sure. Let's meet up at the Desire late tomorrow afternoon for drinks and oysters, and you can give me your answer then."

LEAVING REMY AT THE CAFE, Lily decided it best to take a longer route back to the Carrington. After making sure that she wasn't being followed, she arrived half an hour later than expected.

As she walked in, she found Jordan sitting at the bar, his fingers tapping out an impatient rhythm.

"Well?" he said.

"She wants a day to think about it. I think she's nervous she might be asked to do something she's not willing to do. I reassured her as best I could, but if I'm being honest, I'm not sure she's going to go for it."

"What about her father? Did you get any information about him?"

"No, she alluded to him at one point. Said he had spent some time in Las Vegas, but she didn't really know him during that time. I get the impression he's not in her life."

"Alright, listen. You need to convince her that this is in her best interest. Give her whatever guarantee you have to. And if she still says no, then at least try to get whatever you can out of her about her dad. Maybe strike up a friendship with her at a minimum."

"Sure Jordan. But what's so important about her dad? Who is he?"

"No one you need to concern yourself with."

Not understanding his cryptic explanation, Lily simply nodded in agreement, knowing better than to ask any more questions regarding that subject, and then asked where Theo was. "Back room," the bartender said.

Making her way back, still confused by Jordan's behavior and questions, Lily found Theo at his desk going over the books. At least one of them could stay behind the scenes. While she didn't have the head for numbers like Theo did, Lily had an eye for the details. She knew more than she said and had been compiling information on everyone she came in contact with since becoming acquainted with Jordan and his crew. 'Protect my own,' she reminded herself on more than one occasion.

Smiling at Theo, she plopped down in the chair across from him and waited until he finished balancing the page he was on. When he looked up at her, she filled him in on what had taken place, asking what his impression of Daphne was based on their interaction last night.

"I don't think that's actually her name," he said. "It felt like it took her a little too long when Jordan asked what her last name was. I mean, if it is your name, that's something you don't hesitate answering when asked. Aside from that, I've really got no other opinion. She seemed nice enough, I guess. When are you meeting her again?"

"Tomorrow afternoon. Desire Oyster Bar."

"Good. If it all goes well, I'm sure Jordan will want you to bring her back here. If not, then you and I have a night to ourselves. If I can get through the rest of the mess that is what could be called the finance books of this place."

Lily smiled, understanding that was her cue to leave. Walking around the desk, she gave him a quick kiss and left him to his work.

Throughout her shift that night she still had more questions rolling around in her head. Coming out of the restroom and walking past Jordan's office, she overheard him talking to someone in his office about missing diamonds. Was it possible Daphne had something to do with this and that's why he was being so secretive? How had she pulled that off? From their brief time together, Lily didn't think Remy was that much of a con woman either, if Jordan was able to see through her game at the boutique. No, there was definitely something more going on or some sort of connection, but what exactly it was Lily couldn't quite piece together just yet. Hopefully, she could find out more when she met with Daphne the following afternoon.

Chapter Five

Just as she had done the day before, Remy arrived at Desire fifteen minutes early. She had her suspicions Lily, or rather Jordan more likely, would once again have spies set up to eavesdrop on their conversation. Even if she couldn't figure out who they were. She wasn't sure yet what his endgame was, and wanted to find out as much as possible without giving away too much of her own information. Information is power after all.

Sitting at the last table by the open windows, she figured the crowd noise of Bourbon Street would give her some cover, making it a little harder for anyone to overhear the conversation. It would also give her a good vantage point to see if anyone was lurking outside. Keeping her back to the wall, she sat patiently, waiting for Lily to arrive.

Right at four o'clock, Lily strutted in as if she owned the place. 'The girl certainly is confident in herself,' Remy thought. Waving at her, she watched as Lily made her way across the restaurant, heads turning as she passed the other tables.

"Daphne, you made it. I wasn't sure if you'd show," Lily drawled sweetly.

"I wasn't sure if I'd make it at first either. But then I figured, why not. Let's see at least what you have to say," Remy replied just as sweet.

"Of course. Should we order something first? A couple dozen oysters and Bloody Marys, perhaps?"

Before Remy replied, Lily gave the order to the waitress who appeared at the table, adding on an order of the Cajun fried alligator as well. "Funny, I would have never considered eating alligator before we came here, but now, I can't seem to get enough of it," Lily said, laughing as she caught the look on Remy's face.

"Most people turn their noses up at it. But it is quite good. I don't eat it often myself. Then again, I'm not one to go out to eat very often either. So…" Remy trailed off, hoping Lily would lead the conversation.

After taking a large sip of her Bloody Mary, Lily leaned back in her seat and inquired. "So, tell me more about yourself. Have you always lived in New Orleans, or did you spend some time in Las Vegas too? I seem to recall you mentioned your dad was there for a time?"

Remy raised an eyebrow, considering her answer before speaking. "No, I've lived all my life here. My momma is here, well on the other side of the river. My father's family has been here all my life as well. They've always had a home in the Garden District. But I don't know much about them or the family history. My dad and I aren't especially close."

"I'm sorry to hear that. I was close to my daddy until he passed away a couple of years ago. I guess you could say I was a bit of a daddy's girl. We had a special relationship. I could talk to him about anything and everything. I guess I always assume everyone has had that same sort of bond."

Shaking her head, Remy said, "No. Unfortunately not. He and my momma tried reconciling for a little bit, but it didn't work out, again."

Sensing she was going to have a hard time getting any other information regarding Remy's father, Lily quickly changed the subject.

"So, tell me more about the guy you were with at the party the other night. Have you two been dating long?"

"No. We actually just met. He was a bit full of himself at first, but as the night went on, he kind of grew on me. Still a bit presumptuous for my taste, but a decent enough guy, I guess." Eating an oyster, she continued on. "Not to be blunt, but I really don't think my relationship with Matt, or who my father is, is why you asked me to meet you here. So can we quit beating around the bush and get to the point of this?"

Knowing her facial expressions could give her away, Lily took a moment to compose herself before answering. "Okay. Let me give it to you straight. As I said before, Jordan was on to you the minute he stepped foot in the boutique. Don't ask me how he knew. He just did. He's got a sixth sense about those sorts of things. Maybe it's because he's been around it all his life, maybe it's a natural gift. But he also knows talent when he sees it. And he sees it in you. He really wants you to come join us. Like I said before, to what level you do things is strictly up to you. Me personally, I deal cards, I serve drinks, I smile and talk sweetly to the guys, but that's it. Theo, on the other hand, is behind the scenes, working on the books and has no dealings with any of the clientele. And he prefers it that way. He and I have a solid relationship, and I'm not going to do anything to upend that.

I am not trying to pressure you. Neither is Jordan. He would like you to join us. It would be to all of our benefit, financially and I also think friendship wise too. I like you, Daphne, if that is really your name. It's fine if you don't want to say - " Lily held up her hand in an effort to stop Remy's denial. "But if you are going to work with us, that is one thing you will need to be upfront about. You can use whatever name you want with the clients, but behind the scenes there has to be a level of trust. And that is a deal-breaker."

Tilting her head as if considering all Lily told her, Remy looked at Lily, glanced around the room, then played with the food on her plate. Stalling for time, she debated in her head whether to reveal her real name at this point.

"You've given me a lot to think about. I appreciate the transparency. I'm sure I'll still have questions, but for now, as a show of good faith, my name is Remy Thibodeaux. I'm sure you'll run back to Jordan with that, and he'll run whatever background check he deems necessary. You won't find much. A few misdemeanors, which were nothing more than misunderstandings and have since been cleared up. Aside from those, I've lived a pretty normal, mundane, insignificant life."

"Mundane, sure. Somehow, I think you've had a little more excitement in your life than you're letting on. But that's okay. We're all entitled to keep some information private." Lily replied with as much enthusiasm as she could muster. Still feeling as though Remy was holding something back, she knew better than to push any harder for fear of alienating her altogether. "I will let Jordan know you are thinking about it. Take your time, but not too much time, of course. But if you decide this is something you want to do, come by the Carrington Club tomorrow evening, say around six, and we'll get you set up for the night and you can see how it all works."

Lily waved down the waitress, asking for the check. "It's on me," she said to Remy. "You stay and enjoy what's left. I have to get going. Turns out Theo and I have a free night, which never happens, so we're going to take advantage of that." Scribbling on a napkin, she continued. "Here's my number if you have questions. Though if you can, wait until tomorrow to call, please?"

Taking the napkin, Remy nodded. "Have a great evening. Enjoy whatever it is you guys are going to get up to. Goodness knows there's plenty to do and see in this city at any given time. And I'll give you my answer by tomorrow afternoon."

Watching Lily leave, Remy sat picking randomly at the food left on the table. 'I'm certainly not going to let this go to waste, especially on someone else's dime,' she thought to herself. 'I guess I have a lot to think about and some decisions that need to be made.'

Chapter Six

Leaving the Desire, Lily took her time before returning to the Carrington. She wanted to think over what Remy had shared. While it hadn't been much, she figured out Remy was looking for something more in life. What that was remained to be seen. Maybe coming to work for Jordan would help steer her down a new path. Whether it was the right or wrong path wasn't for Lily to say. So far it had worked out for her, but even she knew her time was limited. This wasn't the life she envisioned for herself and Theo. As much as she liked New Orleans, her heart was still back in Chicago, with family and friends. Maybe one day they'd move back. But for now, she knew she had to get back and report on what she had found.

Hopping on the streetcar heading back to the Garden District, she rode next to the open window, breathing in the smells of the city. The magnolias were in full bloom, and the perfume from them and the other native flowers was intoxicating. She could live without the humidity and the threat of hurricanes, but something about this city definitely had its charm and a hold on her.

Walking in, she found Jordan, Theo, and Marcus sitting at a table, deep in discussion. Taking a seat at the bar, she waited until Theo noticed her. She smiled at him, looking forward to the night they had planned together. When was the last time they both had a night off? She couldn't remember. Jordan quickly interrupted her train of thought, calling her over as he sent Marcus off on a task.

"So tell me, what did you find out? Is she going to join our merry little group? Or did you manage to scare her off?" Jordan sneered.

"Well, you certainly seem to be in a mood this evening," Lily replied coolly. "She's thinking about joining us. I told her to let me know by tomorrow. She was pretty light on details about her family and her life in general. I get the impression she doesn't have much of a relationship with her dad. Like I told you before, it seems he spent some time working in Las Vegas. Came back here and tried to make a go of it with her mother again, but that didn't work out. She didn't say he was dead, so I get the impression he must still be alive. But where he is, I've got no idea. Give me a little more time with her, and I'm sure I can get her to open up. But I also didn't want to scare her away right off the bat."

"Huh. So, in other words, you didn't get much more out of her? You have no idea if she's going to join us, and essentially you failed in the one task I gave you today?" Jordan practically shouted as he rose from his chair. "What good is any of that?"

Theo jumped up, moving closer to Lily. "Now wait just a minute, Jordan. You have no right to talk to her that way.

You asked her to do something, she did it, and now she's here telling you what she found out. What would you have had her do? Take the girl somewhere and torture it out of her?"

"Oh yeah, I almost forgot," Lily interrupted. "Her name is actually Remy Thibodeaux."

"That's the headline you should have led with," Jordan fumed. "What else?"

"That's it. Really. I think she'll show up tomorrow. She seemed intrigued at least. And I feel like she probably needs the work and definitely the money. But Jordan, she doesn't know you from Adam, and your gesture in the boutique kind of set her on guard too," Lily said as reached out, taking Theo's hand, giving it a small squeeze of reassurance.

Jordan, realizing how menacing he was being, stepped back. "Okay. You may have a point. I guess all we can do at the moment is wait to see what she does. But I want you to follow up with her. Even if she doesn't show tomorrow night."

"Sure. Okay. But can you at least tell me what is so important about her? I mean, yeah, she's pretty and all. But from what I can tell, she's no different from any of the other girls you have working here. I just don't see what all the fuss is about?"

"What the fuss is about," growled Jordan, "is none of your business. I have my reasons, and that should be enough of an answer for you."

Nodding in acquiescence, Lily backed away. "If there's nothing else, Theo and I have plans this evening."

Jordan looked at Lily, then Theo, and back to Lily,

waved his hand in a shooing motion, waving them away, as though they were bothersome bugs.

As Lily turned towards Theo, she shrugged and gave him a look as if to say, let's go before he changes his mind.

TURNING BACK TO MARCUS, Jordan barked, "Alright. Enough standing around. Let's get ready for this evening."

Marcus nodded once, turned to the bartender and gave her instructions to pass along to the rest of the staff. Turning back to Jordan, he asked, "Anything else I need to do, boss?"

"No," Jordan snapped. "I'm going to the back and don't want to be disturbed. I'm sure you can handle anything that might come up out here. Short of the police busting down the door, I don't want to be interrupted. Do I make myself clear?"

Not waiting for a response, Jordan stormed off to his office. 'That insolent little bitch,' he thought to himself. 'She didn't get any more information than I already had. I guess if I want anything done right, I'll have to go do it myself.'

Grabbing the phone, he placed a call to a police detective he had on his payroll, gave him Remy's full name and told him to get whatever information he could about her to him immediately. He already knew she was the connection he had been looking for, whether she knew it. Being the daughter of Frank Batiste brought with it a lot of family history and secrets. It was Jordan's job to find where those secrets were hidden.

Chapter Seven

Unsure if she was making the right decision, Remy went to the Carrington club the next evening. Looking around for Lily or any other familiar face, she reminded herself, "beggars can't be choosers. I need the money more than anything right now, and if it doesn't work out tonight, then I'll move on to the next thing."

When she spotted Lily, Theo, Jordan and some other guy sitting at a table, Lily looked up, caught her eye and waved her over.

Making her way to the table, she paused a step away from Jordan, waiting for him to acknowledge her.

Before she could say anything, a waitress arrived, delivering drinks and appetizers. Jordan nodded his thanks to her, then turned his attention back to Remy.

"Daphne, or should I say Remy, welcome to the Carrington. Please have a seat. We were just having a drink and a little bite before the festivities of the evening get under way."

"Thank you," Remy stuttered. She should have known Lily would have told Jordan her real name, but hearing him use it caused her to take a step back for a moment.

"Remy, I'm so glad you decided to join us," Lily said enthusiastically. "I'm sure you remember Theo from the other night, and this is Marcus. He's our bouncer, manager, all around do everything guy. Questions, concerns, anything. He's the go-to guy."

"Nice to meet you, Marcus. I, um..." Remy stuttered. Unable to find her voice, she dropped into an empty chair and looked around the club.

"So, Remy. Are you here to tell us that you are joining our merry band of misfits?" Jordan asked. "Or perhaps you have come to share your deepest, darkest secrets? Maybe something about long-lost stones?"

Looking at Jordan, Remy couldn't quite figure out if he was joking or being serious. And if he was being serious, what secrets and stones was he talking about? How much was he aware of about her and what she had done in the past? And the family story about her dad and missing diamonds, she was sure no one else knew about that. She found herself at a loss for words, something she was not normally accustomed to being.

Quickly finding her voice again, she replied. "I came here to find out a little more information besides what Lily shared, and to give this place a chance. As to stones, aside from The Rolling Stones, or stones used in a lot of the courtyards around here, I have no idea what you're talking about. And yeah, no. My deepest, darkest secrets are mine to keep, thanks."

Jordan laughed. "I'm kidding. Gee, girl. Stop taking

things so seriously. You walked in looking like a long-tail cat in a room full of rocking chairs. I was just trying to lighten the mood."

"Oh, ha ha. Sorry. Yeah, I guess I am a little nervous. Like I said, Lily shared some information with me, but I still have a lot of questions before I commit to anything."

"Here, have a drink. A bite to eat. Settle your nerves, and I'll give you the overview. After that, we'll have Marcus here take you around, show you where everything is, and introduce you to some of the others. Take the night, work a few tables and see how it goes before you make up your mind. Deal?" Jordan said as he extended his hand to Remy.

"Deal," Remy said, shaking it firmly.

One thing she knew how to do was put on the bravado when necessary, and now was one of those times she was going to need it. Observe it all tonight, she told herself, see what you can learn, then make your next move. Cons are always like a game of chess, not checkers. You don't want to rush your next play, nor do you want to give away any of your strategy to the competition.

After a bit more small talk, Jordan explained how he had come to own the Carrington Club. Detailing who some of the more affluent or prestigious members might be in attendance tonight. It was, after all, a members only club, and he was quite proud of who he had attracted to join. Once he finished with the sales pitch, and that's exactly what it sounded like in Remy's head, he turned his attention to Marcus.

"Marcus, will you take it over from here? I need to excuse myself and take care of some other business."

Not waiting for an answer to his question, and with no more explanation or goodbyes, Jordan rose from the table, walking purposefully towards a back room.

"So, Remy," Marcus said, turning his attention to her, "you ready to get started?"

No lead-in, no small talk, just diving right in, she thought. "Uh, sure." She acknowledged. Before she had a chance to say anything more to Lily and Theo, she found herself practically running to keep up with him.

Turning into a small room, Marcus said, "Put your coat and purse back here. They'll be safe, we keep the room locked or at least attended. The room you saw Jordan go into is his office and off limits unless he calls for you. Is that clear?"

Remy nodded, not trusting her voice at the moment.

"Good, now continuing on," Marcus said, on the move again. He toured her through the kitchen, a dressing room, pointed out the restrooms, and two more private rooms.

"Those are always to be reserved before use. Members can use them for whatever they see fit; card games, business meetings, private parties, whatever. They sign up and tell us what they'll need for the time they will be using the room. Food, servers, tables, etc. There's an extra charge to them for cleaning, and anything that would exceed their usual dues. But they can afford it. And of course any gratuities you earn from those gigs are all yours to keep as well."

"Do those rooms get booked often?"

"Often enough. Surprisingly, more so on weeknights. Most of the members prefer the action that takes place in the main room on the weekends. Of course, that's typically when they bring their wives too. Weeknights are when you'll see their other companions." Marcus laughed. "Now, as to that. I'm sure Lily already told you, and I'm going to reiterate it so it's clear. We do not expect any of our employees to tolerate any sort of unwanted behavior. If someone is acting inappropriately or making you uncomfortable in any way, you come to me immediately. And I will deal with whoever it is. Understood?"

Remy, finding herself relieved to hear this reiterated again by someone else, nodded.

"Now, you've had the tour. The only other thing I will tell you is you're going to need to step up your wardrobe. What you have on tonight is barely acceptable. Take a look around at all the other girls and guys in here. Tell me what you see?"

Looking around at all the employees who had arrived since Remy had started her tour with Marcus, she noticed most of the women were in cocktail dresses and the men were in suits, or at least really nice sports coats and pants. Ties seemed to be optional. But Marcus was right. She was definitely going to have to do something about her entire wardrobe if she was going to stick around.

"I, well, that might be a problem. I don't really have a lot in the way of cocktail wear," Remy demurred.

"No problem. Jordan has accounts at a few different places. They all give him a significant discount, and as long as you provide the receipts, we'll reimburse you for any purchases you make. And no, there are no strings attached. It's only one of the benefits he offers to all the employees here. He's a good guy to work for, provided you follow the rules."

She wondered what other rules might have been left

unspoken, but before she was able to ask, one of the other servers came back with a question, putting an end to the tour. Marcus told Remy to go find Tommy, the head server for the night, and he would get her set up with a small section of tables, primarily running drinks and food for the evening.

'Well, I guess I'm doing this,' she thought to herself. 'Here goes nothing.'

Chapter Eight

Working a small section that night, she turned on the charm, hoping to earn higher tips than she was used to. Falling into old habits, she was always amazed at how easily men would succumb to a little flattery and flirting. No matter the education level of any guy she encountered, it always seemed he would think with some other part of his anatomy instead of the brain he was born with.

Once she was in, it took more cunning and conniving to maintain the charade of her interest. As soon as she had gotten what she wanted from them, she would then discard them like yesterday's newspaper, without them realizing it. She was always careful about how she cultivated these relationships and let them go, knowing there was always a chance she'd run into them again.

Working the hotel bars, the circle of men she had been meeting seemed to get smaller. Or maybe it was just that she was being more careful about who she chose to con. But now that she was considering working here at the Carrington, she wondered if maybe this was a step up in clientele she needed. She knew she would have to be careful. After all, these were some pretty prominent members of New Orleans society, and she didn't think Jordan would take kindly to her disrupting his business either.

On the other hand, this new level might open up more avenues and opportunities to meet men from outside the city, maybe even outside the country, who would come in to town on business, being winded and dined by the members that brought them in. If she could ingratiate herself with them, perhaps when they returned they would look her up, shower her with gifts and nights out, only to leave again a few days, or weeks later. Those were the gentlemen she preferred as it led to fewer repercussions in the end.

The one time she found herself on the wrong end of the consequences had been an encounter with a jealous wife that resulted in her being out of circulation for a week while the bruises healed. That woman packed a mean punch. As a rule, she typically avoided married men, not wanting to hurt anyone else who didn't deserve it. But it seemed this guy hadn't been upfront with her either, and in the end they both wound up getting hurt. While hers was only physical, his was damaging both on a financial and reputation level. She supposed maybe a couple of guys in her wake didn't deserve the treatment she dispensed, but as far as she was concerned, all men were just like her father in one way or another, and they all should suffer.

Returning her attention to her section, she was surprised to see Matt seated at a table in a different section. Overhearing Maria, their server, asking flirtatiously, "So, Matt, tell me, what is it that you do?" She watched as Matt explained in more detail than Maria probably wanted, the finer details of money management and trading.

"That sounds really interesting," Maria drawled. "I'd stick around to hear more, but I really do need to get back to my other tables. But oh, Remy, if you aren't too busy, can you take over this table for me?"

Looking up, Matt recognized Remy immediately. "Remy, I'm sorry. I thought your name was Daphne. My mistake. Nice to see you again."

"Likewise. And no, you're not mistaken. A girl can't be too careful in this city, and it makes me cautious about who I tell my name to," Remy laughed, playing off the mixup.

"Ah, sure. I get that. Though I'm not originally from around here, but well, yeah," Matt stuttered.

"Cat got your tongue now?" Remy asked, raising an eyebrow.

"Ha ha. Yeah, sorry. It's been one of those days. And well, I wasn't expecting to see you here, and well, I'm just making a mess of things. Sorry. I think I need to just go."

"No, please don't. Not on my account anyway. I'm just starting out here tonight, and that would look really bad for me if a table just ups and leaves as soon as I start taking care of them."

"So you work here?"

"Maybe. I'm not sure yet. Like I said, this is my first night. I guess it's a trial run for all of us. So how about this? Let's start over again. Hello everyone. I'm Remy. I'll be taking over for Maria and taking care of you this evening. Can I get you all refills on your drinks?"

Matt, looking at his companions, nodded. "Yes, please. Gin and tonics all around. And thank you, Remy. We look forward to your service this evening." Smiling, he nodded at Remy as she turned and made her way back to the bar.

Finding Maria at the bar, she exhaled. "Well, that was awkward."

"Sorry about that. Didn't know you knew Matt. He seems like he'd be one of the good guys. And he's a good tipper too."

While waiting for the drink order to be finished, she peppered Maria with more questions. "So I'm guessing this isn't your first time waiting on him, then? How often does he come in? Who are the others at the table? Any other information I should be made aware of?"

"Whoa, slow down, girl. He comes in on occasion as a guest of other members. He's not actually a member here. But I've waited on him a couple of times. You can identify pretty quick who the good tippers are going to be and who to avoid. Or rather, not expect much of. But why so many questions?"

"Nerves, I guess. I really don't know him. I met him the other night at a party. He came on pretty strong, but after a while settled into himself. Seemed like a nice enough guy. Didn't think I'd run into him so soon again though." Letting her comment trail off, she picked up the tray of drinks and started making her way back to the table.

"Gentlemen, gin and tonics all around. Enjoy. And please be sure to let me know if I can get anything else for you."

"How about a phone number, doll?" One of the other guys at the table slurred. Obviously, he had already had more than his fair share of drinks, she thought. Best to keep an eye on him. Before she could say any more, Matt cut in.

"Dude. Really. That's not appropriate. What would your wife say after all?"

That earned a few laughs from the others at the table and a weak apology from the drunken guy.

Back at the bar, Remy stood next to Jordan. Lost in thought, she didn't hear him asking her how her night was going.

"Sorry. What?" She said, turning to find him staring at her with a look of confusion on his face.

"I was asking how your night was going. And I noticed that the guy from the party the other night is here now too. Is there something I should be aware of?"

"Oh, no, it's fine. Everything is fine. I guess he's here as a guest of another member here, according to Maria. Aside from meeting him at that party, this is only the second time I've ever encountered the guy." Remy rambled and immediately stopped talking.

Jordan laughed, nodding in reply. "Guess you've still got a few nerves to be worked out. Don't worry. Everything is fine. You're doing great. No complaints from anyone yet." He winked. "Give me your answer at the end of the night about what you've decided. If you choose to stick around, we'll get all your pertinent details, cash you out for this evening and get payroll started as soon as next week. Sound good?"

"Yes, that sounds good," Remy absentmindedly replied, not thinking about what she was actually agreeing to. Her mind was filled with thoughts of how she could get Matt away from the other guys at the table and set one of her plans into motion. She knew she had to be careful, especially if he became a member here. That could complicate things.

Jordan broke her train of thought, pointing out her next drink order was ready and wouldn't deliver itself.

"Right. Thanks," she muttered as she picked up the tray and made her way back across the room.

The rest of the night went by without incident. She didn't have time to talk to Matt alone, but he slipped his phone number to her along with a very generous tip. Deciding she would cautiously move forward with a plan for him, she would also keep this job for now too. She was making more money here, and so far there was nothing about it she didn't feel comfortable with.

Chatting with Maria and a few other servers at the bar at the end of the night, Maria asked more questions about her first encounter with Matt.

"No. Oh, this is terribly awkward. And I didn't think I was going to run into him here. And no, before you assume anything, nothing is going on between the two of us. I only met him the other night at another party. Shoot, I didn't even know I'd be coming to work here, much less running into someone who was trying to get me to go home with him."

"So how did you come to find out about us and start working here? Honestly, I didn't even think we were hiring," Maria asked.

"It was all a fluke, actually. I was in this little shop, trying to find a dress for the party I mentioned. I had no business being there or even thinking about going to the party or how I was going to pay for any dress. Honestly, I really wasn't thinking. Next thing that happens, this stranger, who turns out to be Jordan, is buying the dress for me, along with the accessories too. Then I ran into him, along with Lily and Theo, at that party, and well, long story short, here I am." Taking a breath, she looked in the mirror behind the bar and caught Maria giving her an odd look. Was that a smile of amusement or jealousy? She wasn't sure.

"Yeah, sounds like Jordan. He does things like that. I guess he gets some amusement out of it. Who knows? But whatever the reason that brought you here, I hope you stick around. It was fun working with you this evening." Turning to the other girls, Maria said her goodnights, grabbed her bags, and made her way to the door.

The others said goodnight to Remy too, leaving her sitting at the bar by herself. She had already decided what she was going to do. Now it was time to make it official.

Looking around, she saw Marcus come out of what she guessed was Jordan's office. Waving him down, she watched as he approached her.

"Remy, what can I do for you?"

"Is Jordan still around? He wanted me to give him my decision at the end of the night."

"No, I'm sorry. He had to leave about an hour ago. He filled me in and told me to go ahead and pay you for tonight and find out what you decided."

Marcus moved behind the bar to the cash drawer, counting out tens and twenties, before laying them on the bar in front of her. "This should cover your wages. Of course, no taxes tonight because, well, we don't have any of that information." He laughed.

Remy, smiling in return, pocketed the money, replying,

"I won't tell if you don't. And tell him my answer is yes, I'll stick around. I had fun tonight, and it seems like this is a pretty cool place to work. I know I still have a lot to learn, but I'm willing. So I guess my question is, when should I come back?"

Glancing over her shoulder, Marcus looked at something Remy didn't see before answering her.

"Take tomorrow to get things in order. I'm guessing you'll need to get a few new outfits. Come back the day after and we'll have your regular schedule set up then. I'll be sure to pair you up with Lily, and she can show you all the ins and outs you didn't get tonight. You should be up to speed and going fully on your own within the week."

Noticing a slight change in his demeanor, Remy took that as her sign it was time to leave. "Great. Yeah, I'll do that. Thanks again Marcus. I'll see ya'll the day after tomorrow."

Taking one last look back over her shoulder, she saw Marcus move off to a dark corner of the room, sitting down in a chair across from someone she hadn't noticed before. Not wanting to cause any trouble, she knew to keep her questions to herself, and left by the door she had first come in.

Chapter Nine

Waking up late the next day, Remy thought back on all that had transpired the night before. What had she gotten herself into? Was this really the right thing to be doing? She had been making it just fine with her other job and the cons she had been pulling. But what were the chances she was now going to run into some men she had played in the past? After all, a few of them were members of society, the likes of which she had seen last night. Would anyone else like Matt come along and recognize her, calling her by yet another wrong name?

While she had got out of the situation with Matt pretty deftly, some others, who she knew lived in New Orleans, might make her life a living hell. She was going to have to give this job some serious thought now that she had had some time to think about everything.

But first, coffee. Throwing on a sweatshirt and a pair of jeans, she pulled her hair up into a messy bun and made her way downstairs and around the corner to the little bakery and coffee shop she liked to frequent. It was one of the few places that hadn't fallen into the hands of developers, and where she had wonderful memories of times spent with her dad when she was a kid. After he had returned to New Orleans, he would pick her up on Saturday mornings, and they'd start their day here. He'd get the biggest pastry they had in the case, order milk for her and a strong coffee for himself. It was always strong, she remembered, never large, or black, or any of the other ways people would order coffee. He ordered it as though it were some magic elixir that would set everything right with the world. And maybe he was right. Now that she was an adult, she definitely saw the appeal of the dark roast with a hint of chicory you found in most coffee around here.

Smiling at the memories, she placed her order at the counter, then found a table in the courtyard out back. Putting on her sunglasses, she leaned her head back, soaking up the late morning sun, when a shadow passed in front of her. Thinking it was the server setting down her order, she paid no attention until she heard her name.

"Remy. Is that you?" A deep voice asked, interrupting her thoughts.

Turning her head and removing the glasses, she found herself face to face with Theo. Unsure of what he was doing here, she simply raised an eyebrow, considering him before answering.

"Theo. This is a surprise. What brings you here?"

"Same as you. Coffee and some of the best pastries in the city. Lily and I stumbled upon this place when we first came to visit. Now that we're living here, I try to get by every couple of weeks or so. I often pick up an order to go, but thought since it was such a nice morning, I'd take advantage and see if I couldn't find a seat out here and enjoy a treat before I have to go to work. Something about crunching numbers with a full stomach makes it a little more tolerable," Theo said, laughing.

Smiling in return, Remy agreed. "I suppose it would. Though math was never my strong suit, I would be hard pressed to find much of anything to do with numbers, other than a positive balance in my bank account, tolerable."

"I totally understand that. It's not a career path for everyone. But in reality, I don't mind it that much. It's kind of soothing for my analytical mind. Everything adds up as it's supposed to and balances out. Unlike the rest of life. So what brings you here?"

"Oh, I live not too far from here. Didn't feel much like making breakfast myself this morning, so I thought I'd drop in and see what tempting treats they had. I used to come here when I was a kid too." Remy started to say, but stopped herself short before revealing any other details.

"So you're from around here then?" Theo asked.

"Yeah. Grew up in New Orleans. Never saw a reason to leave."

"Is your family originally from here too?"

"Dad's side is. They've been here for what seems like forever. Mom and her family moved here from upstate New York. But liked it so much, they stayed, even after she and my dad split."

Remy noticed Theo biting his lip and nodding as she talked. Was he fishing for information, she wondered, or genuinely interested? Lily had, in a way, broached the same subject. Maybe she was reading too much into it. Then again, she knew always to be cautious too. Deciding to take control of the conversation, she started peppering him with questions about how he and Lily wound up in New Orleans.

When he hemmed and hawed, she knew she had to be careful about what information she shared about her dad and her life in general. He had told her some years back he had done some things he wasn't proud of, and if anyone should come asking about him, to say she didn't know much. Which really wasn't far from the truth. But she was aware of some rumors that were neither confirmed nor denied. Which in her book, was as good as a confirmation.

"Well, I guess I should get going. It was great running into you here. Will we see you tonight at the club?" Theo's question interrupted her thoughts.

"Oh, no, not tonight. According to Marcus, I need to up my game in the wardrobe department first, so I guess today and tomorrow I'll be doing that. I really hate shopping, though. Wish I could just get someone else to do it for me."

"You should call Lily then. She loves it. And she has a great eye for what fits a person. I'm sure she'd love to go. If you want the company that is."

"I, um, are you sure? I don't want to impose on her."

"Tell you what. Let me call her right now. They've got a payphone in the back. If she says yes, where should I tell her to meet you?"

"Here? It seems as good a place as any. I need an hour to run home and get cleaned up. Can't go shopping looking like I just rolled out of bed after all," Remy laughed.

"Great. I'll be right back and let you know what she says." Theo said as he made his way back to the phone.

Remy shifted in her seat, wondering if this was the best idea. It would give her a chance to get to know Lily better and maybe help her decide if it was the right choice to stick around at the Carrington. She figured Lily would be a good source of information on Jordan and the rest of the employees as well, but more importantly, the clients.

Seeing Theo return from the phone with a smile on his face was all the answer Remy needed. She figured Lily would have agreed, though the level of excitement Theo felt about it seemed a bit more than necessary.

"Lily said she can't wait and she'll meet you here in an hour. She really does love to shop, so trust me when I tell you, when you get tired, tell her. Otherwise she'll keep going and going."

"Thanks. I'll keep that in mind. But I best get going if I'm going to be back here in an hour. Thanks again Theo. It was nice running into you. I guess I'll see you around the Carrington later."

Making her way out before Theo monopolized any more of her time, Remy returned home, getting ready for whatever the day was going to hold.

Chapter Ten

As Remy rushed back to her apartment, she didn't spot the man standing across the street watching her. If she had, her plans for the day would have gone in a completely different direction.

Leaning against a wall, just inside the walkway leading back to one of the common courtyards found in this city, Frank was considering what his next plans should be. Remy's mother, Vanessa, had moved on with her life. Marrying and then divorcing that guy. What was his name again? Oh yeah, George Collins. What a boring name for a boring guy. He had at least treated Vanessa and Remy well. Better than he ever had, seeing as how he had pretty much abandoned them. But now that he was back, he was hoping to make some amends, to be at least a part of Remy's life again. It would take some time, but he was willing to put in the work.

Having left behind the old life in Las Vegas, he was trying to start anew here again. He had moved back into the carriage house behind the Batiste family home and begun restoring it to his style and taste. It would take time, which seemed to be a recurring theme. But in the end, it would be worth it. He also knew he had to take it slow, lest he give away to anyone who shouldn't know the fact that he was back again. Few people from the time in his life spent in Las Vegas knew the name Frank Batiste. As far as they knew, he had always been Frank Barnes. And though Nick Costa knew his secret, Frank had been assured that Nick wouldn't have any chance to be dealing with him, as he was locked away in a federal penitentiary serving time for a myriad of crimes he committed while running the Crossroads Casino.

Frank wasn't proud of his involvement there either. Though he avoided most of the dirtier aspects of the job, he had been involved in the theft of *that* diamond necklace. A case that still perplexed officials to this day. Having only recovered some diamonds that had been part of the necklace that graced Marilyn Monroe's neck that night, the rest remained lost. At least, so everyone else thought. Only Frank knew better.

Returning his attention to the present and to Remy, he watched her go into her building, running up the stairs. He wondered what had her in a hurry now. When she left, she had been moving lethargically, as though she had been out too late the night before. He had followed her to the cafe they used to go to when she was younger; the memories of time spent there brought a smile to his face. How he wanted to go in and order their usual, sit down across from her and say, "Hello. I'm home." But he knew he couldn't do that. Not yet. There was still too much he had to do, continuing to split his time between here and Indian Springs.

Did the conversation she had with that man in the cafe

make her nervous or scared? Was that why she was in a hurry? Deciding to stay and watch a little while longer, just to make sure no one else came along, he took another step back into the shadows. When he had thought she was staying in for the day, he was surprised to see her stroll back out again, this time dressed as though she had somewhere important to be.

Again, he followed at a discreet distance. Until he could settle his mind that she was okay, he'd keep an eye on her. When she approached the cafe again, he saw her greet a young woman outside. Overhearing Remy call her Lily, he filed away that information for later research. This had not been someone she had been friends with during her childhood. At least not that he knew. Maybe it was someone from work? Or someone she was running a con with. He wished she didn't take after him in that regard. 'Guess the apple doesn't fall far from the tree.' He thought.

When they turned into a boutique, he figured they must be out for a day of shopping. Knowing this was not something he needed to stick around and watch, he walked on down the block before hailing a taxi to take him home. The less time he spent out in the city right now, the better.

"NO. You listen to me. I want all the information on him that you can get me. And I want it yesterday." Listening to the person on the other end of the phone, Jordan scowled. "Are you not hearing me? Just get the damn information and overnight it. Better yet, fax it to me. And then overnight it."

Slamming the phone down, Jordan rose from his seat, storming over to the window overlooking the street below.

A knock at the door interrupted his derailing train of thought. He barked, "What?"

"Sorry Jordan. I can come back later if you're busy," Marcus said cautiously. He knew when Jordan got into one of his moods, it was best to stay away until he calmed down.

"No, it's fine. Come in. I'm hoping maybe you have some good news for me?"

"Um, not sure if it's good or not. I had a call from Nick's lawyer out in Las Vegas. Seems he has gotten wind of Remy. And before you ask, I have no idea how. I mean, she just showed up here. How does he already know about her?"

"Oh, you'd be surprised at what Nick Costa can find out. He seems to have a pipeline of information running to him in prison. So what did the lawyer want?"

"It seems he knows she's Frank Barnes, Batiste, whatever his name is, daughter. So I guess that's confirmed now, even if Lily hasn't been able to get that out of her."

"Alright," Jordan said, interrupting Marcus. "We're aware of the fact that she's been running cons for a while now. In fact, I'm sure it was her dad who taught her everything she knows. The real question though is, what information does she have about the missing diamonds? And what does she know about me? And who I'm connected to?"

"I don't think she has any idea about you, Jordan. Why would she? The only people in this city who know who you're connected with are in this room. There's no reason for anyone else to know. You've established yourself here, run a clean business, and have not given anyone any inkling to think otherwise."

"Okay. So we have confirmation that she's Frank's daughter. From what Nick has shared with me, he seems to think the diamonds are either in a safe deposit box somewhere, or they've finally been sold off and the money is stashed away. Either way, he wants what is due to him. Both the money and Frank's head on a platter."

"You think Frank is still alive?"

"Oh, I'm sure of it. That supposed car crash in the Nevada desert didn't fool anyone. Well, maybe the cops. But the Costa family? No, they know all his tricks. Frank thought he was so smart. And to an extent, I'll give him credit. He was. He managed to stay out of jail all these years and avoid all the guys who have been looking for him and the attempted hits on his life too. Still, I think Nick got tired of the chase after a while and called most of them off. But he never forgot the betrayal. Neither have I. And now we have a chance to set things right. Money, diamonds, doesn't matter. We need to reclaim what is rightfully ours."

Jordan picked up the phone, then, thinking better of it, set it back down again, and looked back at Marcus still sitting in his chair.

"What are you waiting for? An engraved invitation? We have work to do. I want to know all you can find out about Remy Thibodeaux, Frank Batiste, and anyone else connected to that family. He has a history in this city, and I'm sure there are others out there. Maybe not here. He had a nephew, Neil Evans, who he helped out back in the day too. Became a fairly well-known musician for a time. See if you can't track that guy down as well."

Standing, Marcus nodded, knowing better than to offer any other suggestions. Jordan was definitely in a mood, and nothing he said or did would change that. Not until he had something concrete to share.

After Marcus left, Jordan stood and walked to the window overlooking the street below. Thinking over all he knew, he muttered to himself. 'This is not going to happen quickly. Patience is what you need right now, Jordan. You and Nick have waited this many years; a little longer won't kill you.'

Chapter Eleven

Returning from the bakery, she shut the door behind her. As Remy walked into her apartment, she was wondering what she had agreed to. She wasn't even sure she was going to keep this job for long. Even with the assurances she'd be reimbursed for whatever she bought, because Jordan was such a swell guy, what would happen if she didn't stick around that long? Would they try to recoup those expenses? She had made good enough tips last night, and the pay she received was decent enough too. But something was still niggling at the back of her mind.

Jordan said he was just joking about secrets and stones. And how would he possibly have any idea about the missing diamonds and her dad's involvement? Unless he was connected to that. But she was sure everyone who had any involvement was still in jail or dead. She didn't remember reading about anyone by the name of Jordan in any of her dad's papers either.

Kicking off her shoes, she made her way into the

bedroom and plopped down on the stool in front of her old flea market find makeup table. Seeing the envelope that contained the letters she had brought home, her mind returned to the letter from her cousin, Neil, written to her dad. He mostly wrote about his work in Los Angeles, preparing to go on tour, and how thankful he was Frank had gotten him that opportunity. But then he mentioned the continued questions he had been getting about a missing necklace, and that left him wondering if Frank did indeed have any involvement. He had said he had never opened the letter Frank had left for him since he had received the postcard from Tupelo and was sending it back too. What did that even mean? She wondered. Had that been code for something? Was he in on it too?

Picking up the envelope, Remy shuffled through the papers and found the letter Neil had returned to Frank. No longer sealed anymore since she had already opened it, she pulled it out, slowly rereading it. The first time she read it, she had thought it was just a practical joke. Or it was her dad's way of trying to take credit for something he hadn't done. Though she couldn't think of a reason he would do that, unless he had been in some sort of trouble. She knew he had been involved in some shady deals, but no way he was involved in the stealing of Marilyn Monroe's diamond necklace. But now, as she was reading the letter for the third time, with Jordan's questions lingering, she faced the possibility it was true.

Now with too many unanswered questions and a myriad of unconnected details, she, frankly, wasn't sure how to go about finding out more information.

'Maybe I should reach out to Neil. I'm sure he's still

around. Maybe mom would know how I can get in touch with him,' she deliberated. 'If only I could get in touch with dad. Yeah, because that would be such a good idea.'

Running the brush through her dark hair, she thought over everything that had taken place these past few years. After the divorce between her mom and her stepdad, her mom getting sick was the kicker of it all. Now, if it were true that her dad had stolen the necklace and hidden the diamonds, finding those might be the answer she was looking for. It would allow her to pay for the best care for her mom and stop running all the cons she'd been pulling. Maybe she'd find a job in an art gallery or somewhere else she would actually enjoy and have a normal life.

Right, who was she kidding? She knew she couldn't have a normal life. That definitely wasn't in the cards for her.

Laying the brush back down, she resolved herself to the fact that it was time to pull up her big girl panties and go spend money in order to make money. Not that she was thrilled about it, but a job was a job, and for now this one would pay the bills and allow her to save some money for herself too.

Arriving back at the bakery, she found Lily sitting on the bench out front. "I hope I didn't keep you waiting long," Remy sputtered when she saw her waiting.

"Oh, no. Not at all. I just got here and was enjoying people watching. It's one of my favorite things to do. Especially in this city. It's such a colorful cast of characters between the locals and the tourists. I create stories in my head about each of them. Sometimes I get a little carried away in the process. But at least it keeps me out of trouble."

Raising an eyebrow, Remy considered Lily for a moment, trying to get a read on her. "Or gets you into trouble," Remy joked.

"That too," Lily laughed. "Everyone always told me I had an overactive imagination. Guess I never grew out of it. But enough about made up stories. Shall we shop?"

Shrugging her shoulder, Remy pointed, "Lead the way."

Walking down the sidewalk towards their first stop, Lily chattered on about a whole lot of nothing. 'Boy, the girl can keep a conversation going all by herself,' Remy thought.

"So tell me more about you? What was it like growing up here? I bet you have some great stories about the history of this town and all you've seen over the years. Not to say you're old. Sorry. That came out wrong. See, this is what happens. I've been dominating the conversation and just going on and on. And please, if it gets too much, just tell me to shut up. Theo does. In fact, pretty much everyone I know does." The words just kept tumbling out of Lily's mouth, like the fountain in the courtyard of Pat O'Brien's.

Before she could get a word in edge-wise, they arrived at their first stop. "This place has got some great outfits, and they aren't too expensive either. It's definitely one of my go-to places," Lily exclaimed as they walked in the door.

Overwhelmed by the noise and overstuffed racks of clothes, Remy took in a deep breath before venturing in any further. This was one of those places she hated to shop. Having to shove through pieces that were out of date, mismatched, or just plain awful. Who would wear some of these things, anyway? Plastering on a smile so Lily would think she was enjoying herself, she made her way to a rack she thought might have a couple of pieces to work with.

Lily was buzzing through the store like a bee on speed, grabbing items left and right, with no sense of whether they would work together. Remy was being more methodical, pulling different pieces to mix and match. By the time they both arrived back at the dressing rooms, Lily was out of breath, while Remy was just hoping to get out as quickly as possible.

For the next twenty minutes, Remy tried on and discarded most items. The salesgirl, who pulled the short straw to cover the dressing room, was trying her best to keep up with Lily and her throwing around all the pieces that she deemed didn't work.

Finding only two items, Remy returned her other items back on their hangers to the girl, and made her way to the cashier while Lily continued to reign chaos in the dressing room. As she finished paying, Lily bounced out with her pile of "finds," as she called them, plopping down enough cash on the counter to cover her purchase.

"Oh, it doesn't look like you had much success," she said as she spotted Remy's small bag. "Maybe the next place will have more that's your style."

"Perhaps," Remy replied, noncommittally.

Over the course of the next three hours, they went to four more stores. At the last one, Remy finally found items fitting her style and budget. She pulled together enough items and accessories that she would have two weeks' worth of outfits without repeats. Add in what she had at home, and it should be enough for now. She still wasn't sure this job was going to be a long-term thing, but over the course of the day she decided she would at least give it a month to see how it all went.

The nagging thought of the letters on her vanity still hung in the back of her mind. More than once that day, it took multiple attempts by Lily to bring her back to the present.

"Remy? Hello? Are you there?" Lily called as they made their way out of the last boutique.

"What? Oh, sorry," Remy replied meekly.

"What's going on? You seem to have been lost all day. You're not having second thoughts, are you?"

Weighing her words, Remy turned to Lily. "No. I was just thinking about, well, stuff. It's been a long time since I've had someone to go with me on a shopping trip like this. It just made me think of a friend from school I haven't talked to in a long time." Making up the story as she went, hoping it was convincing enough.

"Oh, I'm sorry," Lily pouted. "It's not easy losing contact with friends like that. And I totally get what you mean. I haven't really had a close relationship since moving here either. So this has been fun for me too. Maybe you could reach out to your friend and invite her to the club sometime?"

"Hmm... yeah, no. I don't think that would be a good idea. She's got her own life now, not one that really lends itself to going out like we used to. But let's change the subject. It's getting all maudlin here. We're two girls out on the town shopping for a new wardrobe. This is supposed to be fun," Remy replied, slightly over enthusiastically.

"You're right," Lily exclaimed. "Let's go grab a quick bite and a drink and we can talk about what's next."

'What's next?' Remy thought to herself. 'That's a loaded

statement if ever there was one.' Pasting on a smile, she grabbed Lily's arm. "Yes, let's."

Settling in at a table in a small cafe, Lily started telling Remy more about the Carrington and all the people she worked with.

"Marcus is definitely the guy for just about everything. You'll see Jordan around most nights, but he's either busy entertaining clients or back in his office taking care of stuff."

"Oh, what sort of stuff?"

"I'm not sure. I mean, from what Theo has told me, Jordan has connections in other cities too. Not clubs necessarily. But some kind of involvement in other places. Mostly Las Vegas, I think? Maybe some sort of family connection out there. He, Jordan that is, doesn't really talk about himself or about where he's from. The guy is kind of an enigma, if you know what I mean."

"No, I'm not sure I understand," Remy said, trying to play dumb and glean any additional information.

When she heard Las Vegas, the hairs on the back of her neck stood up. Was there be a connection between him and her father? She supposed he'd be the right age to have known him. And he never said where he was from before coming here. Perhaps it might explain his interest, and even some of Lily's more probing questions.

One thing Remy noticed about Lily was that, as hard as she tried to be subtle about the questions she was asking, it was obvious to her that this was an information gathering mission as much as it was a shopping day. The question is, who put her up to it and why?

"Las Vegas, huh? Family connection? Are you saying Jordan has mob connections? Lily, I'm not sure I want to come work at the Carrington if that's the case." Remy said, shocked.

"Oh no, nothing like that. Well, not exactly," Lily laughed.

"Not exactly is not exactly reassuring."

Looking around, as if she thought someone might overhear, Lily leaned in closer to Remy as she scooted her chair in to the table. "Okay, here's the deal. Jordan lived and worked at a casino in Las Vegas for a few years. Something big went down. I don't have many details. But the owner, who was somehow mob connected, and a bunch of others got picked up by the feds and thrown in jail for years. Supposedly, there was this other guy who was involved, who they thought had died in a car crash in the desert, but actually, it turns out he gave evidence to the prosecutors, which is what brought them all down. Jordan has vowed to get revenge on behalf of his friends, but he's never been able to find this guy. So, no, technically Jordan is not connected to the mob anymore. But you get on the wrong side of him, and things don't turn out so well."

Raising an eyebrow, Remy looked at Lily, not sure how to respond. Wondering what to believe, she pondered the pieces that had been laid out for her before asking, "So wait, you're telling me what, then?"

Swallowing her drink and setting the glass firmly down on the table, Lily looked her directly in the eye. "I'm not telling you anything. I've said absolutely nothing. If you repeat any of this to anyone, I will deny ever saying it. Do you understand?"

Before Remy replied, the waiter arrived with their meals. After he set each plate down and left, Lily started to say something, turned to look over her shoulder, and stopped.

"Lily? What?"

"Nothing. Forget I said anything at all." Picking up her glass, she continued. "Here's to a successful shopping day. I certainly had fun, and I hope you did too. And I'm looking forward to working with you at the Carrington."

"Cheers. And yes, I had fun too."

"You are still coming to work, right?" Lily asked hesitantly.

"Yeah. Sure," Remy replied as eagerly as she could muster, hoping it was enough to dissuade any speculation that she might have doubts. All the while, all the thoughts of her father's letters swirled in the back of her mind.

Chapter Twelve

Arriving at the Carrington, Remy watched as Lily and the others were busy rushing around, getting ready for the first round of clients, who would stroll in as soon as the doors opened. When Marcus came out and motioned for her to follow him, she learned what she'd be doing that evening.

"So, we'll have you shadow Lily for a little while. I know you saw how things ran the other night, but this is how we train everyone, regardless of their experience. Jordan has his particular way of wanting things done, and we've found this is the best way to show you, and hopefully you'll pick up quickly on everything. And since you and Lily seem to have hit it off already, you two shouldn't have an issue working together like this."

"Sure. I think it will be fine. I defer to her knowledge of how things operate around here."

"Great. Lily, can you join us, please?" Marcus called.

Lily walked over, a tray under her arm, as she's counting out cash and putting it in her order book.

Addressing Lily first, Marcus tells her, "You'll be training Remy this evening. Get her set up with an order book, bank, and whatever else she's going to need." Turning his attention back to Remy, he continued, "Questions, ask Lily. Any problems with a client, come find me. Do not under any circumstance, try to handle the situation yourself. I have ways of dealing with unruly guests. Not that I'm expecting anything, because most of our members signed a contract stating they had read the rules. But on occasion, there are some members' guests who seem to think they know better or that they can get away with, shall we say, inappropriate behavior? They are pretty quick to find out that's the best way to bring their evening of fun and games to an end. And they will not be welcomed back anytime soon. Got it?"

"Yes, sir," Remy replied, standing almost at attention.

Suppressing a laugh, Marcus shook his head as he walked off, muttering to himself. "Oh good. Another smart ass on the staff. Just what I need."

Turning to Lily, Remy smiled. "Okay, boss lady? Where do we begin?"

"Right. Follow me. Kenny will get you set up with your bank, the money you get at the beginning of the night to make change out of. It's not a lot, and if you can't make the change, let the customer know you'll be right back. Take the large bills to any of the bartenders and they'll break it for you. Make sure you don't delay. Even if you have another client trying to get your attention. Tell them you'll be right back with them. We had one girl who was making change, put it in her apron, and then lost the client she was supposed to give the change to. Never found him the rest of the night, and of course it threw off everyone's balance at the end of the night. Not to mention, he came back the next day and raised a stink because he found himself short a bunch of money when he got home. So yeah, that's rule number one. The rest is pretty simple stuff. Self explanatory. You'll see as we go."

For the next two hours, Remy followed Lily around the club, taking drink and food orders, delivering said orders, avoiding grabby hands, and politely smiling at everyone she met. It wasn't until she and Lily had a chance to take a break at the end of the bar that she noticed Matt and a group of members walking in the door.

"Oh."

"What? Something wrong?" Lily asked.

"Just saw someone I recognize," she indicated Matt and his party with a nod of her head.

"Wait? Isn't that the guy you were with the other night at the party? Matt something or other, I think? And then he was here a couple of nights ago too."

"Yeah, that's him. He's a nice enough guy and all. He slipped me his number, but I haven't called yet. Do you recognize any of the others he's with?"

Discreetly looking over the group, Lily shook her head. "Sure, two of them are members. Maybe he's here on business. You said he was some sort of trader or something?"

"Yeah, maybe. And oh, would you look at that? They've been sat in your, or rather our, section. I didn't think we were up in the rotation again so soon."

"Hey, sometimes members will request a particular server or section. Depending on how well they tip the hostesses can determine whether that happens or not. Guess now is as good a time as any for you to go solo. They're all yours, girly," Lily said with a sly smile.

Shaking her head, "Gee, thanks. I'll be sure to return the favor sometime," Remy replied with a little laugh.

Straightening her skirt, Remy approached the table and waited for a break in the conversation. "Good evening, gentlemen. I'm Remy, and I'll be taking care of you this evening."

Before she could continue, one guy chimed in, "You can take care of me anytime, honey," earning him a sharp look from Matt and a slap from one of the other guys.

"Sorry. Please excuse James. He can be a bit of a buffoon," Matt said in way of apology. "Guys, I know Remy, and she's good people. So be on your best behavior, and you better be sure to tip well too."

Laughter and introductions all around were made before drink orders were taken.

"Alright guys. I'll get these in and delivered shortly. In the meantime, if there's anything else I can get for you, please let me know."

Returning to the bar, Remy placed the order and waited for the drinks to be ready. As she was preparing to deliver them to the table, Jordan passed by and asked if everything was okay.

"So far, so good," she told him.

"Good. Glad to hear it. I'll check in with you at the end of the night then. Any problems, find Marcus."

After the first round of drinks were delivered, and food orders taken, Remy found herself back at the bar waiting on her next assignment. Just as Lily was approaching from one side, Remy caught sight of Matt approaching from the other direction. Turning her attention to him first, thinking he may need something for the table, she was surprised by an urgent tap on her shoulder from Lily.

"Sorry to interrupt something more fun. But I need to take care of a large party that came into one of the private rooms. Do you think you can cover our entire section for a bit?"

"Sure. If you're okay with my doing that."

"Of course. You've picked up on everything quick and I have no doubt that you can handle whatever may get thrown at you. Hopefully not literally. If you get in the weeds, grab one of the others. They'll help you out. But most everyone is already taken care of. With the exception of your 'special' table," Lily laughed as Matt came up to them.

Turning her attention back to Matt, Remy asks, "Is there something you all need at the table?"

"Uh no. Actually... I was wondering, well - " Matt mumbled his next few words unintelligibly.

"Sorry, I didn't catch that. If everything is okay with the table, I do need to go check on some others. But I'll be by in a few minutes to check on you again, too," Remy replied as she left him standing at the bar, dumbfounded.

"Sorry man. I dumped my entire section on her. She's still getting her legs under her. Just give her a minute, and I'm sure you'll have a chance to catch her again before she gets back to your table," Lily consoled Matt before she walked off towards one of the private party rooms.

Waiting at the bar, Matt ordered a shot while looking around the club. He had met with Jordan earlier in the day about the possibility of becoming a member. It wasn't a high-pressure sales pitch, yet at the same time, he was left to wonder if things were really on the up and up here. Something about Jordan didn't sit right with him, but he couldn't place exactly what it was during their meeting. The money for the membership wasn't an issue. Yet with all his travels he also thought, would he really be in town enough to make it worth his while? And if he was being totally honest with himself, was he doing it only to get closer to Remy or was it, as he had said to Jordan, 'to wine and dine' the potential clients hoping to make them permanent ones. "Eh, maybe a little of both," he said as the bartender placed his drink in front of him.

"Sorry?"

"Oh, nothing, man. Thanks," he said, tossing back the shot he had ordered and leaving a tip on the bar.

Making his way back to the table and group he was with, he plastered on a fake smile, keeping up with the conversation for the rest of the evening. These clients had the potential to bring in long-term capital to the company. Now was not the time for wallowing in what-ifs and maybes.

As he sat down, Remy returned to check on everyone, clearing empty glasses, plates, and bottles as she went. When she stopped next to him, Matt craned his neck and asked if he could talk to her later, once he wound down the evening with his party.

"Sure. I'll be done around midnight. If you're still here then, or want to drop back by, we can talk then."

"Fantastic. I'll see you then." Then, thinking to himself, *this will give me time to gather my wits and sober up a bit before I make an utter ass of myself.*

THE REST of the night flew by for Remy. With Lily tied up serving the private party, Remy found her stride taking care of all the tables she had to cover. Aside from one wrong drink, everything else went smoothly, and she wound up with a generous amount of tips for the night. 'A girl could get used to this kind of money,' she thought to herself.

Cashing out her bank and putting her apron in the dirty laundry bag hanging in the employee room, she gathered up her things before returning to the bar, where she found Marcus, Lily, Theo and Jordan.

"How'd the evening go? No problems, I'm guessing, since you didn't have to come find me at all," Marcus asked.

"It was all good. The customers were great. The other staff helped out when I got a little behind. But I think I found my rhythm, and if tips are like this every night I work, I can't see a reason not to stick around."

"That's what we like to hear," Jordan chimed in. Lily had a huge smile plastered on her face, while Theo shook Remy's hand in congratulations.

Seeing Jordan raise an eyebrow, Remy turned to find what he caught his attention, when she saw Matt approaching their group.

"Oh, right. I forgot he was coming back. Said he wanted to talk to me. I hope that's not a problem?" She asked the group.

"No, not at all. I was surprised to see him back again. I knew he had been in earlier in the evening with a group of guys he was trying to land for a business deal. He is definitely an interesting character," Jordan replied.

"Okay good. Yeah, not sure why he wanted to come back. But I'll go talk to him. Thanks again, all of you. I'll see you tomorrow night then."

Making her way across the room to Matt, Jordan turned to Lily and said, "Start slow, but encourage her to get to know him better. He's got deep pockets, and I'm sure she wouldn't have any trouble charming him. He seemed hesitant about joining as a member when I met with him. And that's fine. If she can pull this off, that won't matter."

Chapter Thirteen

As Remy approached, Matt felt the nerves in his stomach increasing. What was it abut her that made him feel this way? He negotiated with the best of them, bringing businessmen and their lawyers to their knees in the boardrooms, but her? She practically took his breath away and made him forget what he wanted to say. Trying to steel himself, he took a deep breath, hoping to appear nonchalant.

"Matt. Hey, you made it back," Remy said as she approached.

"Yeah, I, um…" Matt stammered. "Sorry. Got a little tongue tied. Must have had a little too much to drink this evening."

Laughing, Remy nodded. "Yeah, you and those guys put away a few cocktails tonight. Hopefully, all the business dealings went well?"

"They did. Thanks for asking. But that's not why I am here."

"No, I guess not. So what was it you wanted to talk to me about?"

Shuffling his feet, Matt looked around. "Can we go somewhere else to talk? I mean, if you want to stay here, I get that. If it would make you feel safer or whatever. But if you wouldn't mind, I'd rather go somewhere we can sit and get a drink or even a bite to eat and have a conversation."

"Uh, yeah, sure. Let me get my coat, and we can go down the street. There's a little diner that's open. They're got the best late night breakfast platters. If that works for you?"

"That would be great."

After grabbing her coat, Remy found Matt waiting outside. "Mind walking? I could use some fresh air after being inside a smoke filled room all night," she asked.

Matt nodded as he offered his arm for her to hold on to.

"And a gentleman to boot. Not something you see much these days," Remy giggled.

Making their way down the street in silence, Matt ran through a litany of things he wanted to ask her. Entering the diner, he took a moment to take in the place's ambiance. It was as though they had jumped back in time. Old-fashioned tabletop jukeboxes, chrome detailing, even the old linoleum floor. It all made you feel you had left the hustle and bustle of the real world behind. All they needed were servers on roller-skates and the picture would be complete. And wait, there she was. At least one server, anyway, took their role seriously.

Settling in at a table, Matt and Remy took their time reading over the menus. Periodically, Matt stole a glance at

Remy, smiling to himself and wondering how he got so lucky to get her to agree to go out with him.

Laying his menu down on the table, he raised a hand to a server, letting them know they were ready to order. Continuing in his chivalrous mode, he allowed Remy to order first. A bacon, lettuce and tomato with well-done bacon, a side of French fries, and a coffee to drink, made him like her even more. She wasn't afraid to eat, unlike so many of the women he had known. Ordering a large breakfast for himself, he thanked the server and turned his attention back to Remy.

"So, thank you for agreeing to come out after work tonight. I'm sure you're exhausted after your shift."

"Actually, I'm feeling quite invigorated at the moment. Must be my third wind. Seeing as I had my second wind a couple of hours ago," Remy smiled. "But I'm sure if you ask me again in fifteen minutes I might give you a different answer then."

"Well, if you do find you are winding down, please don't hesitate to tell me. I don't want to keep you any longer than you want to be kept." Matt said before realizing how his words came out. "No, wait. Sorry. That didn't sound right. I don't mean to imply you're a kept woman."

Remy interrupted, "Oh my gosh. You're funny. I didn't get that at all. But now that you've said it, well maybe being a kept woman wouldn't be so bad." She grinned.

Shaking his head, Matt mumbled, "I'm such an idiot."

Looking at him seriously, Remy asked, "Why would you say something like that? From what little I know of you, I would never make that judgment. You seem quite the opposite of an idiot. A successful businessman, wining and dining the clients tonight. I'm guessing they became clients anyway, based on how jovial everyone was at the table. And certainly handsome enough. You carry yourself well. So please tell me why would you think yourself an idiot?"

"Wow. You really know how to make a guy feel better, don't you? You're right. On many accounts. They were potential clients when we walked in, and by the time the night was over, I had a verbal agreement for a contract which will be quite lucrative for me and the company. As for the rest of this, well, a lot of credit goes to my assistant, Ella, and a stylist she brings in to keep me in the latest fashion. Honestly though, I'm more comfortable in a pair of jeans, boots, and t shirt. Put me on a horse out on the plains in Wyoming and I'm happy as can be."

"Right. You mentioned something about Wyoming the first night we met. I'm not sure I could live out there, with all that wide open space."

"Really? Why?" Matt asked, leaning in to hear her better over the noise of the diner.

"Oh, I'm a city girl at heart. I've lived here all my life. And well, I feel like if I can't find it here, then I don't need whatever it is I was looking for. I suppose that's a bit naïve and close-minded. Maybe that would change if I had the chance to travel more. But I've got family commitments keeping me here and close to home," she said wistfully.

"That sounds a bit ominous. Hopefully nothing too serious."

"Sorry. It's not that bad. Well, my mom is sick and requires a lot of doctor's appointments and medications. She does pretty well on her own, but I like to be around to check on her and make sure everything is okay and taken care of. A lot of what I make helps with her bills too."

"Oh, I'm so sorry to hear that. What about your dad? Is he around too?"

Remy leaned back in her seat, wondering what the sudden interest everyone was taking in her father. Maybe this was Matt being nice. After all, it was the first time he had asked about Frank, and it was in conjunction with her mom's illness. But again, the nagging feeling in the pit of her stomach returned.

Finally, she replied. "He hasn't been around much. Honestly, I don't even know if he's dead or alive. But let's talk about something more fun. We didn't come here to discuss all these depressing topics. I get the feeling you had something you wanted to say earlier."

Just as Matt was about to ask her out for an official date, the server rolled up on her skates, deftly delivering their plates, before gliding away again.

"It amazes me how she can do that," Matt laughed. "I'd be flat on my butt if I tried to go from one end of the room to the other."

Remy laughed, which quickly turned into her almost choking on the bite of food she had taken. Managing finally to swallow, she sat back, looking at him, and waiting for him to continue.

"Right. So now that I've managed to embarrass myself by putting that awful image in your head, and make you choke on your food, I suppose I should tell you why I wanted to see you tonight."

"I was starting to wonder. I mean, I am wonderful company and all." She smirked.

"Yes, you are. And that is the reason. We've met a couple of times now. But I wanted to do the right thing and ask you out on a proper date. I feel like I came across a bit obnoxious the first night we met, and really, that's not who I am. At all. I get anxious in social situations like that, and well, I acted like an ass. So, all that being said, what would you say to a proper dinner date?" Matt asked, holding his breath while waiting for her to respond.

"I'd say I think that would be very nice," Remy replied as she saw relief spread across his face. "Did you have somewhere in mind?"

"I do. But I wanted to check with you what your schedule might look like first before I make the final arrangements."

"Don't you mean reservations?"

"Um, sure. Those too. So when do you next have a night off?" Matt said, not wanting to give too much away.

Part of the reason he was so nervous was the details he was keeping to himself about where the dinner would be. Knowing now that Remy had never had the chance to travel, he wanted to do something special, and what was more special than dinner in New York City?

"Well, normally I work Mondays at a little place called the Blue Pelican, but I'm sure I can take next Monday off. That is if where you're planning on taking me is open. After all, a lot of places around here are closed on Mondays."

"Oh, the place I have in mind will be open. So let's plan on Monday then. I'll pick you up around 4:00 if that's okay. It will take us a little while to get where we're going."

Raising an eyebrow at the time he suggested Remy said, "Okay, that seems a little early for dinner. I mean, how long is it going to take? And what should I wear? Are we talking about something formal here?"

"It will give us some time to chat and get our appetites ready. Dress, I'd say the little black dress you wore to the party the other night would be fine."

Shaking her head at how vague he was being, she threw her hesitation aside and agreed to go along with whatever he had planned. After all, guys like him with money to burn, there was no telling where they would wind up.

"Okay then. I guess we have a date for Monday then. I'm looking forward to seeing where it is you're taking me."

Not saying anything more, Matt grinned at her as he devoured the rest of his breakfast platter.

Chapter Fourteen

Matt arrived at her door promptly at four o'clock. Walking outside, he directed her into the waiting car, nodding to the driver, who apparently was in on the plan and knew where they were going. As they settled back into their seats, Matt turned to her. "I hope you're hungry. The chef has a special meal planned for us tonight."

Her curiosity now peaked, she glanced out the car window and saw they were heading away from town. "And just where might you be taking me?"

"Can't say. I don't want to ruin the surprise," Matt grinned.

As they drove through an open gate on the edge of the airport and stopped next to a private plane waiting on the tarmac, Remy turned back to him.

"We're not staying in New Orleans for dinner, are we?"

"No, we're not. I hope you don't have any fear of flying. I suppose I should have asked before, but also didn't want to give anything away either."

"I don't think I do. I mean, I've never flown before, so I have no frame of reference."

"Just think of it like riding in a really comfortable car. Only up in the sky."

Shaking her head, she took in everything around her. The bright blue afternoon sky without a cloud in sight, the plane in front of her, and the hangar behind them. She felt like it was a dream she didn't want to wake up from. Walking up the steps into the cabin, the pilot and a flight attendant greeted them. The co-pilot was in his seat, already running through a pre-flight checklist.

"Welcome aboard. It looks like we've got a good tailwind that will make our trip to New York City a little shorter than normal. Settle into your seats, and we'll be underway shortly," the pilot said to them both.

As Matt directed Remy back to the seats, the attendant followed with two glasses of champagne.

"Anything else you need right now, sir?" she asked.

"No, thank you. I'll let you know if we do," he said while keeping his attention on Remy. He was enjoying watching her take it all in, seeing the realization dawn in her eyes of where they were going.

"Matt, I don't know what to say. I mean, this is too much. For a first date, really? Dinner in New York City. I won't even bother to ask where we're going, because I wouldn't have any idea what to expect, anyway."

"Good. At least that can remain a surprise then. And honestly, it's not like I do this often. I wanted to do something special for you. It sounds like things have been kind of rough lately, and I think everyone deserves to be spoiled at least once in their lifetime."

"I think this goes beyond spoiled. But sure, why not," she said with a huge smile on her face.

The time spent in the air passed quickly, the two of them talking about any subject that came to mind. Matt shared how he had started out doing the most menial tasks in the company that he now ran. The owner was so impressed with his work ethic; he promoted Matt through the ranks until the day when the owner decided he wanted to retire and enjoy life. He made Matt an offer to buy the company, and without a second thought; he jumped at the chance. Now here he was, a few short years later, running not one, but two offices, and getting ready to launch a third.

"It keeps me pretty busy. New York was the first office, and that's where I got my start. A little over a year ago, I opened the New Orleans office. And now we're about to launch a West Coast division too. It's both exhilarating and scary at the same time."

"Wow. I can't even imagine. When do you sleep? Much less have time to take an impromptu dinner in New York City?" Remy asked, still trying to wrap her head around everything that was happening.

"It's important for me to take time for myself. I could easily work around the clock, but thankfully I have people around me I trust and who will also call me out and tell me I need to step away for a while. Trust is a big deal for me. I've been burned a couple of times in the past, so I'm wary going into any new relationship, whether it's business or personal."

As they began the descent into New York, Remy spent the remainder of the time looking out the window and considering what Matt had shared with her. While she barely knew him, there was something about him she connected with and couldn't bring herself to treat him like so many other men in her past. When she first met him, she thought he'd just be another easy con. She'd have some fun, get what she could, and leave him brokenhearted. But after everything he had shared, she was having doubts.

'Maybe the best thing to do is put a stop to this before it goes any further. At least then it won't hurt him nearly as much.' Deciding since they were here now, and how excited he was to show her even a small part of the city, she would tell him on the flight back to New Orleans. She hoped the pit now sitting in her stomach would resolve itself. She really wanted to enjoy what was to come.

Chapter Fifteen

After her whirlwind trip to New York the thought of returning to work now felt a bit like a letdown. While they had only been in the city a few hours, it whetted her appetite to travel and see more of what she had been missing out on. Matt had been so effusive talking about all the places he had visited for business and pleasure, and how he would love to experience them again, through her eyes.

By the time they had returned to the plane for the flight back, it was well past midnight, and she was barely able to keep her eyes open. The talk she had wanted to have never took place as they both dozed off as the plane departed. When he dropped her off at her apartment early that morning, he was still talking about where their next trip should be. She knew she would need to have a hard conversation with him before he started making too many plans, but now, back in reality, she had to shake herself out of the daydream as she walked up to the bar to check in with Marcus.

"Where do you need me tonight?" she asked.

"Hey, Remy, glad to see you back. Uh, Jordan wants to talk to you first. After that, how about jumping in as a floater. We've got a couple of different groups scheduled to be in tonight, and none of them ever seem to stay put at their tables. They always seem to bounce back and forth between the tables or even try to take over one that they're not even assigned to. I didn't think they even knew each other, but apparently this is something they do regularly, mixing it up and creating chaos for the rest of us."

"Sure. Any idea what Jordan wants to see me about? I don't want to walk in blind," she nodded her head at his door.

"Dunno. I think he's got a project he's wanting to get you involved in. It's all good, though. Nothing to be worried about," Marcus said a little too nonchalantly.

Remy turned, making her way back to Jordan's office, when she was about to knock and Lily came walking out with a scowl on her face.

"Hey Lily, everything okay?" Remy asked.

"Huh, oh, Remy. Yeah, fine. Just was talking to Jordan about something he wants Theo and I to do. Well, more Theo than me. But, sure. Everything's just peachy," Lily said with more than a hint of sarcasm in her voice.

"Uh, okay. Well, I guess I'll see you when I'm done here then. Let me know if you want to talk later."

Lily stomped off as Remy heard Jordan call for her to come in and close the door behind her.

"Remy, glad you're back. Did you have an eventful trip?" Jordan said, not looking up from the open ledger on his desk. It had his attention more than what was currently going on in his office.

"You could say that. But I'm guessing that's not what you called me in to talk about. Um, so Marcus said you wanted to see me about a project? Is there some event coming up you need me for?"

"Not exactly. Have a seat, and I'll explain," Jordan said as he looked up, his attention fully on Remy now.

Remy sat down on the edge of the chair, still unsure of what to expect, especially with the way Jordan was staring at her.

"I'm guessing you saw Lily leaving just now?" Jordan asked nonchalantly.

"Yes, she seemed a bit out of sorts."

"Hmm… I thought she was on board with what we discussed. Maybe I'll have to check in with her again. Okay, well enough about her, back to the matter at hand. I need you for a special project I've got in mind."

"Sure. Anything I can do to help around here. Is it a big private party or something?" Remy was eager to help however she could. Especially if it was a private party. Tips and pay for those were always better than a regular night, and the extra money right would come in handy now.

"It's something else. Outside of here. It won't involve much. I need you to run an errand, but it will pay well if it all goes according to plan."

"Uh, okay, I'm not sure I understand," Remy said.

"I'll give you more details later. I first wanted to see if you were interested. Once I've got everyone on board, then we'll meet up and I'll give everyone assignments and details of what they need to do and where they need to be."

"So it's nothing here at the club then?"

"No. All I can say right now is it's going to happen over in Metairie. Early next week, probably. No later than the week after. Right now, I simply need to know if you're willing to help." Jordan said, leaning forward on his desk.

The look he was giving Remy told her she didn't have much choice in the matter, so she just nodded.

"Great. Let me talk to the rest of the guys, and then after work tonight we'll all meet back here, and I'll fill everyone in on what's going on. Now, go on and get back out on the floor. We're gonna have a busy night tonight. Should be good for tips for you all too."

Remy quickly left his office, more confused than before she had gone in. Was this what Lily had been alluding to when she came out? She'd have to corner her at some point this evening to compare notes. Remy had an uneasy feeling about whatever it was Jordan had planned, but she also knew she couldn't back out now.

Later that night, once things had settled down to a manageable pace, Remy found Lily in the back hall.

"Hey, any idea of what Jordan is cooking up? He was pretty light on details, but told me you and Theo were on board already."

Lily shuffled her feet, looked down, then back up again, and sighed. "Yeah. Some. But I'm not supposed to say anything until after we all meet later tonight. He said he'd fill everyone in. What I can tell you is we've got the easy part of the job. A distraction, if you will. It's the guys who will be in more trouble if it goes sideways."

"What kind of trouble? The way he was talking, it

sounded like this was a one-off event or something. What you're saying doesn't make sense."

"Oh, it's an event. But not like what you're thinking. And you're right. It doesn't make a lick of sense. He was pretty light on details when he talked with us too. But," she stopped to look over her shoulder and make sure no one else was listening before continuing, "and please don't tell anyone else I told you this, but Theo and I are looking to leave here. New Orleans actually. We were hoping to get out by the end of this week, but now with whatever this is that Jordan has got in the works, it's not looking like we're not gonna be able to do that anytime soon."

Just then, Marcus came around the corner, barking at them to get back on the floor. Hurrying to get back, Lily whispered, "We'll talk later. After the meeting. Plan on coming over to our place unless you have other plans."

THE REST of the night flew by, the entire staff was in constant motion, until the last guest left and the all the glasses had been washed. Flopping down into a chair next to Lily, Remy kicked off her shoes, as she heard Lily let out a long sigh. Before they had a chance to get comfortable, Jordan came out with Marcus, Theo, and Tommy.

"Okay. Great, we're all here now. Let's get started," Jordan said, launching into discussion mode with no thanks for a good night's work.

"So, I know Marcus is aware of this, but for the rest of you, here's a quick rundown of what's coming up. Next Tuesday, the Metairie bank is going to be getting its normal morning delivery of cash, and we are going to go help ourselves to some of it."

Remy, suddenly no longer tired, sat straight up in her seat, suddenly aware of what Jordan was suggesting. Still unable to figure out how she and Lily were going to play into his plans, she listened more closely as he continued.

"You girls will be our distraction. What I need you to do is go in and get the manager involved in some sort of convoluted task. I'll leave it up to the two of you to figure out what that looks like. But keep him busy, so he can't see what's going on with the tellers. Marcus, you and Theo are going to come in five minutes after them, and give your notes to the tellers at the same time. Only two of them will be working then, so make sure you both coordinate your walk up to their stations. The only option they'll have is to fill the bags with the money, since the manager will be too busy, and they can't leave their windows when customers are in front of them. As soon as that's done, you stroll back out of the bank, and Tommy will be waiting to drive you off. Don't peel out like you did something illegal. Drive off normal, take side streets, and head back to Marcus's place. Once you're there, drop off the bags and split up. Go on with your day as normal. Girls, you can stick around until the cops show up. Give your statements if they want them. You didn't see anything. You were there on normal banking business. Once they've let you go, go home. Or go shopping. I don't care. Just don't do anything you wouldn't do any other day."

Tommy interjected, "What car am I supposed to use, boss?"

"I don't care. Not your own, obviously. Pick up a rental,

or borrow one from a friend. A friend you don't like that is. Steal one if you have to. Make sure it's nondescript. Once this is done, leave it over in Belle Chasse or somewhere else where it will take them a while to find. Oh, and one other thing. No weapons. Politely tell the tellers this is a stickup, hand over the cash they have access to, and that's it. It won't be a big haul. But that's okay. That's all you need to be concerned with."

Shaking her head, Remy looked at the others. Theo and Lily both looked dejected. Marcus sat with his arms crossed as though this was something he did frequently. Tommy shrugged his shoulders. Jordan stared down each one of them, daring anyone to ask any questions.

"Alright. Go home. We had a good night here tonight. Be back tomorrow, ready for a busy weekend. We'll be closed on Monday. So that should give you all plenty of time to prep whatever it is you need to."

Grabbing her things, Remy left saying nothing to anyone else. She wasn't sure if she should go to Lily's now, or go straight home. Either way, she faced a dilemma and no chance of turning back.

Chapter Sixteen

As long as you behaved and didn't act like an ass, you were always welcome at the Blue Pelican. Walk into any bar in any town, and you'd find them, the regulars, the bar-flys, the "Cliff and Norm of Cheers". Call them what you will, they were always present. The Blue Pelican was no different. Most of the clientele were the folks always in their regular seats, no matter the band playing and no matter the weather. Short of a hurricane blowing through, they were there. On the off chance a hurricane was coming, they were probably showing up to help board up the windows and then have a hurricane party. Just another one of the odd traditions in New Orleans, throwing a party when a life-threatening storm was approaching. And the drink named *the hurricane* - well, let's say you'd probably feel better after surviving the lashing of wind and rain of a category 3 storm than you would after one or more of those drinks.

At the end of the bar sat Brendan and Colin, occupying their usual seats. God help anyone who stumbled in and sat on one of their stools. They really should have brass plaques mounted on the bar with their names etched in fancy script, at least then people would know not to sit there or risk their wrath. All in all, they really were gentle souls, a little rough around the edges. They'd come in after work, and stay until closing time, and yet somehow walk out on their own every night.

Aidan, another regular, was a local cop. Remy always felt a little safer whenever he was around. The bouncers were great guys, but they only had so much they could do within the law when it came to rowdy customers. At least Aidan had the authority to actually arrest someone, or even threaten arrest, causing most people to back down and behave.

As she came up to the bar to place another order, Remy heard Aidan sharing another one of his work stories. "Yeah, it's kind of jacked up the way it works. It's no wonder they never get caught."

The quizzical look on her face gave away the fact she was eavesdropping. Turning her way, he explained, "I was telling Mike about the latest bank robbery. Last week, these guys walked into a bank over in Metairie. They handed both tellers a note demanding whatever they had on hand. As per the rules, the tellers comply. These two guys walk out, get into the waiting car and take off. Now here's where it gets ridiculous."

Remy interrupted, "Can you hold that thought for a minute? These drinks won't deliver themselves, and I really want to hear how this turns out."

Shrugging, he takes a sip of his beer and nods that he'll wait. It doesn't take her long to deliver the order and come back with three more. Aidan picks right back up where he left off.

"So the tellers, adhering to the directive they have to follow, now have to wait until the schmucks are gone. Then they can get the manager to call it in to the main office." Noting the look of disbelief on both Mike and Remy's faces, he continues. "Before you ask, this is bank policy, definitely not what we would recommend. According to this policy, they have to call the main office first. Then the main office puts in a call to the local police department. By which time, these guys are on a plane to the islands or somewhere lost in the swamps where we can't find them. Yeah, there's surveillance tape, so we have a grainy image of what they look like, but all we can do now is set up around town, hoping maybe to catch a glimpse of one of the guys, and pick him up on suspicion of being the bank robber and possibly busting him for something else."

As he finished, Mike returned with her latest round of orders. "Crazy. I'm in the wrong business," Remy declared. "Basically, you're telling me that if I want to commit the perfect crime, it would be to rob a bank? What do you think, Mike? You want to go in on this together?"

Mike laughed as Aidan finished his beer and only replied with a grin, "I heard nuthin."

Walking away, Remy was certain he had to be talking about the robbery she had taken part in. While she was relieved to hear she and Lilly weren't suspects, she wondered if they were on the surveillance tape too. Aidan hadn't mentioned anything about anyone else being in the bank, but was he holding back, to see what her reaction was?

Returning to the bar, she turned back to Aidan with an idea of how she might get more information.

"Did they mention anything about witnesses?"

"Oh sure. The manager had been busy with another customer, but aside from that, no one else was there. Why do you ask?"

"I think I might have been there. I was with a friend who was trying to set up a safe deposit box, and the manager was helping her. We must have been in the vault when it happened because I don't remember seeing any of this. But when we came back to the manager's desk, a teller came over. She seemed a bit nervous, like she wasn't sure what to do with us still being there. The manager thanked us for our business, and we started to leave since we were done. But now that I'm thinking about it, as we were walking out I thought I heard him shout something about the main office was going to be pissed. I honestly had no idea though any of this took place."

"Did you go to the cops?" Aidan asked.

"Why would I?" Remy shrugged, trying to play it cool.

Shaking his head, Aidan agreed. "Yeah, guess you wouldn't have any reason to. You sure you or your friend didn't see or hear anything?"

"No. I wish we had. She was busy filling out paperwork, and I was sitting next to her, holding the bag with her grandmother's papers and jewelry. Then we went back to the vault, put the stuff away, came back out, she signed something else, and that's when we left."

"Alright. Well listen, if you think of anything, reach out to me, will ya?"

Remy agreed, picking up her next round of drinks and

winding her way back to the waiting tables. She knew she'd have to talk to Lily and Theo about this. But should she say something to Jordan too? How would she explain her relationship with someone in local law enforcement? She was sure he wouldn't be happy to hear that.

Dropping off the last drink, the gentleman sitting by himself paid and gave her a handsome tip.

"Thank you. Um, sorry, I didn't get your name," he said as he handed her the money.

"Remy. And thank you. I appreciate this," she smiled.

"Of course. I'm Rick. Nice to meet you. This is my first time here. It's a nice little place. Wish I had known about it sooner."

"You must be new to the area. It's been around forever."

"Something like that," Rick replied noncommittally.

"Well, welcome to the Blue Pelican. It's not much, but we like it here. Come back again and you'll be considered one of the regulars, just like those guys at the bar," she indicated with a tip of her head.

"I'll just have to do that. Thanks again," he said with a grin.

Turning her attention to another table, Remy found herself overcome with an odd sense of familiarity. Unable to place where she knew him from, but something about Rick reminded her a little bit of her dad. Well, at least the memories she had of him. But those were from years ago, before he disappeared again. The last time she asked her mom about him, her mother told her he had left New Orleans and she was guessing he was probably dead. Whether or not he was, she couldn't fathom a reason he would show up here under a false name. No, it must be one of those doppelgänger moments where you meet someone who is eerily like someone else you know.

Returning her thoughts to what was more pressing, she ducked into the back and used the payphone to place a quick call to Lily. Briefly explaining what she had learned, they agreed it would be best to tell Marcus the next night at work. Let him deliver the news and suffer the tirade Jordan was sure to throw.

Chapter Seventeen

Fortunately, for all concerned, it was quiet at the Carrington when Remy arrived for work. The only party on the reservation books wouldn't be coming in until later, and the stormy weather rolling in seemed to keep everyone else away for the moment.

Finding Lily in the staff room, she gave her the rest of the details she had learned from Aidan, and they agreed Marcus should be the one to hear it first.

"But I also have to tell you something else," Lily whispered to Remy. "Earlier today, Jordan called me at home. He was asking whether you had told me anything about your trip. And he was also fishing for more information about Matt. Like I would have any idea about the guy. But long story short, he's wanting you to get some er, financial information for him."

"What kind of financial information? And from who? Matt? Why would he think I'd have access to anything relating to his business? We've only been on two dates, really. I mean, yeah, he flew me to New York for dinner.

And it was great and all. But are you asking me to do what I think you are? You want me to run a con on him?"

"Not me. This is coming from Jordan. He thought you'd take it better if I suggested it. I'm sorry. I don't like being in the middle like this. Honestly, if I were you, I wouldn't. But with what he's got hanging over our heads now, I don't think you have a choice. Even if he doesn't go to the cops, he could just as easily tell Matt and ruin any chance of you having a relationship with him."

"Sure. But if he did that, then he kills the chances of getting whatever it is he wants out of this. Really, how does he expect me to do this? And in what time frame? It's not like we're living together or even in a serious relationship."

Lily looked dejected as she sighed. "I have no idea. Honestly, I just want to be done with it all. Theo is so stressed out lately, he's not sleeping. I can hardly eat. Every time I think about what we did, and well, all the other stuff in the past… I want to not do this anymore. But I also see no way out."

Slamming the cupboard shut, Remy looked around, making sure no one else heard what she was about to say. "Here's a thought. Maybe we don't say anything to Marcus. Maybe this is our ace to hold on to until the time is right. Or maybe we go to Aidan and tell him you saw something after all, and we give him just enough information so they can investigate further. Or maybe Theo steps up and, oh, hell. It is a lot of maybes. But…"

Throughout the evening, Remy and Lily exchanged glances, each one trying to decide what the next best step would be. At the end of the night as they were cashing out, Remy had an idea. Leaning over to Lily, she said in a low voice, "Don't say anything to anyone for now. I'll play along and see what I can get out of Matt. Though I won't try very hard either. But this way you can tell Jordan you told me and I agreed. If he thinks we're doing what we're told, then maybe he'll let his guard down. In the meantime, it will give us more time to figure out what to do next with the information we have."

Lily scrunched up her face as though she had sucked on a lemon and barely nodded. "I don't like it, but okay." Her only response before she walked away, leaving Remy alone at the bar.

'Huh. Not the reaction I was expecting,' Remy thought to herself. 'I'm starting to wonder if she's simply putting on an act for my benefit and maybe I'm the one being conned here.'

Before giving herself a chance to wallow in these thoughts anymore, she handed over her money to Kenny and said her goodnights. She would have to come up with a contingency plan of her own if this all went sideways for her.

Arriving back at her apartment, she found a bouquet and a note outside her apartment door. Opening the envelope, she found a handwritten note from Matt.

Remy,

I hope you've had some time to rest after our excursion and dinner. I also hope that I didn't scare you off either. I had such a wonderful time and really would love to see you again. I will be out of town for the next two weeks, finishing up the final details at the West Coast office. But when I return, I'd love to make plans to take you on the trip to Jackson Hole I mentioned the first night we met. All you need to do is say yes, and bring yourself. Everything else will be taken care of. Give me a call and let me know what you decide.

~ Matt

SHAKING HER HEAD IN DISBELIEF, she couldn't believe how fast he was moving. He barely knew her, and yet here he was inviting her on an all expense paid trip to go skiing, something else she'd never done before, somewhere she's also never been. If anyone was counting, this would only be their second or third date, if you counted the meal at the diner as a date.

Lying down in her bed, her mind was racing with thoughts of all the events that had taken place since she first met Matt, which in part had been because of her meeting Jordan in that boutique. Fate certainly was being a little troublemaker right now, and she was left wondering if she should get out while she could, before she found herself getting in too deep.

Chapter Eighteen

After having met Remy at the Blue Pelican under the guise of the newcomer Rick, Frank returned the next night. When he asked about her, Mike told him she only worked one night a week, more for the fun of it than the money, since she now had a regular job over at some exclusive members-only club in the Quarter. Trying not to press and raise suspicions, Frank didn't ask what the name of the place was. It was probably best he found another way. The last thing he wanted was for news of his asking probing questions to get back to her. As far as she knew, he was just another customer, and not her long-lost father.

Frank had moved back to New Orleans the month before while still keeping his house in Indian Springs, Nevada. In the past years, he spent most of his time traveling the country, keeping tabs on both her and his nephew, Neil. He was proud of both of them, and how far they had come in their lives. Neil had chased his dream of musical stardom and found success. Twenty-plus years after signing his first record contract, he was still writing music and playing sold-out shows. Following the route of his latest tour had been one thing Frank had really enjoyed. Though Neil was never aware he was out in the crowd, Frank always made sure to document the occasion with a picture of himself under the venue sign. Someday he hoped he could share these with Neil, but first he had to set things right with his daughter, Remy.

Unlike his brother and other family members she grew up around, he had not been a stable presence in her life. Having left New Orleans for Las Vegas when she was little, he returned after she started middle school. They reconnected, much to the chagrin of her mother, and had a complicated relationship for a few years. Whenever she asked, he was always vague about what he had done in Las Vegas and any supposed involvement he had with the theft of Marilyn Monroe's diamond necklace. But the one thing they did bond over was the love of music. When she was barely sixteen, he snuck her in to see her cousin Neil play a show at a club on Bourbon Street. Having managed to get her backstage, introductions were made, and this was a chance for Frank to reconnect with Neil too. Their time together was short-lived, as Neil was back on the road, and Remy returned to her teenage life.

Frank continued to drift in and out of her life until a year after she graduated high school, when he caught wind of the fact that some of the Costa family members were being released from jail. Nick Costa, the head of the family, was still in jail and would be for the rest of his life. But

Michael Leon, Nick's second in command after Frank's betrayal, had been released. Frank couldn't be sure, but he had heard rumors that Michael had been seen in New Orleans asking people about Frank's whereabouts. Deciding it was best for the safety of both him and his family, he left town again. This time with no forwarding address, no indication of where he was going or if he would return.

He knew Remy would be dismayed, and her mother would simply say, I told you so. He hated leaving without a proper goodbye or explanation, but it was best for everyone in order to keep them safe. But now that he was back, he found himself more concerned about Remy's well-being than he ever had been before. From what little he had gleaned, he found out she was running her own cons. Most were successful, albeit small time. At least she hadn't been caught yet, and that was most important.

After his latest visit to the Blue Pelican, he spent the next week visiting various clubs in the Quarter and the Garden District, when he found out by sheer coincidence she was working at the Carrington Club. A friend of a friend shared he knew someone who was a member who mentioned her by name. Not being familiar with it or who owned it, Frank knew he couldn't try to walk in off the street. Members only places like this, you either had to go as someone's guest, or you had to be invited to visit as a potential member. A visit to the city clerk's office told him the Carrington had only been around for a couple of years. The new owner had taken over the space of another members-only place, which had closed due to mismanagement. At least, that was the public story. When he tapped into his network of people who knew the behind-the-scenes details, he found out the previous owners were shut down for tax evasion, and not paying off the right people at the right time. The new owner, one Jordan DuBois, was a transplant to the Crescent City. Not much information existed regarding who he was or where he came from, which raised more red flags for Frank. It was bad enough for an outsider to come into his city and try to take over a piece of its history. But not being able to find out details about who he was, set off alarm bells. Somehow, he was going to have to get in. But how remained the question for the moment.

Deciding to drop in at the Blue Pelican the following Monday when he knew Remy would be working, he took a seat at the bar, doing his best to blend in with the rest of the patrons. Not wanting to risk her spotting him, he kept a baseball hat on, pulled low, with his shoulders hunched, nursing a beer. He was close enough to the waitress station to overhear conversations between her, the bartender, and the regulars.

His attention was drawn away from her and further into a conversation off to his left when he heard a couple mention an upcoming party they were to attend at the Carrington. Casually inserting himself into the conversation, he introduced himself. "Pardon the intrusion. I'm new to town, only been here a couple months now, but did I hear you mention the Carrington Club?"

The gentleman turned, stuck out his hand in greeting, and replied. "Hello. Yes. We've never been before. My girlfriend here got invited to some work event they're hosting. Why do you ask?"

"My apologies. My name is Rick. I wasn't meaning to intrude. When you mentioned that place, my ears perked up. I think I may know someone who works there, but haven't been able to get in touch with them. It's been a few years since we last spoke, and I don't have their current contact information. As it's a private club, I haven't been able to get in either. You mentioning it struck me as a lucky chance that I couldn't pass up. Not to be too bold, but any chance I might tag along?"

"Rick. Nice to meet you. I'm Alan, and this is Delilah. It's a private event for Delilah's company and its clients. I'm not sure we can bring anyone else who's not on the guest list."

"Of course. I understand. I thought I'd try. If you don't mind my asking, what sort of business is it that you work for, Delilah?"

Delilah leaned over, replying, "I work for an investment firm, Crescent City Brokers. One of the partners, George Collins, wants us to wine and dine some of our bigger clients. Not something I normally get to do, but I recently landed one of the bigger ones, so lucked out and got an invite."

Frank nodded, sipping his beer, not wanting to appear too interested, but thinking of how to use this to his advantage.

"Ah, I see. Well, thank you. I appreciate you taking the time to talk to me. I guess I'll just have to find another way to get in touch with this friend."

"Oh, sure. Sorry we weren't more help. I hope it works out for you." She drawled, turning her attention back to her drink and her boyfriend.

Slapping a five dollar bill on the bar, Frank nodded to Mike and the couple next to him as he made his way back towards the front door. Stepping out into the early evening air, a plan started to form in his mind of how he might get himself invited to this upcoming party.

Chapter Nineteen

Two and a half weeks after receiving the flowers and note from Matt, Remy found herself back on Matt's private plane, their destination a long weekend ski trip to Jackson Hole. As promised in the note, all she had to do was show up, and everything else was packed and waiting for her. All the clothes and equipment, he assured her, were already tucked in the luggage compartment, and she would get to see everything once they landed and settled in at the lodge.

Looking around at the luxury she found herself in again, she still couldn't help but gawk a little bit. While she had been to some high-class places, and had worn some fine jewels, this was next level comfort she didn't think she would ever get used to.

Matt reintroduced her to the pilot, first officer, and flight crew from their last flight, telling her, "I've flown with this group more times than I can count. We're in expert hands here. Anything you want, you just ask."

Putting his arm around her waist, he guided her back to

two seats, this time replete with pillows, blankets, an eye mask, and a table set with drinks and finger foods.

"Matt, this is too much," Remy drawled. "I mean, it's not like we're flying around the globe. The flight can't be that long."

"Around three and a half hours, depending on if we catch the wind right. But at least for the time being, we can enjoy ourselves," he said as he waved his hand around the cabin. "Now, settle in, buckle up, and we'll be on our way."

The flight time passed quickly. The crew were discreet and kept out of the way for most of the trip. On one occasion, the pilot came out and asked if Remy would like to sit in his seat and see the view from there. Following him into the cockpit, she sat down, amazed by all the controls, which she made sure to keep her hands far away from. Looking through the windshield at the stunning view of the countryside below them differed completely from the view she saw out of the small airplane windows.

Walking back to her seat, she pinched herself as a reminder of what her true intentions were supposed to be. She knew she shouldn't allow herself to fall any deeper into this relationship, as much as she wanted to. This was a make or break moment where she was faced with having to make the hard decision. While she had initially agreed in theory to get the information Jordan wanted, she was still having second and third thoughts, wondering if she should cut ties now and admit her failure to all involved.

Touching down in Jackson Hole, a chauffeur met them on the tarmac with a four-wheel-drive vehicle that would transport them to the lodge where they were staying. Taking in the surroundings, Remy turned to Matt and smiled. "Thank you. This is already an amazing weekend, and it's only getting started."

Over the course of the weekend, Remy and Matt spent their time skiing, eating, enjoying a relaxing massage and soak in a private hot tub, and leaving all the cares of what was going on in New Orleans and the world behind them. Only once did Matt take a call from his secretary, Ella, where she overhead him repeat an account number twice. Whether this was the specific account Jordan wanted the number for, she didn't know. But she kept repeating it over and over in her head until she could discreetly write it down on a piece of the lodge stationery and tuck it into the pocket of one of the suitcases. Somehow she was going to need to find a way to separate herself from him and call Jordan to give him this information before they returned to New Orleans.

After a leisurely run on the slopes, Remy found her chance when Matt suggested an afternoon cocktail and bite to eat. Suggesting he get them a table while she freshened up, she returned to the room where she placed a quick call, leaving a message with Marcus, detailing what she had found out.

"We won't be back until Monday night, so Jordan should have time to get whatever he needs to do, done. Matt mentioned he won't be back in the office until late Tuesday morning, and I'm sure he'll be swamped with whatever he missed these past few days. Hopefully, he or Ella won't detect anything amiss for a day or two if we're lucky."

Hanging up the phone, she had a moment of panic, questioning what she had just done. Knowing she couldn't stay in the room any longer she returned to where she had left Matt, only to find him settled into an overstuffed leather chair by the fireplace, Remy sat down next to him with a sigh.

"Everything okay?" he asked.

"More than okay. I can't tell you how much I've enjoyed this. It's exactly what I needed."

"I'm so glad. As I said before, I'm not expecting that you feel the same way, but I have to tell you, Remy, I know it's been fast, but I think I'm falling in love with you."

Biting her lip, Remy tried to control the storm of emotions that suddenly surged inside of her. "I, um…"

"Don't say anything. I just had to tell you that. I don't want you to feel you have to say anything in return you're not ready to say." Matt said, taking her hand in his. "Now, sit back, enjoy the drink; food is on the way."

Trying to settle further into her seat, Remy turned her head away from Matt, fearing if she looked at him, he would discover her secret and what she had done.

When the weekend came to an end, Matt and a bellhop took their bags down to the waiting car, while Remy finished getting ready. Joining him shortly after, she sat in her seat as they began the drive back to the airport. Sad to see the weekend ending, they were both quiet. Matt read over a few phone messages the desk staff had given him before leaving, while Remy stared out the window, watching the vast scenery speed by.

Boarding the plane, the crew welcomed them back, warning of some possible turbulence ahead. "It looks like we're going to be flying through some storms. Should be cleared up though by the time we land," the pilot told them before takeoff.

Knowing what she had done and what she would soon face at home, Remy wondered if this was an omen of the upheaval that she would soon be experiencing.

Arriving back in New Orleans, they touched down smoothly, taxiing to the hangar. Stepping off the plane, Remy was accosted by the humidity hanging in the air. Feeling as though all the breath was being pushed from her lungs, she grabbed hold of the stair railing as she came off the last step.

"Everything okay?" Matt asked, coming to her side.

"Fine. Just had a moment where I couldn't breathe. Guess I got used to the clean mountain air we've been experiencing. This all feels a little bit much now."

Guiding her to his car, Matt opened the passenger door and waited until she was inside.

"Give me a moment to get your suitcase, and then I'll take you home."

As Remy sat, waiting for him to return, she remembered the paper she had written the account number down on was still in the front pocket of her suitcase. Had she stuffed it down far enough so he wouldn't find it when he put the bag in the trunk? Her heart started beating staccato as sweat beaded on her neck. Seeing him stalking back towards the car, her thoughts turned to the worst case imaginable, when her door flung open. Waving a piece of paper in her face, Matt grabbed her arm, pulling her out of the seat.

"What is this?" he demanded.

"I, I can explain," Remy stammered.

"I think you better. What are you doing with one of my accounts written down and shoved in the pocket of your suitcase? Are you trying to fleece me? Do you honestly think you'll get away with this? No, you know what, never mind. Don't try to explain." Matt's face flushed red, a vein bulging in his neck. Reaching into the car, he grabbed her purse from the seat and threw it at her. "I can't believe I thought that maybe we could have something together. That after I told you how I felt that maybe you were starting to care about me, even if only a little bit. I guess I was wrong."

Storming back to the driver's side of the car, he got in. Giving her one last look, he put down his window far enough to shout at her. "You can walk your long legs right out of my life!" The car's tires squealed and smoked as he sped away.

Left standing in the hangar, her purse at her feet, Remy looked around to see the staff averting their eyes. Knowing she'd get no help from anyone there, she slowly made her way to the terminal to find a taxi to take her home.

Arriving back at her apartment, Remy dragged herself in through the door. Not turning on any lights, she walked to the kitchen, grabbed a bottle of wine from the refrigerator and a glass from the drain rack, before walking out onto her balcony. Sliding down into the chair, she uncorked the wine, poured a large glass and drank half of it down in one gulp.

She had thought she would have had a little more time before he found out what she did, at least until the following day. In hindsight, it was foolish of her to leave the paper where she did. Had she just burned it in the fireplace when she hung up from the call with Marcus, none of this would have happened. But at the same time, it didn't surprise her it all fell apart as quickly as it had. Matt had been clear from the beginning about his trust issues, and she took no time in breaking his trust and his heart.

For a moment she considered calling Jordan to tell him what had taken place, but instead decided to let him find out on his own. This was just another thing that he had gotten her mixed up in, and she would not be the only one to take the blame. She was sure she would be getting a call from the police tomorrow, if not sooner. Knowing that's what she deserved, she drank the rest of her glass of wine, then poured another, as she sat and watched the traffic on the street below.

After finishing her second glass, she decided that was enough to drink and made her way back into her apartment. Walking into the bedroom, she laid down, taking only enough time to kick off her shoes before she passed out.

Chapter Twenty

When she woke the following morning, the first thing she did was check her answering machine for messages. Finding none, she glanced at the clock, surprised to find it was just after eleven. She had been sure she would have heard from either the police or maybe even someone from Matt's office by that point. But no calls, no notes slipped under her door. No indication of anything out of the ordinary.

After taking a shower and getting dressed, she took her time getting ready for the day. Checking the kitchen, she noticed she was out of most breakfast items. Breakfast at the cafe down the street for a quick bite would be her first order of business. Grocery shopping would have to wait a little longer.

As she came out her front door, she saw a pickup truck parked across the street, when a fleeting thought of having seen it before she left on her trip crossed her mind. The only reason it stuck out to her then was the way it had been awkwardly parked. Just as it was now. As though they pulled in only to be able to leave in a hurry. Surely traffic control would be by to give them a ticket if it persisted, so she didn't give it another thought.

Coming back home from her lunch and grocery run, she noted the truck was gone. 'Guess it must have been someone who stopped for a quick errand or delivery,' she thought to herself.

On edge most of the day, she unpacked her groceries and took time getting ready for work that night. Still no calls or visits from the police left her wondering why not. Surely Matt or someone at his office would have reported what she had done by now. Perhaps Jordan hadn't had the chance to do anything with the information and Matt's accounts were all still intact. That was the only reason she could conceive for him not pointing a finger at her. Whether or not she liked it, it was now time to face Jordan and find out where things stood.

Arriving at work, she walked straight to Jordan's office, and knocked hesitantly, waiting until he called out for her to come in. Once inside, she stopped and stood in front of his desk, waiting.

"Remy, nice to see you back. I'm guessing you had a good time on your little trip?" The sarcasm dripping from Jordan's tone was unmistakable.

"It was very nice. Thanks for asking," Remy replied, waiting for him to lead the conversation rather than volunteering any information.

"Uh huh. Sure. Well, the account number you got for me didn't do us any good. It would seem the account was closed before we could gain access. Any idea as to how that happened?"

Remy stood still, considering what he had said. Unable to piece together how that had happened so quickly when Matt had only confronted her about it the previous night. Had he found out sooner and kept his cool the entire day and flight home? Was he better at hiding things than she gave him credit for?

"I have no idea what happened. Maybe it was set to be closed before I got the information? I mean, I guess that could have been what the phone conversation I overhead was about. He did repeat the number a couple of times."

"Well, regardless of if it was to be closed or not, I'm going to need you to spend a little more time with Matt and try to gain access to another one, some other way."

Shuffling her feet, head hanging down, she looked back up at him and said, "I don't think that's going to be possible."

"What do you mean?" Jordan growled.

"I mean, Matt ended things with me last night. Just after we landed, as we were about to leave the airport, he confronted me about finding the paper I had written the number down on and essentially left me stranded."

Before she finished, Jordan exploded. "He found the paper? Just how stupid are you? Never mind. Don't answer that. Get out. Go home. Take the next couple of nights off." Pushing back from his desk, he rose. Sensing it wouldn't do her any good to say anything more, Remy turned and rushed out of the office and the club.

Choosing to walk around the neighborhood first before returning to her car, she wondered if the life she was leading was really best for her now. Even though she hadn't admitted it to him, she had found herself falling hard for

Matt and was devastated by the hurt she had caused him. Unlike any of the other guys she conned in the past, he was different. He had been a gentleman, always taking her thoughts and feelings into consideration when making decisions affecting the two of them. He had lavished her with trips and gifts she knew she didn't deserve. Unlike any other man in her life, he was genuine.

Maybe now was the time to cut ties with the Carrington and these cons she found herself mixed up in. Even with Jordan's threats hanging over her head. She could move back in with her mom, take care of her when needed and possibly even go back to school. Find a respectable career to pursue, settle down, have kids and a dog. Laughing at herself, she realized it was all a far-out dream. There was no way out of this. Not an easy way anyway.

Despite New Orleans being a large city, the community she had been involved with was well connected and would do their best to bring her down if she should betray them. The only way out was to leave New Orleans altogether, and that definitely was not an option right now.

Returning to get her car, she drove back to her apartment, where she saw that truck parked down the street. Once again it was parked at an odd angle, as though the operator didn't know how to drive. Surely they must be accumulating a trove of parking tickets. And how many times now had she seen it? It was never at the same time of the day, and she had no idea how long it had been parked. There had been one day, right before this last trip with Matt, she thought it was following her, but then he turned off down another street, only to catch up with her again a few blocks away. Was it intentional? Trying to make her think he wasn't following her? Or was it just another coincidence? Who was she kidding? She didn't believe in coincidences. She'd keep an eye on whoever it was, not sure who they were yet, or who they might be working for. But she had to watch her back from here on out.

Chapter Twenty-One

After being off work for two days, Remy was surprised to get a call from Marcus telling her she was needed that night. No other explanation or sign to say Jordan was no longer mad. Deciding she would play it cool, she dressed and showed up for work as though nothing had happened.

A few hours into her shift, she came up to the bar, setting her tray down in order to reset her order tablet and glass that held a small amount of bills for customers to make change if needed. Not seeing anyone behind the bar at first, she startled when Jordan stood up from behind the bar and said, "Remy, can I see you in my office when you have a minute, please."

"Sure. Let me ask Lily to cover my tables, and I'll be right back," Remy said with a note of hesitation hanging on the end of her reply. After his kicking her out the other night, she was reticent now, wondering what he was going to do or if he was going to try to rope her into something new.

Knocking on the door, she heard Jordan call out, "Come in". Entering, she found it the same as before, with no one else in the room, aside from him behind his desk and her standing in front of him.

"Please sit down. Make yourself comfortable. Take a minute to get off your feet. As it's been pretty busy tonight."

"Uh, thanks. I suppose it has been. But I'd rather be busy than stand around doing nothing. So I don't mind." Remy was trying not to ramble, but was finding it difficult to keep her thoughts straight.

"I'm sure you're wondering why I called you back here."

Nodding, Remy didn't trust herself to say anything, so she waited for Jordan to continue.

"First off, the bank job is in the clear. From what I've heard from my contacts, the cops have no idea who was involved. They don't suspect you or Lily either."

Letting out a slow breath, Remy nodded, still saying nothing, waiting for what was to come next.

"No, the reason I wanted to talk to you, is it has come to my attention you haven't been completely honest with me," Jordan said in an even tone as he leaned back in his seat, keeping his eyes on Remy, while waiting for a response.

Realizing she had to respond, she took a beat before saying, "I don't know what you mean."

Sitting straight up in his chair, he replied. "No, Remy, I think you do. Now, I know you weren't honest with me when we first met. You gave me a different name, and you were more than happy to take what I bought for you and use it to your advantage. But we've moved past that now. I know who you say you are, and what you've done before when it comes to conning men in our fair city. But what I'm referring to now is, you haven't been truthful with me about who your family is."

Now Remy was confused. What did her family have to do with anything? Jordan knew her mom was sick, since that's why she agreed so readily to this job. Was he be talking about her dad? But what did he have to do with anything as far as Jordan was concerned? He'd been gone for years.

Seeing she wasn't going to respond, Jordan leaned in closer. "Your father. Frank Batiste."

"Yes, that is or was my dad. But what does he have to do with anything? I have no idea if he's dead or alive."

"Stop playing games with me, Remy. You know who your dad is. Was. What he did all those years ago when he was working in Las Vegas."

Shaking her head, she looked at Jordan, trying to determine his angle and how he knew anything about her father's time in Las Vegas.

Deciding her best course of action was to play coy, she replied. "Yes, he worked in Las Vegas some years ago. He came back here after that, but I was still pretty young then. What little I heard about his time spent out there was he worked security for one of the casinos. He got to meet some famous people and reconnected with a cousin of mine. But that's it. Anything else you think I might know, I don't."

Jordan's fists clenched the edge of his desktop, as he glared at Remy. "Stop lying. One of those famous people he met was none other than Marilyn Monroe. I'm sure you've heard the story about how her diamond necklace went missing after she performed at the Crossroads Casino. The casino where your dad worked. He was a part of that. And I know you know where the missing diamonds are."

Remy sat back in her seat, her stomach now in knots, and her knee beginning to bounce rapidly. Trying to keep her composure, she started, stopped, and started again. "I, no, Jordan. No, I don't know anything about missing diamonds. Yeah, I heard a story about how he met Marilyn as part of his job. And I heard something about the missing necklace too. But as far as I know, he didn't have anything to do with that. The cops never charged him. If they thought he was involved, don't you think he'd have been in jail? And more importantly, do you really think I'd be working here if I had those missing diamonds? Shoot, if that were the case, my mom would be receiving the best medical care, and I'd be off on a beach somewhere enjoying life."

Taking a deep breath to steady herself, she stood, then continued. "I'm not sure I belong here anymore. If you believe what you do and won't take my word for it, then maybe it's best we each go our separate ways. I'll finish my shift tonight, you or Marcus can pay me out, and we'll never have to see each other again."

Jordan stared at her, the look in his eyes burning into her. "No, Remy, that's not going to happen. Even though I said we were in the clear, you see, there's still the evidence I have of this little thing at the bank you were involved with. And I'm sure if the cops were to find out, well they'd be at your door quicker than you can say bon ton roulet. So unless you want that to happen, and the result being no one around to take care of your sick mother, then you will keep working for me. And you will find out where the missing diamonds are and share that information with me. Do you understand?"

Backed into a corner with no possible way out of the situation at present, she sighed in agreement. "Fine. But I'm telling you, I don't know anything about the diamonds. If my dad did have them, he must've hidden them really well or taken them with him to wherever he wound up."

Jordan returned his attention to the ledger on his desk while waving his hand in dismissal, sending Remy back out to the floor. Knowing she was stuck, she would have to visit her mom tomorrow and see if there was anything she hadn't told Remy about missing diamonds and her dad's time in Las Vegas.

Chapter Twenty-Two

When Lily saw Remy coming out of Jordan's office, she tried to get her attention, but Remy passed her by, not saying anything to acknowledge that she had even seen her. Lily had overheard Marcus telling Remy that Jordan wanted to see her, and now she was left to wonder if she would be called in next.

When nothing more happened, she returned to the bar, and caught Theo's eye, raising her eyebrow in an unspoken question. He shrugged in response. 'Well, that's weird,' she thought. Picking up her tray, she made her way back to her assigned tables, checking in with all the customers, delivering drinks and settling tabs. The rest of the night went by without incident and no further interactions with Jordan or Marcus. Unsure what to make of it all, Lily shelved her questions for now until she and Theo got home and compared notes on what took place that evening.

"Hey Remy, do you want to stop by for a late bite?" Lily called out as she saw Remy putting on her coat.

"Thanks Lily. But I think I'm going to head home. I'm pretty tired tonight. Maybe another night though," Remy replied without enthusiasm.

"Sure. Go home and get some rest. I'll see you tomorrow," Lily said as she watched Remy hurry out the door. Turning to Theo, she asked, "You ready?"

"Yeah, let's get out of here," he said as he placed his hand on the small of her back, leading her to the door. Leaning closer to her ear, he continued, "We've got a lot to discuss and some decisions needing to be made. It's probably best she didn't come over tonight."

Lily looked up at him with a question in her eyes. Theo shook his head as if to say, wait until we're home. Saying their goodnights to Marcus and Jordan, they quickly left, making their way out into the late night air.

"Don't say anything until we're home," Theo muttered. "We've got company."

Lily tried to glance over her shoulder, but couldn't see who might be following them. The late-night crowd was still spilling out onto the sidewalk. While it wouldn't give them enough privacy to have a conversation, it certainly would make it easier for someone to follow without being obvious.

Reaching their apartment, Lily dropped her purse and jacket by the door, making her way to the bedroom where she changed out of her work clothes. Theo double checked the locks, then wandered around the apartment, raising windows to let the night breeze in while looking outside for anyone who may be lurking. Making his way back to the bedroom, he sat on the edge of the bed, turning his head towards Lily.

"Something is definitely going on, Lily. I'm not privy to all the details about what Jordan's up to, but I'm not liking it. I know we talked before about getting out of here sooner rather than later. But now, I'm not so sure if we're going to be able to do that at all."

Lily, pulling a t-shirt over her head, agreed. "Any idea why Remy got called back into the office tonight? She seemed off the rest of the night after that. But wouldn't say anything to me about what happened either."

"I don't know. Both Jordan and Marcus were pretty tight-lipped all night."

"Hmmm…" Lily murmured.

Hearing a bang out on the balcony, Theo jumped up to go investigate, calling over his shoulder to Lily. "I don't know what's going on. But something is definitely up."

Opening the French doors, he looked around, not finding anything out of place. 'Must've just been the wind,' he thought to himself.

Returning to the bedroom, he found Lily shaking and crying, holding a crumpled piece of paper in her hand, with a large rock on the bed next to her.

"Lily? What's wrong? Where did that come from?" Theo demanded as he ran towards her.

"It, it was wrapped around this rock. Came through the window right after you walked out. How it didn't break the glass is beyond me. It's like someone was standing outside and just tossed it in," she stuttered.

Theo, taking the paper from her hand, read the typewritten words.

KEEP YOUR MOUTH SHUT. DON'T GO ASKING QUESTIONS YOU DON'T NEED TO KNOW THE ANSWERS TO.

"What the hell?" Theo shouted. "How? Who?" That must have been the noise he heard, a distraction created by someone outside, prompting him to leave the room before they made their move to scare him and Lily into silence.

Pulling Lily into a hug in an effort to calm her shaking nerves and his anger, Theo ran through everything he could think of since they first met Jordan. They hadn't really known much about him when they first met him and seemed to know little more now, even after all this time.

"Lily, what do you know about Remy's dad?"

"Uh, not much really. Remy and I were chatting one day when she mentioned the fact he had spent some time in Las Vegas. She really didn't say anything more. Nor does she really talk about him. I get the impression he wasn't around for much of her childhood. She talks more about her mom than anyone. Why?"

"I don't know. Something about it seems too coincidental, maybe? Do you think you could ask her more about him?"

"I guess I can try. I have to be careful, though. She seems to keep parts of her life pretty closed off. I know she was born and raised here. Her mom still lives in the house where Remy grew up. Aside from that, I don't know much else. But let me call her tomorrow and see if I can't get her to meet me. Maybe I can get her talking some more."

"I think that would be a good idea. We need to find out what's going on before we can make any plans to get out of here. I suspect Jordan is going to hold this bank job over all of our heads. We just have to not get involved in anything else he might decide to plan."

"Like that will be easy," Lily scoffed.

Theo nodded. "I don't know what else to do for now. I guess we keep our heads down and do our jobs. Come on, let's get some sleep. I think tomorrow is going to have even more in store for us."

Chapter Twenty-Three

"Mom, you here?" Remy called as she walked in the front door.

"Out in the backyard, le petite amie," she barely heard her mom say.

"What are you doing out here? This damp is not good for you. Not to mention the heat. You should be inside where it's comfortable, Momma."

"Now listen here, young lady. I'm fine out here. The doctor says I need to get out more. So, I'm out. You forget, I've spent more years in this climate than you have," her mother said, waving her hands around. "But that's not why you're here. Come sit down. Grab a glass of lemonade and tell me what's on your mind. Because I can see from clear over here, something's got you in a state."

Remy walked over, gave her mom a kiss on the cheek, poured a glass of lemonade and settled down into the glider across from her.

"Oh, Momma, I'm not sure where to begin. Life has gotten kind of out of my control lately. And, well, crap."

"What is it? You can tell me anything," her mom said, looking at her with concern in her eyes and on her face. Even with the silk headscarf covering her forehead, Remy saw the worry lines forming.

Remy knew she shouldn't be here, burdening her mother with all this. She should find a way to deal with it on her own. Her mother's health was fragile at best, and this added worry would only burden her more.

"No, it's nothing. I shouldn't have brought it up."

"Remy Francine Thibodeaux Batiste, I am still your mother. And I know something is bothering you. You didn't come all this way just to have a glass of lemonade with me. Now, tell me what's going on."

Curling her legs up under herself, Remy took another sip before telling her mother what transpired with Jordan the night before.

"Is there any truth to this? Did Daddy really have something to do with the theft of the necklace? And if so, where are the diamonds? I mean, surely if he had them, we would have found them by now, right?"

"Remy, darling. There's a lot you don't know about your dad. I suppose I should have told you long ago. But I didn't want to ruin your idea of him. Even though he wasn't around much, you still idolized him. And well, I couldn't be the one to destroy the image you had built up."

"What do you mean? Are you telling me that it's true? But then who is Jordan to him? And how does he know about all this?"

"That I don't know. I've never heard your dad mention that name before. Before he disappeared this last time, some guy he had been mixed up with had been released from jail sooner than he ever expected them to be. I think that's one reason why he's not around now. He's trying to keep us safe. But now with what you're telling me, it sounds like that isn't the case either."

Vanessa Thibodeaux Batiste picked up her glass, took a small sip, before carefully setting it back down again. Remy saw her mom's hand shaking, but wasn't sure if it was because of her illness or if the conversation they were having caused it.

"In the back of the guest room closet is an old hatbox. Go get it, bring it back out here, and I'll tell you the rest of the story."

Walking through the house, Remy wondered what her parents had been keeping secret all these years. Surely her father wasn't mixed up in organized crime. She knew he had done some illegal things in the past, but something to this degree was beyond what she wanted to believe about him. Then again, maybe that's where her con artist skills came from. Were they hereditary? She laughed to herself. Finding the box tucked back in the corner of the closet shelf, she pulled it down, but didn't open it. She'd respect her mother and wait until they were together in order for her to tell whatever tale was about to unfold.

The screen door slamming behind her as she came back out onto the porch startled her mom from what appeared to be an impromptu nap.

"Sorry, Momma. Didn't mean to disturb you."

"No, mon cher, it's fine. I was just resting my eyes," her mom said, using the pet name she had for Remy when she was a little girl. "Sit down and open the box. I'll explain as we go through each of the things in there."

As Remy pulled the lid off the box, she found it stuffed with letters, newspaper clippings, a few poker chips with The Crossroads emblazoned across them, and another small envelope with her name on it. Picking it up, she felt something hard inside, but her mother stopped her from opening it.

"No. You need to wait a minute on that one. First, you need to hear some history."

Setting the envelope down on the table and the rest of the papers back in the box, Remy gave her mother her undivided attention.

"The time your dad spent in Las Vegas was pretty benign. He stared off at a rather shady place and then got out of there pretty quick too. He always told me there was a line he wouldn't cross, and that was physically hurting people. I have no reason to believe he didn't keep his word. When he found a place where he felt like he belonged that was the Crossroads Casino. Was he involved in the theft of the diamond necklace? If I had to guess, I'd say yes. He never confirmed it to me. But from what he did share about other thefts he was involved in while working there, it wouldn't be a stretch of the imagination. But this idea that he made off with the diamonds and hid them away somewhere, no. I don't think there's any truth in that. He did make a deal with law enforcement in order to avoid jail time. And yes, he did stage the accident to make it appear as though he died. He thought it was the only way to keep us safe and to get himself out from the criminal family he found himself tied up with."

Catching her breath, Vanessa looked off in the distance,

as if remembering another time and place. Continuing, she finished her tale.

"The envelope with your name on it has a key to a safe deposit box. What's in the box, or even where the box is, I have no idea. Your dad wasn't always forthcoming with details. And honestly, Remy, if I were you, I'd just forget about the whole thing. But you and your dogged determination, I know you won't. Especially now that you have your boss threatening you too. So, I will be honest and answer whatever questions you may have if I can. But anything more, I'm afraid you're on your own. Maybe reach out to your cousin Neil. I think he's still in Los Angeles, and I have a number for him somewhere. He knew your dad back then and may have some information I don't. But right now, I think I need to go lie down for a bit. This trip down memory lane has tired me out more than I thought it would. Take as much time as you need to go through the box. Take it home with you if you want. If not, that's fine too. Stick it back in the closet. It's been on the shelf all these years. A few more days or weeks isn't going to change the contents."

Vanessa stood and slowly made her way out, heading back towards her bedroom, before Remy had a chance to ask any questions. Now faced with sorting through years' worth of papers, letters, and more, she wondered if she shouldn't just put it all away and not think about it ever again. But as her mother pointed out, once she got a hold of an idea, she had a hard time letting go. Instead, she settled into her seat and began the search for clues and, hopefully, answers to all the questions she now had.

Chapter Twenty-Four

After the day spent with her mother and learning more about her dad, his family history, and the time he spent in Las Vegas, the more confused Remy found herself. Flipping the envelope containing the safe deposit key back and forth in her hands, she knew she had to find a good place to hide it. Maybe she should have left it at her momma's house. Shoved everything back in the box and turned her back on it all. Instead, she brought it home with her and left it to sit on the coffee table, where it continued to vex her.

Perhaps it was a good idea her mom suggested, to reach out to her cousin Neil, and see what other information he might have. It had been years since she had seen or talked to him. He still sent postcards from some of the more exotic places his tours had taken him. Despite the fact that she didn't usually respond, he did his best to maintain a relationship with her. She felt guilty now, knowing she was his only family left, both his mother and father dead and her dad who knows where. She wasn't sure if he had stayed in touch with the rest of the Batiste family, as she had lost touch with most of them too. From the stories she heard about Neil's mom, she was sorry she never met her aunt Celeste. Apparently, she was a force to be reckoned with and had been the keeper of the family history, which really would have been helpful right now.

Picking up the phone she dialed the last phone number she had for him. Surprised the number was still in service and she had reached his answering machine, she left a message.

"Hey Neil. This is your cousin Remy. Um, I'm not sure where you are at the moment. If you're on the road, or maybe you're home for a while? Anyway. Give me a call when you get a chance. I've got a couple of questions about Frank. I'm hoping you can answer. Okay, thanks. Bye."

Hanging up the phone, she wondered how long it would be before she'd hear from him. When it dawned on her that she hadn't left a phone number, she started to pick up the phone to call back, but then wondered if it was fate's way of telling her to let it go. If Neil couldn't get back in touch with her, then she couldn't get answers to the questions and life would go on as it had been.

Who was she kidding? Life was not going to be the same moving forward. She had Jordan and his threats hanging over her head. In addition to all these other unanswered questions. Resolved, she picked up the phone again, calling Neil back, expecting to get his machine again. Much to her surprise, he answered after the third ring.

"Hello."

"Neil. Hi. This is your cousin, Remy. Sorry to call back again so quickly."

"Remy, hey. I just got your message. But you didn't leave a number. I was hoping you'd call back," Neil laughed, putting Remy immediately at ease.

"Ha ha. Sorry about that. I'm terrible when it comes to leaving messages. Especially to someone I haven't talked to in years."

"Hey, we've both been busy with life, you know. So what's going on? You said you had questions about Frank. How can I help?" Neil asked.

No beating around the bush, she thought. "You must be busy, so I won't keep you too long. I was over at my momma's house the other day, and she pulled out an old box of stuff about Frank. Inside was a safe deposit box key, some newspaper clippings, and letters he had written. To me, her, and also to you." Swallowing a couple of times, she continued. "There was one letter in particular, addressed to you. And well…" she drawled out the well, trying to figure out how best to ask her next question.

When Neil interjected. "Oh. Yeah. I'm pretty sure I know the one you're talking about. I thought your dad had destroyed it. Seeing as how it had become irrelevant and possibly a bit incriminating too." Neil replied with a note of regret in his voice.

"Incriminating? Are you saying what I think you're saying? I thought it was just a joke, or a family legend," Remy exclaimed.

"You read it then? Right. It wasn't a joke. Do you have a few minutes? I don't think this is going to be a quick conversation."

"I have all day if that's what's necessary."

"I don't think it will take that long," Neil laughed before

continuing. "Do you have the letter with you by any chance?"

"Yeah. I wish I didn't, but Momma suggested I bring the box with all the papers home."

"Alright, I guess you may as well open it then. It will probably answer a lot of questions, and then I can fill in the blanks."

Picking up the envelope, Remy carefully pulled the letter out again

> Neil,
>
> If you're reading this, then I'm probably dead. I was hoping it wouldn't come to that. But as I told you when we were in Las Vegas, the Costa family is not one you want to be on the wrong side of.
>
> As you may have heard, yes, I was involved in the theft of Marilyn Monroe's diamond necklace. You may have also been told I went to the cops and shared with them everything I knew. That's a big part of why Nick and the rest of the guys were picked up and hopefully now serving long sentences. Also, Sharon wound up doing the right thing and turned state's evidence. I have no idea what's happened to her. As far as I know, she left town after she was done talking to the cops. At least I hope she has. For as much trouble as she caused you, it was unintentional, and she felt bad about it.

But if it weren't for her, we wouldn't have had the time together that we did.

Now, what I need you to do, if you're willing, is look in the back of your dresser. You'll find a small envelope taped to the back of the drawer. You may have also already found the other package in one of your socks. Keep that hidden for now. In fact, keep it hidden as long as you can. However, the envelope contains a safe deposit box key I want you to hold on to for Remy. She's too little to do anything with it now. But when she's old enough, give it to her. Or give it to her mom, Vanessa.

I'm sorry things turned out this way. I really thought the staged accident would be enough to thwart Nick and the guys. Guess that wasn't the case.

I love you, kid. Always have. And keep chasing that dream of yours. I have faith you're going to make it big one day. Just wish I had been around to see it happen. Instead, I'll be here in heaven with your mom and Grandpa Joe, cheering you on.

Love,
Frank

Holding the phone between her ear and shoulder, she set the letter back down on the table. Holding back a sob, she heard Neil ask if she was still there.

"Yeah. I'm here. I guess I need to open this other envelope and see what else is in there besides a key."

While Neil waited, Remy open the other letter and read.

> Dear Remy,
> I am so sorry for not being there to see you grow up. I'm sure you've become an amazing young woman and have a bright future ahead of you.
> Inside this envelope is a key to a safe deposit box in Indian Springs Nevada. There you will find an account in your name. Its contents includes a deed to a house out there, some other important papers and other things that I won't mention now but you'll understand why when you get there. You are the only one who has access to this box. When I set it up, the bank manager was under the impression I was a lawyer representing you. Since you were a minor, the only signature on file is mine. You'll need to present identification to prove who you are. But once you've done that, everything in the box is yours to do with what you like.
> I love you Remy and your mom too.
> Love,
> Dad

Finished reading, Remy swallowed back the tears and asked, "where the hell is Indian Springs Nevada?"

Chuckling in response, Neil told her about the drive he and Frank had taken around the town one day.

"It's not much of a place. At least it wasn't then. Back then, it was known for folks taking vacations to come watch the atomic testing in the desert. Now that's not a thing anymore. Though I think there might still be a military base out there. I'm sure the town has been built up since then too. But if you want, I've got a few days off. I can take a quick drive over."

"No, I couldn't ask you to do that. Besides, you wouldn't be able to get into the box or even know where the house is. And what am I even supposed to do with a house there? Shoot, it's been more than twenty years. Is it possible it's still standing?"

"Good question. Obviously, at least at that time, Frank wasn't dead, but he also didn't reach out to me to get that letter back. As to where he is now, your guess is as good as mine. Unless you've heard something?" Neil asked hopefully.

"No. Nothing. This is all so much. But let me ask you this. What was the package in your sock?"

"Oh, that. It was five small diamonds. I'm guessing they were from the necklace. I accidentally found it one day shortly after I moved to Los Angeles, and as soon as I saw what it was, I shoved it back in and haven't looked at it since. I didn't want to believe they were real and didn't even want to think about how they had gotten in there. I didn't suspect Frank at all. In fact, I wondered if the two guys who helped me move had been responsible. But that didn't make a lick of sense either. So I did my best to ignore it."

"Really?"

"I was so busy in those early days trying to make my way. And I didn't want to take a chance Mr. Costa or anyone else might find out. I mean, I never had a problem with him. But one guy he had working for him, Michael Leon, he was one to stay clear of. I heard he got out of jail a couple of years ago. If I had to guess, I'd say he's probably still searching for the diamonds."

"Do you know where he wound up?"

"No. I heard he was in Las Vegas for a while. But that was the last I heard. I can ask around, see if any of the guys from the Tru Tones might know."

"Thanks. I'd appreciate it. I don't know what to think right now. I guess I'm going to need to make a trip out to Nevada though."

"Hey, if you decide to come out this way, let me know. I'd love to meet up with you. Maybe spend a little time catching up over some better memories. Any help I can be, I'm here for you."

"Thanks, Neil. I don't know what to say. I'm so confused. But yeah. If I come out, I'll be sure to get in touch. Thanks for taking the time to talk today."

After saying their goodbyes and making promises to stay in touch regardless of what she decided to do, Remy sat back on the sofa and had a long cry. Everything she thought she knew about her dad was now in question. If he had been involved with the mob, what else could he have done?

And more importantly, who was this Michael Leon, and did he know about her? Did she have yet another reason to be worried now?

Chapter Twenty-Five

Remy paced back and forth, wondering what to do next. Now faced with yet more decisions to make, she was thankful to have the night off from the Carrington. In an effort to distract herself, she decided she'd go try to pick up a shift at the Blue Pelican this evening. Maybe it would help her forget everything she had just read and heard.

Arriving at work, she saw Mike already busy behind the bar. Aidan and the other guys were in their usual spots. Going into the kitchen, she dropped off her bag, grabbed an apron and headed to the bar to pick up her bank for the evening.

"Remy!" Aidan called out, echoed by Brendan and Colin.

Waving hi to them, she turned her attention back to Mike. "What's new this evening?" She asked as he counted out the cash and change into her waiting hand.

"Same old, same old. Though some guy was in here asking about you the other night. Said his name was

Rick, I think? Someone I need to keep an eye on for ya?"

"Huh. No. Just a customer from a few weeks ago. Guess I must've made a good impression on him. Did he say what he wanted?"

"Nope. He was asking if you were working. I mentioned you worked at some other swanky place most nights, but didn't give him the name. Didn't think you needed him coming around there looking for you too. If nothing else, at least here you've got a cop and these other clowns looking out for you," Mike laughed.

Hearing his profession referenced, Aidan leaned over. "Something I need to be aware of?" he asked.

"Dude. I swear you've got ears like a cat," Mike said, turning to him. "It was just some guy asking around after our girl here."

"You point him out to me if he comes back again and I'll get the message to him, loud and clear," Aidan said, sitting up straighter on the bar stool.

Remy laughed, shaking her head at both of them. "Guys, it's fine. He was harmless. And I can handle myself, thank you very much."

"Of course you can. But you know we're here for you. No matter what," Aidan said reassuringly.

"Actually, Aidan, I think maybe I could use your help with something. You got a minute to talk?" Remy asked, her tone turning more serious.

"Sure. Whatcha got on your mind?"

Unsure of how much information to share with him, after all he was still a cop, she asked if he knew of a way to find out about a cold case in another state. Not giving any details about it being the high-profile theft of a diamond necklace, she made up a story about a cousin who had been robbed while in Las Vegas.

"You could reach out to the police where it happened. But if it's a cold case, then I doubt they'd have much they could share. You want me to try to find out for you?"

"No, thanks. You're probably right. There's nothing that can be done about it now. I happened to be talking to him recently, and we were reminiscing. He shared a story with me I didn't know had happened to him and my dad. Thought maybe something might have turned up after all this time. But it was a long shot."

Sensing she was holding back, Aidan leaned in closer, his voice lowering so no one else would hear. "Is something going on you need some help with, Remy? You in some kind of trouble?"

Shaking her head no, she laughed nervously. "If there was, I'd be the first to tell you. No, really, everything is fine. It was just my curiosity getting the better of me."

"I'll take your word for it, for now. But if you need help, you know where to find me, right?"

"I do. Thank you Aidan. You're a sweetheart, despite what those other guys say," Remy laughed as she turned to grab a tray and get to work.

The rest of the night passed without incident. Rick, the mystery man, didn't come back in looking for her, and the other customers were the distraction she needed to clear her mind of everything else going on.

Returning home that night, she quickly showered and climbed into bed. Mulling over the past couple of days, she fell asleep, dreaming of bomb blasts in the desert, raining down diamonds instead of fallout and debris.

When she bolted awake from her vivid and definitely weird dreams, Remy tried to corral the thoughts that disrupted her sleep. Something about Jordan and Las Vegas kept ringing in her head. Knowing she wouldn't be sleeping anymore that night, she stumbled into the kitchen, flipped on the coffeepot, then sank down to the floor waiting for it to finish brewing.

Once able to pour the first cup, she wandered back into the living room, opened the doors to her minuscule balcony and looked out over the neighborhood. Taking the first scalding sip, the intensity of the dark roast cleared the cobwebs as she gave more consideration to what it was her thoughts and dreams were trying to show her. Jordan had to somehow be connected to the crime family her dad worked for in Las Vegas. That was the only logical explanation for why he knew so much about Frank and the necklace, and Frank being her dad. But was his name really Jordan Dubois? Or was it possible he was the guy Neil mentioned? Taking another large sip of the coffee, she found her train of thoughts now running straight down the track, one idea falling into place after the other.

"Ugh," she shouted in frustration, startling a pigeon strutting around on the balcony next door. 'Maybe Aidan could be helpful after all,' she thought. 'If I could somehow get him to run a background check on this guy who was released, that may answer a lot of questions. And maybe give me some leverage too.'

Walking back into the apartment, she glanced around, trying to decide if this really was the right course of action to be taking? It certainly would get her deeper into the family secrets and all the consequences that might result from finding answers.

Maybe instead of getting Aidan involved, she should take a few days off, travel out to Nevada and see what she found out there first. After all, if it's nothing more than a deed to a house in the safe deposit box, then that puts an end to all this speculation about the missing diamonds.

But what if she finds the diamonds too? Then what does she do? It's not like she could just walk into a jewelry store and say, "hey are you willing to buy these?" Even after all these years, someone would have to recognize the stones, right? But what if they were willing to buy them? No questions asked.

The train of thoughts that had been so linear suddenly took a wild turn and derailed. Now, ideas of what she could do with all the potential money started running wild. Get her mom the medical care she needs, making sure she was comfortable and well taken care of. Quit her job, change her name, travel the world. Leave all these small time con jobs behind.

Who was she kidding? If Jordan was in fact this guy Michael, and he still had connections to the mob, then she wouldn't be protected anywhere. How did her dad do it? How did he disappear off the face of the earth? She still wasn't convinced he was dead, despite all her mother said. Add into the mix what connections Lily and Theo had to all this? Were they part of this all along? Should she even trust sharing any of this with Lily? She really needed to talk to someone about this right now. But who?

Determining her best first step should be to contact

Diamond Masquerade

Aidan, she quickly dressed and made her way down to the precinct where she knew he worked. Under the pretense that this was related to her cousin, she said she had come across a name in some old letters and wondered if he might run a check on it. She promised she wasn't going to do anything illegal and wouldn't try to contact them. She wanted only to satisfy her curiosity, and hopefully it would help to answer some of her questions.

Aidan was skeptical at first, but agreed. "Listen, you can't tell anyone I did this for you. Understand? I could lose my job over this," he implored.

"I promise. I won't say a word. And thank you. I appreciate this so much." Remy said, sitting next to his desk, while he placed a call to the Las Vegas police department. While on hold, he also thumbed through the records they had locally. Coming across a liquor license for Jordan Dubois, he noted the connection to the Carrington Club. Turning to Remy, he quizzed her, "Isn't that your other job?"

Sheepishly she replied, "Yeah. I didn't think anyone at the Blue Pelican, well aside from Mike, knew about that."

Just then, someone came back on the line, returning Aidan's attention to the phone call. "I see. Yes. Thank you for your help. Much appreciated. If we can ever do anything for you here in New Orleans, please don't hesitate to reach out. Right. Bye."

Hanging up the phone, he turned to Remy, a deadly serious look on his face.

"Do you have any idea of the can of worms you just opened here?" he asked, not taking his eyes off her.

"What? Um, no," she stuttered.

"From what they told me, it appears Jordan Dubois, owner of the Carrington Club here in New Orleans, is a possible alias for Michael Leon of Las Vegas. He has extensive connections to the Costa family. One of the major crime families back in the early heyday of the Las Vegas strip. It seems he got out of jail a few years ago and, after some new trouble out there, he skipped town, and it looks like, he wound up here. Though why no one caught this when he applied for the liquor license is beyond me. Now, are you sure you don't want to tell me what's going on?"

Remy heaved a giant breath, shoulders slumping, as she slid down in her seat. Unsure of what to do next, she looked at Aidan and said, "I don't know. I found out some things about my dad, and well, it's just all so far out there. I don't have any proof of anything. It's all hearsay. Family legend, if you will. But based on what you told me, I think I need to go home and make some decisions."

"Are you in trouble, Remy? Do I need to put you in touch with a lawyer? Or a bodyguard?" Aidan asked, concern lacing his voice.

"That's sweet of you to offer. No, I'm okay. At least for now anyway. I promise if anything changes, you will be my first call." Remy stood, dusting her hands off on her jeans.

Aidan walked her to the door, giving her a side hug as he murmured, "Stay out of trouble."

Arriving back home, Remy sat down on her couch, picked up the hatbox and placed it on her lap, removing the lid and setting it to the side. Pulling out the letter to Neil, the safe deposit box key, and letters her dad had written her while she was in high school, she sat and read through them all again. Noting a couple of the postmarks were from

Indian Springs, it made more sense now. Realizing she'd have to go out there, she placed a call to Neil and filled him in on her plan.

She'd work tonight, act as though everything was normal. When she found herself chatting with Lily throughout their shift, she mentioned in passing that she was going to take a few days off, but didn't go into any detail about why.

Only at the end of the night did she tell Marcus she would need some time off to take care of her mother. She gave him the excuse that they were traveling to see a doctor in Baton Rouge for some new tests. If all went well, she'd be back for her shift Saturday night and was sorry she would have to miss the costume party on Friday. She had been looking forward to that ever since finding out about it.

Having kept her distance from Jordan all night, she breathed a sigh of relief when she clocked out and didn't find him at the bar where he could normally be found after closing. The last thing she wanted to think about right now was what might happen if things didn't go well. Or if Jordan caught wind of where she was really going.

Chapter Twenty-Six

Not wanting to raise any flags with Delilah at Crescent City Brokers, Frank, under the guise of Rick, set an appointment with another advisor in the office. Posing as a potential client with a copious amount of money he wanted to invest discreetly, he quickly gained an invitation to the upcoming costume party at the Carrington Club.

"Sorry for the short notice, but as a potential new account holder, I think this might be something you'd enjoy attending. A lot of our senior vice presidents will be there, along with some of our other top tier clients. This will give you an opportunity to meet with them and get a better feel for our company and how we take care of everyone, too," the advisor said in his sales pitch.

"Of course. That would be great. I appreciate the invitation. You said it's at the Carrington? I'm not familiar with that place," Frank said.

"It's a private club, quite strict with its membership. George Collins, one of our partners, is among the first members. Unfortunately, he's out of town. Otherwise, he'd be there too. But the club owner, Jordan Dubois, has promised to take excellent care of us. I expect it to be a top-notch party."

Hearing Remy's former stepfather mentioned a second time in relation to the brokerage, he was thankful George was going to be absent from the party. While they had only met twice before, the last thing he needed was for George to unwittingly blow his cover story. If George was going to be attending, Frank might have had to rethink his appearance.

"Fantastic. Well, I appreciate your time today, and look forward to the party Friday night then," Frank said as he gathered up his briefcase and paperwork before walking back out into the late afternoon. Putting on sunglasses to shield himself from the glare rising from the street and any potential prying eyes, he strode off with purpose before hailing a taxi, hoping to send anyone who may be following him off his tail.

He hadn't spotted anyone, but based on what he was finding out from other sources, he was sure it wouldn't be long before word got around that he was back in the city. As much as he wanted to reach out to Remy again, he had to make sure who Jordan was before he felt confident in his next steps.

As far as she still knew, he was some guy named Rick, and he was hoping to keep it that way as long as possible. Of course, if she was scheduled to work the costume party, that would add a wrinkle to his plans. Despite giving the brokerage his Rick Stratton alias, which would appear on the guest list, would she recognize him, even hidden behind the mask? And more importantly, would she put it all together that he wasn't Rick, but actually her dad? Resigned to the fact that there was only one way to find out, he would attend the party Friday night and let the chips fall where they may.

Returning to the hotel he was using as Rick's place of residence, instead of the carriage house back in the Garden District, he made his way to the bar to grab a bite to eat and a drink to help calm his nerves. These next few days, he'd have to spend off the radar of everyone, either as Rick or Frank. But tonight he wanted to at least enjoy one more evening observing what all the city had to offer.

Friday morning Frank left his room to pick up his tuxedo from the dry cleaner and a mask from one of the many tourist shops lining Bourbon Street. While it wouldn't be as elaborate as some others he was sure guests would wear, it fit with the narrative of him being invited to the party last minute. Had he shown up in something more elaborate that would have taken much longer to design and make, it would have raised questions he didn't want to have to answer. If New Orleans excelled at one thing, it was throwing outrageous parties where no expense was spared when it came to presentation.

He was surprised to find himself nervous about attending the party this evening. More so because of the unknowns he could be walking into than anything else. If Jordan really was Michael, living here under an assumed identity, then he would be entering a viper's nest with no clear idea of how he'd get himself out. If Remy recognized him, he hoped it would only be as Rick. But that was a whole other set of circumstances he didn't want to find himself in either.

Arriving at the Carrington after the party had already started, he presented the invitation to the doorman, relieved to find it wasn't anyone he knew from his past life here or in Las Vegas. Walking in, staff from Crescent City Brokers greeted him, handed him a glass of champagne, and told him to enjoy his evening. Meandering around the room, he took in as much detail as possible without being overt. Waitresses wandered through with trays of hors d'oeuvres and more champagne, while busboys came close behind, picking up empty plates and glasses. The bartender paid attention to the customers, but Frank knew he would also step in as needed muscle should anyone get out of line.

Not seeing Remy amongst the servers, he overheard another waitress talking to someone called Marcus about where she was. He was obviously in charge when the boss wasn't around, but he was also not someone else Frank recognized. Maybe he got lucky and no one here was connected to his past and all the suppositions he first came in with were unfounded. Overhearing Marcus say she was taking care of her mother, Frank breathed a sigh of relief, knowing there was one less chance of being discovered this evening.

Just as the thought crossed his mind, he turned to see a face he had not expected to ever see again in his life. Michael Leon, in the flesh, here in New Orleans. Coming out of the hall that Frank assumed led to offices and the restrooms, Frank watched as he started making his rounds. Shaking hands with people he knew, introducing himself as Jordan Dubois to those he hadn't met before. Frank quickly ducked behind a busboy, using him as cover to make his way to the opposite corner. Trying to put as much distance between himself and Michael, he continued moving until he made his way back towards the door.

Trying to leave without being seen, he stumbled when Delilah stopped him, thankful she hadn't recognized him since his mask was at least hiding half of his face.

"Leaving so soon?" she purred. "The party is just getting started."

"I'm sorry to say, yes, I must go. Something has come up requiring my attention," Frank said, glancing over his shoulder. Seeing Michael coming his way, he nodded to Delilah as he reached for the handle.

"Please don't go yet," he heard an old familiar voice say to him. "You'll miss out on all the excitement we have planned for the evening."

Without turning back, he mumbled in response. "Right. Well, maybe another time," as he pushed through the small crowd entering at the same time.

Finding himself back out on the sidewalk, he hurried away, not wanting to take the chance anyone might have followed him out. Leaving his mask in place until he was sure he was clear, he turned the corner and leaned up against the wall. Understanding exactly how close he had come to being face to face with Michael, he knew he would have to work fast if he wanted to stay more than one step ahead of him and keep Remy safe.

Chapter Twenty-Seven

Touching down in Las Vegas, Remy found she was having second and third thoughts about whether this trip was the right thing to do. 'Maybe I should just leave well enough alone. Neil and I can meet up, share some family memories and then I'll head back home,' she thought as she walked down the jetway and into the terminal. Hearing her name being called pulled her out of her ruminating, as she looked over to find her cousin, grinning from ear to ear. Not much changed since the last time she saw him.

Smiling in return, she resolved to see this wild goose chase through. It's what her dad wanted for her, even if he didn't come out and directly tell her. And who knew, maybe this was what she needed in her life right now.

"Neil. My gosh, you still look the same!" she exclaimed as they hugged.

"And you're all grown up. Geez, how long has it been?" he laughed.

"Too long. I'm sorry about that. I should have been better about staying in touch."

"No, the fault is mine. Your dad wanted me to look out for you, even if it was from afar, and I neglected to do that. I'm sorry. But let's not stand around here in the airport. I've already got a car ready for us."

"Great. Let me grab my bag, and we can go. Maybe along the way you can tell me all about what you've been up to these years."

Making their way through the airport, amid the cacophony of tourists and slot machines, Neil filled her in on what life as a musician had been like for him. Telling her if it hadn't been for her dad, he wouldn't have found himself where he was today.

"He took me on an impromptu trip to Los Angeles and set up some meetings with record executives. It all happened so fast, I could hardly believe it. Then everything that happened with the missing diamond necklace, his car wreck, and the Crossroads getting shut down. For a minute there, I wasn't sure which end was up. But I landed on my feet, and your dad turned out to be alive. And I guess everything else kind of took care of itself. At least up until now."

"Yeah. Dad and I reconnected a couple of times over the past years. But then he disappeared again. Momma seems to think he's dead. But I don't know. I don't think that's the case. I mean, wouldn't we have heard something? I guess I'm not sure what I'm hoping to find out here."

"Well, whatever it is, I'll be here with you. We'll get through it together."

Remy smiled as she handed her bag to Neil to put in the

car. "Thank you. I really do appreciate your coming here. I imagine it's strange for you to be back after all this time too."

"A bit. I often wonder what would have happened if I hadn't gotten on the bus with that stranger, or wound up here. But that's another story, I'll tell you on the drive. So sit back, relax and prepare to be entertained."

As they drove to Indian Springs, Neil shared more of how he first wound up in Las Vegas and then regaled her with stories of various tours he had been on over the years. She told him about her life in New Orleans, how she was taking care of her mom and was hoping if nothing else, maybe sell this mystery house and use the money for her care.

As they pulled into town, Neil noted how much it had changed and yet stayed the same. Billboards and signs of the old atomic tourism which had been so heavily promoted years ago were still around, though no one really came here on family vacations any more. Now, the population consisted mostly of military families and folks who worked in supporting businesses living here. It wasn't close enough for most people to commute to work on the Strip, though he was sure plenty of people drove over there at any time to take advantage of all it offered.

Parking in front of the bank, Neil got out of the car while Remy paused before opening her door, in an attempt to gather her nerve to face whatever it was her dad had in store for her here. Approaching a teller, she asked to speak to someone about accessing her box and was shown to a waiting area.

A small, old man approached, his hand extended in

greeting. "Miss Thibodeaux, welcome. I was wondering if I'd ever have the chance to meet you. I'm Mr. Barnard."

"Mr. Barnard, a pleasure. This is my cousin, Neil Evans."

"Of course. Please follow me. I'll take you back to your box. I only met your lawyer the one time, oh, more than 20 years ago now. When he first set up the box. I was starting to doubt we'd ever get to see him or you after all this time."

Remy tilted her head in question. Thinking it had been her dad had been the one to set up the box. "My lawyer? Oh, yes, of course," she said, wondering what else her dad had neglected to tell her.

"Yes. He had set up a savings account for you as well. To cover the cost of the box as long as it was needed. I can check the balance of that account as well, if you like." He said as they entered the vault.

Finding the box, he placed his key in the first lock, then waited for her to insert her key into the second. Once the door was unlocked, he removed the box, placing it on a table in the middle of the room.

"I'll give the two of you some privacy while I go retrieve that information for you. Just come to my desk when you're done and we can take care of the rest."

"Of course. Thank you," Remy replied as she stared at the box on the table.

"It's not going to bite," Neil joked as she stood there.

Unable to move, she looked at Neil. "Would you open it, please? I don't think I can. I need a minute."

"Are you sure? We can wait until you're ready. It's not like there's any kind of rush of others waiting to get in," Neil said, trying to lighten her mood.

Taking a deep breath, she nodded. "Okay. I think I can do this. After all, what could it possibly contain besides some papers and oh, I don't know, a missing diamond necklace?"

Stepping up to the box, she lifted the latch and raised the lid. On top of everything was an envelope addressed to her. Setting it aside, she then pulled out a deed to a property in Indian Springs, followed by a small black velvet bag. Holding it reverently in her hand, she trembled before setting it on the table and opening the drawstring.

Both she and Neil gasped when they looked inside. Finding more than a dozen diamonds of various sizes, Remy began laughing hysterically until tears ran down her face, and she began hyperventilating.

"Remy, are you okay? Take a deep breath," Neil said, concern lacing his voice.

"Fine. Fine. Well, no, not really. I mean, what are we looking at here?" She gasped. "All these years, and these have just been sitting here. In this town in the middle of the desert. What the hell?"

Glancing out to the lobby, Neil shook his head, lowering his voice so only she heard what he had to say. "Listen, I think you need to put this stuff in your purse, and we need to go. While you do that, I'll go out and talk to Mr. Barnard. I'm guessing you'll want to close out the account along with the box too?"

"Yeah. I don't really see a reason to keep either one anymore. I mean, if this is everything. Maybe we can go find the house though?"

"Of course. You take your time here. Meet me in the

lobby when you're ready." Neil said, walking out to the manager's desk.

Remy carefully drew the drawstring back and placed it in the bottom of her purse. She couldn't believe she was walking around with Marilyn Monroe's missing diamonds. How much were they possibly be worth now? Looking over the deed to the house, she found it was paid off, her name listed as the owner of record. The envelope with her name sat practically shouting at her, but she couldn't yet bring herself to open it. That would have to wait until later. When she was alone in the hotel room, maybe.

Walking back out into the lobby, she found Neil in conversation with Mr. Barnard. Waving her over, he pointed to some papers on his desk.

"Miss Thibodeaux, in order to close everything out, I'll need your signature in a couple of places. But before you do, are you sure you won't keep your account with us?"

"Thank you, Mr. Barnard, but no. I don't live around here," she drawled, letting her southern accent slip. "I was only here settling some things I discovered with my father's estate. I'm afraid I need to be getting back home soon."

"Of course, I understand, and my condolences as well. Give me a moment and I'll get a cashier's check drawn up for you as well," Mr. Barnard said as he made his way over to the tellers.

Remy turned to Neil, raising an eyebrow as if to say, now what, but said nothing else. As soon as Mr. Barnard returned, she signed all the necessary paperwork and thanked him again for his help.

Walking back out into the desert heat, she slipped a pair

of sunglasses on to hide the tears forming. She wasn't sure why she was suddenly so overcome by emotion, but here it was, along with a million new questions rolling in its wake.

Chapter Twenty-Eight

Returning to the hotel, Remy and Neil went to their respective rooms to decompress, and most importantly to give Remy the time and privacy she needed to read over the letter she had just found. Neil suggested meeting for dinner later to discuss what next steps she wanted to take.

Propping up the pillows behind her back, Remy tried to make herself comfortable on the bed, holding the letter addressed to her, and studying her dad's handwriting. She knew if she opened the envelope, it would be another step in this journey she wouldn't be able to come back from. Slowly she pulled out the sheets of paper contained within. The first was a letter, addressed to her, and written some years ago. The other had what appeared to be a house key taped to it, with an address scrawled underneath. This must be the house here in Indian Springs. 'Well, if it's still standing,' she thought.

Setting the key aside for the moment, she started reading the letter. It was from her dad, an apology mostly, for missing out on so much of her life. He hoped the contents of the box would make up for a small part of that. He knew it wasn't enough to replace the memories they should have made together. But he hoped she could find solace in the home and financial support from whatever she did with the diamonds. He listed a couple of names of people she should get in contact with. One was a lawyer here in Las Vegas who would handle any real estate legal matters. The other was someone he said she should trust to handle whatever she decided to do with the diamonds.

"Whatever I decide to do?" she scoffed. "I'm sitting on stolen property, with the potential to wind up in jail. And he's just casually offering me names of what - criminals - to help me."

She knew she was going to have to talk this over with Neil. There was no way she'd be able to keep it from him. Maybe he would have an idea for a way to get out of this absurd situation she found herself in.

Going down to the restaurant, she found Neil sitting at the bar nursing a beer. Taking the stool next to him, she waved to the bartender for two of what he was drinking.

"Did you get any rest?" Neil asked as he turned to face her. Seeing the look on her face, he continued. "Oh, I guess not based on that look. You read the letter then?"

"I did."

"And..."

"I'm even more confused now than I was before. I guess our plan for tomorrow will be to go find the house. Aside from that, I really don't know what to do," Remy said, throwing her hands up in the air. "I never thought I'd find myself in a situation like this."

Neil nodded, unsure of what to say. Laying down money on the bar to cover the cost of the drinks, he said, "Let's go get a table and get some dinner. Maybe the distraction of a meal will help clear your head a bit. We can talk about plans for tomorrow and not worry about the er, other items, until later."

Following the hostess to a booth, neither of them said anything. After perusing the menu and placing their orders, Remy let out a long sigh.

"So, I found a key and an address along with the letter. From what I can tell on the map, it looks like the house is on the other side of town in a neighborhood. So if I had to guess, it should still be there."

"Good. Well, after breakfast tomorrow morning, we'll take a drive over and see what we find. I would wager it's empty, since the deed is in your name and no one else was around to do anything with it. Did your dad say anything in the letter about it being taken care of by anyone in the meantime?"

"No, nothing about that. Mostly him apologizing for not being in my life. He hoped you and I stayed in contact. Guess neither of us did that very well," she smiled. "Gave me a couple of names too. One for a lawyer here, Patrick Leary, and another guy who I should contact to handle the other items, as you called them."

"Patrick is a good guy. He helped me out with all the trouble I found myself wrapped up in when I first got here. He'll do right by you. He's straightforward with his advice, and unlike some other lawyers, he's honest. I'm glad your dad put you in touch with him. Who is the other guy?"

"Someone named Jimmy. He didn't give a last name.

Just an address. He's over in Las Vegas proper, if he's even still around. I feel kind of weird though just showing up at his door after all these years. I mean, who is he, and what connection does he have to my dad? Or to the folks my dad used to be involved with?"

"If Frank said you can trust him, then I have to guess he's not connected to the Costa family. After all, I would think they're probably still looking for the missing diamonds too."

"You're probably right. Still, is going to him what I should do right now? I kind of feel like I need to keep these close for now."

Remy hadn't told Neil about her conversation with Jordan. She still had doubts in her mind about who he was and how he knew her dad. Maybe he had just heard the stories and was trying to shake her down for whatever he could get out of her. Was it possible Lily and Theo had stronger ties to Las Vegas than they let on when she first met them? Perhaps their trip had been more about them living a life out here, and when they wore out their welcome, they decided on New Orleans as their next place to run their games.

Unable to finish her dinner, she pushed her plate away. "I think I'm going to head back up to my room and take a bath," she told Neil. "I'll meet you down here tomorrow morning for breakfast?"

"Sure. I'll see you then. Try to get some sleep tonight," Neil encouraged as she left the table.

After a long, hot bath, Remy climbed into bed, running over everything in her mind again. Had it been a coincidence all those months ago when she first ran into Jordan in that boutique? Or was it a setup from the beginning? And the truck that's been parked on her street lately. She was sure she saw someone sitting in it for hours on end. Why would they do that if they were supposedly visiting someone in the neighborhood? Or maybe it had been a shadow, and her mind was playing tricks on her. If it was really someone, who were they and what connection did they have to her and all of this?

How different would life have been if she hadn't gotten roped into running a con on Matt too? She knew he really cared for her, and she broke his heart. Still surprised at how much that one hurt her the most. Usually, the guys she conned deserved it. Or at least they weren't as wrapped up in the relationship as he had been. No, this happened all too fast, and she knew she went too far with. And she'd carry that guilt for the rest of her life. Maybe she wasn't cut out for this kind of lifestyle after all. Her dad had obviously gotten out of it. But why had he even gotten into in the first place, she wondered? Had it been because of the circumstances he found himself in when he was living here in Las Vegas. She imagined it was probably hard to avoid back then. After all, if the stories were to be believed, the mob ran the Las Vegas casinos for many years. Whether or not you wanted to be involved, if you were working at one of them, you found yourself tied into that life at some level.

'One step at a time,' she thought to herself. Rolling over, she set the alarm to give herself plenty of time to wake up and get ready in the morning. She was going to need it for what she would have to face next.

Chapter Twenty-Nine

Driving over to the house, Remy found her stomach in knots, that morning's breakfast threatening to return. Her mind kept going to the darkest places, wondering what they would find? Would the house even be worth anything if she sold it? Or should she think about keeping it? So many questions about what her next steps should be. After all, she had a life in New Orleans, and it wasn't as though had the ability to easily pick up and move out here. What would she even do for work if she did? Indian Springs wasn't a booming metropolis. And life in Las Vegas didn't much appeal to her either.

No, if anything, she would try to sell the house. At least then she could use the proceeds to help take care of her mom. And quit the Carrington too. Find a normal nine-to-five job, nothing that would involve her in any illegal activities anymore.

Winding through the neighborhood, Remy saw what looked like a picture of Americana in front of her own eyes.

Houses with white picket fences, flags proudly flying, flower beds abundantly blooming. Even here in the desert, somehow these homeowners made it look like Main Street USA. That definitely sealed it for her. This was not a place she wanted to live. A cookie cutter life, with a husband, kids, and a dog, was not the life she was now imagining for herself.

As Neil parked in the driveway, Remy fished in her purse for the key. Looking around, she was sure a nosy neighbor would soon approach, so she quickly made her way to the door, inserted the key and went inside. It was blissfully cool, chilling the sweat that had formed on her neck and face. Walking into the living room, she turned on a light and looked around. It was a cozy enough home. Minimally decorated, but obvious that someone had lived here. And from what she saw when she walked into the kitchen, it had been fairly recent too, finding condiments in the refrigerator, and food in the freezer. Dishes in the cabinets, a coffeemaker on the counter, pots and pans stored next to the stove.

Moving into the main bedroom, she found a closet containing men's clothes and shoes. The dresser held socks, underwear, and T-shirts. While the hamper was empty, it was becoming more and more apparent the thought of her dad being alive might not be unfounded.

Turning to Neil, who had been silently following her this entire time, she said, "If no one else knew about this place, do you think it's possible Frank was living here all this time?"

"It looks like it could be. I mean, these clothes certainly would fit him. And he is the only other person we know who would be aware of this house. Should I go ask one of the neighbors if they've seen anyone around?"

As they moved into the next bedroom, Remy found a room decorated for a young girl. It looked as though it hadn't been touched in over a decade or more. A dresser with a jewelry box on top, revealed a dancing ballerina when she opened the lid. A built-in bookcase stocked with titles any girl would have loved to read. A pink gingham bedspread and white decorative pillows covered the bed. The lamp on the bedside table, just within reach to shut off after a night of reading under the covers, completed the room. As a tear formed in the corner of Remy's eye, she wondered what life would have been like had she and her mom lived here with Frank.

Shaking her head to clear that thought, she agreed Neil should be the one to go talk with any neighbor who might be home. Hoping it would raise less suspicion, she was not in any frame of mind to answer the questions that would follow.

"I'll be back shortly. Why don't you get a glass of water and go sit down in the living room?" he suggested.

Agreeing, she followed him back down the hall, turning towards the kitchen as he went out the front door. When she noticed another door, she opened it and found it led to the garage. An old Ford Galaxie parked in the middle, with a workbench running down the far side. Tools were hanging on a pegboard above the bench. Everything neatly stored in its designated place. The entire vibe of this house did not gel with the man she knew as her father. Sure, he had been a mostly steady presence when he had been around, but he was also social, outgoing, and a little bit messy too. Now she was seeing another side. Not only was he leading a double life, but one so out of character from what she thought she knew.

Hearing Neil come back in, she quickly went back to the kitchen to find out if he had any answers as to who might have been living here.

"Well, it turns out a guy named Rick Stratton was living here. Supposedly an airline pilot, so he wasn't around a lot. But the description the neighbor gave me sounds an awful lot like your dad. The last time she saw him was a little over a month ago, she thinks. Saw him get a cab, which she thought odd. But he had a couple of suitcases with him and was dressed in normal clothes and not his pilot's uniform. That's why it stuck out to her. Usually when he left, he took an old car from the garage."

Waving at the door, Remy said, "Yeah, it's out there. I'm guessing it's vintage 1950 something. I don't think I've ever seen one like it before."

"Right. Well, that at least answers that question then. I guess this is where your dad has been keeping himself hidden. Does the name Rick Stratton mean anything to you though? I've never heard it before."

"Uh, maybe," she blurted. "I think he might have come into the Blue Pelican, this little neighborhood bar I work at, one night a week. The only reason I remember is because he left me a really generous tip. I wasn't complaining. I just thought it odd. But why wouldn't he have told me who he was? This is making less and less sense now, and also, I'm starting to get scared."

"Scared? Why? What's going on? Is there something you

haven't told me?" Neil's voice rose with concern as he directed her towards the sofa.

Sitting down, she filled him in on everything she had been doing for the past six months. Ending with Jordan and his most recent accusations about knowing who her father was and what he was involved with when he lived in Las Vegas. She finished by saying, "I feel like I've dropped into the twilight zone, and I have no idea how to get out of this."

"What does this Jordan guy look like?"

"Tall. About the same height as you or Dad. Italian descent based on his coloring and definite Roman nose. Which always struck me as odd. His name definitely doesn't fit how he looks. Salt and pepper hair. Always dressed well, expensive looking suit and tie, but I figure that's part of the job. Why? Who do you think he might be?"

"Based on the description you're giving me, and the fact that it's been more than twenty years since I saw the guy, it sounds like it's Michael Leon. One of the guys your dad worked with at the Crossroads. And one of Nick Costa's enforcers. Remy, if this is the case, then yeah, you have reason to be scared. He also would have been one of the guys involved in the theft of the necklace."

"Wait, what? You don't think he was one of the ones who was released early? Do you think he knew who I was all those years ago and has now found me in New Orleans? Neil, what am I going to do?" Remy cried.

Reaching over and taking her hand, Neil tried to comfort her. "First, you're going to take a deep breath. You're safe right now. You are practically on the other side of the country from him, and there's nothing he can do to you here. Does he even know you're here?"

Remy shook her head. "No. He thinks I took my mom to Baton Rouge for a doctor's appointment."

"Good. So what we're going to do is a more thorough search now, to see if maybe this is where your dad has been living all these years. Once that's done, we'll lock it back up. I think for now it's best if you don't do anything else with the house. The last thing you want to do is draw any attention to it. Listing it for sale would increase activity, not to mention the legal paperwork it would trigger too. And if Frank has been staying there, that might make it harder on him too."

"How would that make it harder on him? Didn't the neighbor say it's been more than a month since he's been here?" Remy said.

"They did. And maybe that means he's back in New Orleans for good. As for the Rick guy who paid you a visit at work being Frank, I think it's quite possible that was him. He was probably checking up on you to make sure you're doing okay and didn't want to bring any trouble to your door. Especially if he knows Michael is out and in New Orleans too. Do you think he's been to the Carrington at all?"

"No. At least not when I've been working. It's a private club after all, so it's not the easiest place to get into."

"Okay. Then, hopefully, he hasn't encountered Michael in the wild yet either. As for the other items," Neil lowered his voice, still not wanting to mention the word diamonds specifically, "do you have somewhere safe back home to keep those? Another safe deposit box, maybe even at a bank outside of the city?"

"No. I never needed one. I pretty much live paycheck to paycheck, and I don't have anything of value. Well, I didn't until now. I think maybe the Batiste family keeps a couple of boxes. Momma mentioned something one time about some of Dad's family papers, an old journal I might be interested in reading someday, along with other family history. I guess I could get in touch with one of Victor's kids. Gosh, it's been ages since I've even seen any of them, too. Guess it's time for another family reunion?" Remy laughed. "But what do I tell them? I can't exactly share with them what I want to add to the box. What if one of them got curious and went looking one day?"

Neil sat for a minute, contemplating the logic she put forth.

"No, I wouldn't put it in their box. But maybe they could arrange another box for you. Under the Batiste name. It would at least be somewhat separate from your name. Then again, if Michael is familiar with Frank's real name besides the name he went by when he was living out here, then that wouldn't work either."

Sitting in silence, both Remy and Neil contemplated what the next steps should be. Deciding to take one room at a time, they started their search for more information.

Returning to the kitchen, Remy concluded that, yes, Frank had been living here, and fairly recently too. He hadn't left any pictures on display, so no one would find any visible signs it was him. But mail and a magazine subscription in the name of Rick Stratton answered the nagging question that had been lingering. Frank was her customer Rick. She chastised herself for not recognizing her own father. When Neil reminded her, it had been years since she had last seen him, and they both had changed during that time.

"Still. I should have known it was him. I guess that's why he felt so familiar," she lamented.

"It's not worth beating yourself up over. At least you know now he's still alive and safe." Neil told her. "Now, let's get locked up here and get back to the hotel. You've got an early flight to catch tomorrow."

The following morning, as Neil drove her to the airport, he tried to fill the silence in the car with talk about his upcoming tour.

"Hopefully, I can get them to schedule at least one night in New Orleans soon. If that happens, I'll call you with the date and put your name on the guest list. In the meantime, keep me updated, please. Even if it's just a message on my machine. I call and check them even when I'm on the road. And if you should happen to see Frank, tell him his nephew misses him too."

Arriving at the terminal, Neil handed her suitcase to an attendant to check in. Remy held her purse close, keeping hold of the diamonds. She was not letting those out of her sight. Hugging Neil goodbye, she made her way into the airport, stopping in the bathroom to transfer the diamonds to her pants pocket. The security magnetometer wouldn't detect those on her body, but they sure would have been visible in her purse going through the X-ray machine. Once she cleared security, she would move them back to the hiding spot in her purse, which would remain with her at all times.

Touching down in New Orleans, she was glad to be back home on familiar territory. She couldn't understand how her dad had lived all those years in the desert like that. Even with the chaos of parades, the heaviness of the humidity and the destructive storms that blew through the city, she wouldn't trade this place for anywhere else. It was home.

Chapter Thirty

Returning to work at the Carrington club the next night, everything appeared normal at first glance. Marcus was helping behind the bar, while she, Lily, and another new hire Lily was training, were busy all night. With not having much more than a chance to say hello in passing when picking up drink orders, it wasn't until the end of the night when Lily cornered Remy, asking how her mom was doing.

"Oh, the appointment went fine. There's not much to report right now. The doctors ran some new tests, but it will take a while to get all the results in. Once they do, I guess they'll let my mom know. Hopefully, she'll share that information with me too. But I wouldn't be surprised if she didn't either. She can be evasive sometimes," Remy said pointedly. Seeing Lily didn't get the jab, she continued on. "So, how were things while I was gone? I see we've got another new hire."

"Yeah. Maria quit right after the masquerade party. I guess one guest got a little too handsy with her, and it was the last straw. So far, Francine is doing all right. She caught on quickly, but I'm not sure how long she'll last either. I'm not sure she has the stones to do what Jordan wants."

Hearing the word stones come out of Lily's mouth made Remy pull back. Was that her way of alluding to knowing Jordan's suspicions about her? Using it as a segue, Remy clucked her tongue.

"Huh. Yeah. I guess it does take someone with a certain level of acceptance of illicit behavior to work here. After all, look what we got roped into. I still don't feel good about having that hanging over my head. I'm sure it's even worse for you and Theo too."

"Theo is really upset about it. He's wanting to leave New Orleans altogether now. But I really like it here. And I like working and hanging out with you too. It wasn't the same while you were gone."

Seeing this as her in, Remy suggested they meet up for lunch the next day. "Yeah, I don't see me leaving New Orleans. This is definitely home. But I do have my doubts about this place. Maybe we can discuss it over lunch?"

"That would be perfect. Anywhere in particular you had in mind?" Lily smiled.

"Why don't you come to my place? I'll make us something special. And we can talk without worrying about anyone else hearing anything."

Lily reached over and gave Remy a quick hug. "I'm so glad you're back. See you tomorrow."

"Sure. See you tomorrow," she called in return as Lily made her way out the door.

The next morning, after a quick run to the store to get the ingredients for their lunch, Remy started preparations, while rehearsing in her head how she was going to approach this subject with Lily. Knowing she had to be cautious with what she shared and she needed to let Lily divulge what she knows without too much prompting on her part, she decided having a couple of glasses of wine with their meal might be a helpful lubricant as well.

Just as she finished setting the table, she heard a knock on the door. Opening it, she found both Lily and Theo standing there.

"Oh, hi. You're both here. Please, come in," she said, the surprise in her voice evident.

"Sorry, I was dropping Lily off. But I wanted to tell you something too, if you don't mind the intrusion," Theo said.

"No, of course. Can I get you something to drink?" she asked as she closed the door behind them.

"I won't be too long. But you girls go ahead. I see you've already got a couple of wine glasses out."

"Lily, can I get you a glass?"

Lily nodded, turning her head to Theo as if to say, go on and tell her.

Stepping a little further inside, Theo began talking fast. "I know Lily mentioned to you last night about me wanting to leave New Orleans. I said that only in passing. I'm frustrated at how things went down with that bank job, and I didn't think Jordan was going to hold it over our heads like he is. And well, I'm ashamed to admit it, but I've had trouble with the cops in the past. Not here, but in other cities when I was younger, before I met Lily. I was really hoping to turn over a new leaf with us moving here. But now, yeah. That was all I wanted to say. Just wanted you to hear my side of things. And if you have any questions, please come ask me. I'll tell you what I can."

Once finished, he gave Lily a quick kiss and made a beeline for the door. Not waiting to hear Remy's response or Lily's side of the story. Lily turned back to Remy, apologizing. "Sorry. He was a bit abrupt in his leaving. He's not very good when it comes to having hard conversations. He was nervous the entire way over here. He kept rehearsing what he was going to say. And now here I am rambling on. Oh, Remy, I'm sorry. I feel like this is all my fault now."

Handing a glass of wine to Lily, she motioned to the couch. "Let's sit down a minute and talk. Lunch can keep. I feel like there's something more you want to say, maybe?"

With shoulders sagging, Lily lowered herself down into the corner of the couch. "I feel like I owe you an apology and an explanation. There's a lot you don't know about how you wound up with the job at the Carrington. Well, actually, even before that. The black-tie event where we first met was all a part of this grand plan of Jordan's."

Remy sat looking at Lily, trying to make sense of it all. "What? I don't understand? What grand plan?"

Shaking her head, Lily began explaining to Remy what took place.

"So, yeah. I guess I should start at the beginning. Jordan meeting you at that boutique wasn't just a coincidence. He had me following you for a couple of weeks before. Learning your routine, where you worked, lived, and so on. When I saw you heading out shopping that day, I called him from a payphone down the block and told him the general area where you were. I don't know if he managed to get the girls to talk about the party so you'd overhear or maybe that part was a coincidence. He said he was close by. The number I called wasn't the club. So I guess that's how he got there so quickly after you did. Anyway, when he first told me to follow you, he gave me a story about how you were the daughter of someone he used to work with. But you wouldn't have known who he was, and he wasn't sure how to go about meeting you. I mean, for all you knew, he was a total stranger."

Stopping, she took a large sip of her wine. Seeing Remy wasn't going to say anything, she resumed her story.

"So our meeting that night at the party, he orchestrated that too. And he wanted me to offer you the job, knowing you'd probably jump at the chance to make better money than what you had been at the Blue Pelican. He also said he knew you had pulled some small cons and those skills would help you fit in with us too. I had no idea he had plans for the bank job in mind when all this happened. I just thought he was going to have you con these guys out of their money. I mean, you've seen how they throw it around at the club. Anyway. I didn't expect things to get as involved as fast as they did with you and Matt either. I feel really bad about how that all turned out."

Remy tipped her head to the side, responding, "Yeah, that kind of sucked."

"Sure. So fast forward. The day after the bank job, Jordan came back to me and told me a little bit more about how he knew your dad. Said something about their having worked together years ago in Las Vegas. But I guess your dad knew him as someone else? He didn't give me a name. But he said they were involved in some heist together, and he thought you might have some idea of what happened to whatever it was they stole. He didn't give me any detail what it might be. And to be honest, I don't think I want to know. The deeper I find myself in this mess, the worse I feel. I admit, at first I didn't think much about you personally, it was a job needing to be done. But now I've gotten to know you, I feel like we've become pretty good friends. And I don't want to see you get hurt. I don't trust Jordan. Never have. But Theo and I are in too deep to him now. I don't see us being able to get out. You, on the other hand, could probably make a relatively clean break. Maybe? I'm so sorry."

Lily hung her head in shame as she reached for her glass again. Drinking down the remaining wine in one big gulp, she got up and grabbed the bottle from the counter, refilling her glass, before sitting back down again.

Remy sat, thinking over everything Lily had dumped on her. It was a lot to take in, and some of it didn't make complete sense. Yet it also gave weight to some of her suspicions that Jordan was in fact Michael Leon. Which brought back full circle the information Aidan had shared with her too. Feeling betrayed and even a little sorry for Lily, she didn't think it wise to share any of this information with her either.

Shaking her head to clear her thoughts, she said, "Come on, and let's eat. I've got a few things I think I need to tell you too. Maybe we can find a way out of this for both of us. Well, all three of us. Okay, four of us."

Seeing the look of confusion on Lily's face, she continued. "I'm counting my dad as well. I thought he was dead. Well, at least missing again, presumed dead by everyone else. But I've recently found out he's still very much alive."

Over the course of the meal, she told Lily a story about her cousin learning about the house in Indian Springs and the idea that Frank might have been living there. She glossed over what she knew of the time he spent working in Las Vegas. Giving Lily the excuse, she only had a vague memory of hearing about his working at one of the casinos and all the famous people he had the chance to meet.

"I'm not sure about his connection to Jordan and whatever this job is they may have worked together. After all, we only have Jordan's word to go on. Maybe he's making it all up as a way to try to coerce us into doing something else. But I agree with you. I don't trust him. And I think the sooner we're done with him, the better."

Chapter Thirty-One

After her lunch with Lily, and having some of her fears confirmed, Remy received a call from her mother's doctor. The most recent tests they had run did not show any improvement. In fact, he was worried that she might have taken a turn for the worse.

"But how can that be? She's been feeling fine. She's been going outside every day. She even went and ran a couple of errands. Close to home of course, but she did it on her own," Remy lamented.

"I wish I had better answers, but I'm afraid there's not much more we can do here. There are some treatments she could try either in Atlanta or Rochester, Minnesota. But those would cost money out of your own pocket. The insurance will only cover so much, and we're creeping close to the maximum they'll even cover here. I'm sorry, Ms. Thibodeaux," The doctor said as he disconnected the call. Leaving no chance for other questions or discussion about next steps.

Remy sat back, the darkness of the news settling in as

the afternoon sun slid behind a cloud, casting shadows across her apartment. Now she faced an even bigger dilemma. How was she going to come up with more money to take her mother somewhere else to get the possibly life saving treatment she needed, and get away from Jordan at the same time? If she tried to do anything with the diamonds here in town, it would only be a matter of time before word got back to him, or other unscrupulous players. They would find out the missing stones were in play once again, and that she had them all along.

If only she could find her dad and ask him what to do. Because apparently he had more connections in the darker parts of the city who were adept of handling something like this discreetly. 'I guess the apple doesn't fall far from the tree in this case,' she thought to herself.

This was not the life she had imagined for herself growing up. No, right now, if her life had gone according to her childhood dreams, she would live in a house in the Garden District, married, and making a living painting and finding joy in that creative outlet. Instead, all of her art stuff was piled in the corner, and she was too busy working two jobs, hustling for tips, and taking care of her sick mother.

Life had been so much simpler when she was young. When her parents were together, and they would have family gatherings at the Batiste household, she knew it would always be beyond what she could imagine. The house was always impeccably decorated for whatever event or holiday was being celebrated. The food was sublime, and the staff they had working for them had been with the family for years. Handwritten recipes passed down from one generation to the next. This was not your average meal for the kids and something fancy for the adults. No, everyone was served on the fine china and with the family silver, and ate all the same things. She grew up on everything from red beans and rice to crawfish étouffée and raw oysters harvested fresh from the Gulf that morning. Somewhere she had copies of some of the recipes. Not that she had the time or space to cook meals like that for herself. But she had dreamed of doing just that for a family someday too.

Now, none of those dreams would come to pass. If she didn't find another way to take care of her mother, she'd lose her soon for sure. And not knowing if she'd even see her dad again, she was distraught at the thought of being an orphan.

Shaking herself out of this spiral of doom and gloom, she looked at the clock and realized she needed to get ready for work. It was going to be tough going in knowing what she did now, but she would have to face Jordan at some point. She only hoped she could continue to pull off the deception of not knowing anything for a little longer.

Arriving at work, she found the Carrington surprisingly empty. On a Friday evening, she had expected to see more people already starting their weekend. After putting her personal items away in the staff room, she made her way to the bar to talk to Kenny and find out her section for the evening. Not seeing Lily or Theo anywhere, she asked if they were around.

"Lily is in one of the private rooms setting up. A last-minute call to schedule came in this afternoon. Not sure who it is. It was all rather hush-hush, and Jordan handled it himself. But hey, I'm just the bartender here, right? As long as I keep the drinks flowing, that's all anyone cares about," he joked. "You and Francine can split the tables between the two of you for now. It's weird that we don't have a lot of reservations for tonight."

"I was noticing that. Maybe it will pick up more later. At least I hope it does. I need it to be a good tip night."

"Anything you want to talk about," she heard come from behind her. Spinning around, she came face to face with Jordan, with Theo a couple of paces behind him. "We didn't get a chance to talk last night. It being your first night back after taking your mom to see the doctor in, where was it again? Baton Rouge, I think you said." The sneer in his voice set her on edge.

"Jordan. Hey. Um, yeah. I, uh, heard from the doctor today. It's not good," Remy stammered in response.

Eyeing her as if trying to catch her in a lie, Jordan nodded once. "Sorry. Well, things should pick up in a couple of hours. I just had a call about another group coming in. Some brokers and clients from the party the other night while you were gone, want to come in again. I'm sure you'll be able to handle them when they get here. Let the hostess or Kenny know where to seat them," he said, turning to go back to his office.

Theo, not having said a word the entire time, looked at Remy as though he wanted to both hug her and push her away at the same time, before he turned to follow Jordan. Wondering what the look he had given her was, Remy overheard Jordan questioning Theo about an entry in a ledger he was holding as they walked back towards his office.

Turning her attention back to the tables, she considered

where it would be best to have the group seated, while also replaying that exchange in her head. Something was definitely going on. Had Jordan pressured Theo and Lily before she got there? Did Lily share something with him about her or even the fact her dad was alive, and now Jordan was trying to catch her in a lie? Tonight was going to be harder than she first thought. Gathering herself, she showed Kenny where the group should go, placing a reserved sign in the middle of the table as Francine arrived and helped set up the rest.

Chapter Thirty-Two

The group from Crescent City Brokers came in, boisterous and talking non-stop about the masquerade party and how much the clients enjoyed it as well. It even helped them land a new client, one Rick Stratton, who they seemed to think was going to have the potential to be a bigger client than they first expected, Remy heard one of them say as they sat down at their assigned table.

"Good evening, everyone. My name is Remy. I'll be taking care of you this evening. Did I hear you talking about the costume party the other night? It sounds like ya'll had a good time. Hopefully tonight will meet or exceed your expectations as well."

"Remy. Darlin', you weren't here the other night, were you? I think I'd remember those eyes, masks or no," one broker flirted.

"No, I'm afraid I missed out on all the fun. I had a family matter I had to attend to. But you don't want to hear about that. So, what drinks can I get started for everyone? And then we talk about food, games, and more if you like."

Agreement all around the table led to everyone talking at once. Remy quickly made note of who wanted what drink and excused herself back to the bar. Placing the order with Kenny, she added, "I think we're going to have our hands full with that group tonight."

He winked in acknowledgment. "I'll make Marcus aware too. Maybe we'll need to move them into their own room if it gets too out of hand."

Returning to the table with a tray full, she made her way around, making sure the right drink was placed in front of the right person. The leader of the group slipped her a generous tip with the request to keep the drinks coming. They had plenty to celebrate this evening, and it appeared as though no expense would be spared. Turning his attention back to the table, he mentioned the commission they would earn from Rick Stratton's accounts would pay for this night's frivolity, prompting Remy to hover close by.

Hearing what she was guessing was her dad's alias mentioned, now she knew her dad had found a way into the club while she was gone. Was he there looking for her, or had it just been a coincidence? No one here had mentioned anyone asking about her. Maybe she should check in with Mike and the others at the Blue Pelican tomorrow, see if maybe he came back since her last shift. Hopefully, his showing up at the Carrington was a fluke, and he'd go back there instead of coming here again. Knowing who Jordan really was made her think the last thing she needed was for him to recognize Frank. There was no telling where that would lead.

Still distracted, Francine interrupted her thoughts, asking if she should pick up the table that was just seated. "Uh, yeah, go ahead. I think this group is going to keep me running for a while. Holler at me if you get in the weeds and I'll help out. Lily should be back out soon too. At least I think she will." Stopping her rambling, she headed to the table again, when she turned back. "Hey Francine, was anyone asking about me the night of the masquerade party?"

"No. I don't think so. At least no one asked me. But I'm so new here, I wouldn't have known who you were anyway. Why?"

"Oh, no reason. Like I said, if you need any help, shout."

Remy strolled back to the table of brokers, checking on drinks and taking orders for appetizers. Another account rep, who appeared to be a junior to all the others here, was mentioning how fast everything seemed to transpire with Mr. Stratton gaining an invitation to the party the other night.

"I thought we weren't allowed to invite anyone else after the RSVP date. How did he swing that?"

"Money, honey," the leader of the group leered at her. "When someone comes in with that much money they are looking to invest; you do whatever they ask. He did seem pretty insistent on getting the invite. Not sure why? With his bucks, he could simply apply for membership here. Whatever. It's good for us any way you look at it."

Hurrying back to the kitchen, Remy was now sure he had been here looking for her. Did he also know who Jordan really is? Maybe that's why he took the opportunity to come in disguise. No one would figure out who he was while wearing a mask. It would have offered the perfect cover to observe everyone here. And she knew Jordan was probably on the floor for most of the night. With all that money and potential new members floating around, he wouldn't miss a chance to schmooze as many of them as he could. Before she could stop herself, her thoughts suddenly took a turn, running down paths which led to Jordan finding out it was really Frank, and what he might do. Now more than ever, she knew she had to find her dad. Let him know she had gone to the safe deposit box, and knew the whole story. But was it really the entire story?

Lily returned to the main floor an hour and a half later, at which time, Remy and Francine had most things under control. She was told to pick up the few tables of the late guests who wandered in. Counting up tips at the end of the night, Remy was pleased to see it had been a profitable night for everyone. This extra would go into her mom's medical expenses account. While it wasn't enough to cover all the new bills she knew would come, every little bit helped.

"Hey Remy. Thanks again for lunch today. It was nice to hang out," Lily said once Francine had left. "Both Theo and I feel a little better about where things stand now."

"Yeah? You sure about that? When I saw Theo earlier, he didn't look so good. He was hanging behind Jordan like a dog who had been kicked one too many times, but still was loyal to its master."

"Hmm… I'm not sure what happened then. He was fine before we came into work. I haven't had much of a chance to talk to him this evening. Being busy back in the private room and then out here the rest of the night. He was supposed to be going over the books with Jordan."

"Oh, that makes sense. Jordan had a ledger in his hand when I saw them both. Maybe that's what it was, and I'm reading too much into it," she assured Lily, not believing a word she was saying. "Well, I need to get going," she said as she quickly made her way out of the club before anyone else stopped her.

Arriving at home, she made a cup of tea and went out onto her balcony, watching the late night party goers stumble down the street. Despite all the parties and fun this city offered, it also had a dark side most people didn't experience. And she was finding herself mired in it deeper than she wanted to be.

Reflecting on her conversations with Lily over lunch and that evening, she got an uneasy feeling in the pit of her stomach again. Was Lily trying to convince her of her altruism, or was she playing a long con, trying to make Remy feel comfortable enough to share more information about her dad and his past? Puzzle pieces were falling into place, but there were still more that had yet to be revealed.

As the hours rolled by, she continued to sit, forming a plan in her mind. First, she would find her dad and set things right with him. However that turned out, she knew she had no control over. But at least she could move forward once she talked to him.

When she found her thoughts turning to Matt, she found she still felt awful about the way things unfolded and ended with him. He deserved so much better and also to know it hadn't all been just a game to her. Maybe she should reach out to him and see if he'd be willing to meet with her. Allow her to explain her side of the story and try to apologize. Maybe he could even be helpful in exposing Jordan once and for all.

With all these maybes and what ifs running through her head, she made her way to bed. It was going to be a busy day, and she needed to get at least a few hours of sleep.

Chapter Thirty-Three

Waking from a fitful sleep, Remy poured her first cup of strong, black, chicory laced coffee, hoping it would help her get through the day ahead. Thankful she didn't have to think about dealing with Jordan today, she set her focus on finding her father and getting the nerve to call Matt.

After a hot shower, two more cups of coffee, and a few deep breaths, she picked up the phone, dialing Matt's number. She was surprised when he answered the phone instead of getting his voicemail.

"Matt Hanson speaking," his all business voice came through the handset.

"Matt. Hi. This is Remy. Remy Thibodeaux," she said.

After what felt like one of the longest pauses in history, she heard him take in a breath.

"Remy. To what do I owe the honor of this call?" he sneered.

Hearing the derision in his voice, she knew he was still

dismayed at how things turned out. Deciding to throw herself at his mercy immediately, she apologized.

"Matt. I am sorry. Truly. I did not mean for things to go the way they did. I was in a really awful place when we first met and found myself mixed up with some folks that I have since learned didn't have my best interests at heart. It's no excuse. And if you want to hang up now, I'll understand. I felt like I had to call and try to apologize one more time. And if I'm being honest, I kind of need your help."

Stopping to take a breath and a sip of water, she wasn't sure if Matt was still on the line or if she was talking to no one when she heard him respond.

"Remy. While I appreciate the apology, it feels a little late and a bit disingenuous. Especially if you are also asking for help."

"I just, well. This would be so much easier in person. Can we meet? Please? Somewhere of your choosing. Please hear me out. If you decide you want nothing else to do with me, I'll understand. I just really need to talk to someone right now."

"Could you be any more vague? Can you give me some ideas of what this is regarding?" Matt's voice gave away the frustration he was experiencing.

"It has to do with Jordan and, well, something from my past. Or rather, my family's past. I don't really want to say much over the phone."

"Fine," he spat. "Meet me at Armstrong Park in an hour. I can give you 15 minutes, but that's all. I don't have time for any more of your games, Remy."

"Thank you. I promise. No games. I'll see you there," Remy sighed as she hung up the phone.

Unsure if she would be able to convince him to help her in such a short amount of time, she would have to make her point clear, while still holding back some vital information. She knew he'd sense if she wasn't being one hundred percent upfront, but that was a risk she had to take right now. Afraid that if she shared too much, she'd be putting him in harm's way too.

Arriving a few minutes early to the park, she wandered around until she found a bench in a shaded area with as few people around as possible. Looking around, she spotted him coming across the green, as handsome as he had been the last time she saw him. 'Why did I do what I did to him,' she chastised herself. 'We could have really had something.'

Standing up and waving at him, she saw him nod in acknowledgment as he made his way to her. Sitting down on the bench, she left room between the two of them to start.

"Thank you for coming, Matt. You look well."

"Your fifteen minutes have already started, Remy. Are you sure this is how you want to spend them? I thought you had something you needed to tell me."

Short and to the point, she thought. "Right. Okay. First, again, I'm sorry. I know it's just words and nothing I can do will make up for the hurt I caused." Seeing he wasn't going to respond, she scooted a little closer, lowering her voice.

"So, the reason I called you is I recently found out Jordan Dubois isn't who he says he is. Long story short, I think he might be someone my dad knew in his past. From what I can piece together, they worked together years ago in Las Vegas. I guess there was something shady going on back then. It was, after all, the early 1960s, when the mob ran the town. Somehow Jordan found out who I am and the connection to my dad, despite us having different last names. And he seems to think I have knowledge of the location of some missing diamonds. I didn't know any of this when you and I got involved. This all only came to my attention in the past couple of weeks."

"Involved. Sure, that's one way to put it. So how does this affect me? I mean, so far, yeah. I don't see any point."

"Right. Well. I need someone with outside connections. With no ties to him or his business. And I need someone who is honest. Someone I can trust. I don't have anyone here I can turn to. I've got a cousin out in California, but he's on the road, and well, that doesn't matter. Sorry. I'm getting off track here."

"What sort of outside connections? I'm just a businessman after all. I'm not sure what I can offer you," Matt replied, shifting in his seat.

"That's where you're wrong. You see, because you're in business, you have ways and connections to find out information on other businesses and the owners, and well, I don't know what all else. And since Jordan was essentially responsible for the mess between us, and all that resulted, I thought you might like to get at least a little revenge on him."

Sitting back, Remy realized how stupid this all sounded now. Feeling like she hadn't really thought it through, she said, "No. Never mind. This was a bad idea. Please. Accept my apology and forget you ever knew me. I'll figure out a way to deal with this on my own."

Before she picked up her purse, Matt placed a hand on

her arm. "Wait. I accept your apology. Really, I do. I can tell you feel awful. And I remember you telling me about your mom and how sick she was. I'm sure that had something to do with why you did what you did."

Nodding, Remy looked at him, unable to find any words to respond to the unexpected kindness he was showing her.

"Yes, I would like to get back at Jordan for what he did. Not necessarily to me because nothing really came of it. But for what he made you do and I'm guessing is continuing to make you do?"

Shaking her head, "I can't even begin to tell you what else has happened."

"Okay. I won't pry right now. But at some point, you are going to have to tell me everything. For now, tell me what you can."

Leaning over and giving him a quick hug, she explained, "I've confirmed with a friend from the police department that he was from Las Vegas, having come here a couple of years ago. And I have an idea of how he and my dad might be connected, if he is the same guy and doesn't share a name in common. If there's some way for you to find out anything about the history of how he came to own the Carrington or any other businesses, he may be involved in. Anything like that. I would be ever thankful."

"So what are you going to do in the meantime? Are you sure you're still safe working there?"

"I don't have a choice. I need the money, and as long as I can play along, drag this out, he won't suspect anything else is going on. If I quit now, it would throw up too many red flags and put more people in harm's way."

"Good point. But if anything changes, I want you to reach out to me. Immediately. I admit I'm still hurting from what happened, but I also still care about you too. And now with what you've told me, if something were to happen to you, I don't think I'd forgive myself."

"Matt. Oh, I'm so sorry, again," Remy sobbed.

Putting an arm around her shoulder, Matt pulled her in close, letting her cry.

"Well, that was embarrassing," she sniffled.

"It's nothing to be ashamed of," Matt told her, holding out his handkerchief. "How about we get some lunch and talk about next steps?"

Chapter Thirty-Four

After her lunch with Matt and his reassurances that he would help however he could, Remy walked around the French Quarter, taking her time, distracting herself by observing all the tourists. Wondering how many of them would get conned today. It was always simple for her to spot an easy mark. They all had the same appearance. An expensive camera hung around their neck, stopping in the middle of the sidewalk to consult a map, then looking up and around with overwhelm showing on their face. New Orleans was definitely a city like no other, and she wouldn't trade it for anywhere else.

As she walked along, she noticed what had changed and what had remained the same over all the years she'd lived in the city. Some places had historical value and would never be allowed to close or be modified without going through all the proper procedures and channels. Others came and went with the seasons. At one time, The Gibson, a club her dad had told her about, stood on this spot. It had been closed for some years now. But it had been a favorite of many in the Batiste family over generations. She had heard the story of a time back in the 1920s, how a serial killer had been stalking his victims there. Bodies had been found in courtyards nearby. One maid who had worked for the family almost became a victim of his. Yes, her family definitely had its history in this city. And it would now seem that would continue for some time to come.

As she was admiring the architecture of the building where the Gibson used to be, she didn't catch that someone had walked up and stopped right behind her. Stepping back, she bumped into them. Turning around to apologize, she instead came face to face with her father. Before she had time to react, he started speaking.

"Remy. What an unexpected surprise to run into you here. I stopped by the Blue Pelican the other night, but you weren't working. I'm not sure if you remember me, Rick Stratton." He said, extending a hand.

"Hi dad," she deadpanned, waiting for him to respond.

A minute passed, feeling more like an hour, as he looked down in defeat and back up again.

"Right. Okay. Well, if you have a few minutes, let's go somewhere a little more out of the way, and talk. I have a feeling you have a lot of questions," he said as he offered her his arm and led them around the corner. Finding a coffee shop, mostly empty, they walked inside, placed an order and found an out of the way table.

"So, how long have you known?" He asked with little surprise in his voice.

"This is how we're going to do this?" she jibed. "No, hey, I'm sorry for disappearing again. Making you and your mom think I was dead. And oh, by the way, I left you a house in Nevada. Along with some other items that I now have no idea what to do with."

Picking up his coffee cup and setting it back down without taking a drink, Frank looked overwhelmed. "Remy, I'm sorry. I did it to protect you both. Granted, it wasn't the best way of handling things. I know that now. I just reacted in the moment."

"The moment," she practically shouted before lowering her voice again. "What moment? I thought life was going along just fine. I was in school, Mom was healthy, and you were living back in the carriage house at the Batiste house. What happened that caused you to suddenly up and disappear? And I guess move to some town in the middle of the desert where they are known for their atomic testing? Am I going to have to worry about you getting sick now too?"

Tears were forming in her eyes, and she quickly brushed them away, not wanting him to see how upset she really was. She had already cried once today and wasn't going to do it again.

Frank reached over and took Remy's hand gently in his in an effort to comfort her. Clearing his throat, he replied. "Since you found the house, that means you've been to the safe deposit box. Where you found the, a... Which, by the way, where are they now?"

"Hidden away" was all the answer she would give him right now.

"Uh, okay, that doesn't exactly sound safe. Maybe you should think about another safe deposit box. And one more question before I tell you what's been going on. Has anyone been asking about them? Or me?"

Taking her hand back, she sat upright in her seat. "Yeah. My boss at the Carrington. Jordan Dubois, but I think you may have known him by another name, Michael Leon. At least according to Neil, anyway."

Seeing this was not the answer to the question he was expecting based on the look of surprise on his face, she continued.

"I found some old letters, one of which was addressed to Neil. I hadn't talked to him in years, but decided to reach out after Jordan started making some weird accusations about knowing who you were and what you did. I had no idea what he was talking about then. Now, I have more puzzle pieces, but still not the entire picture. I guess now that we're here, you can fill in the blanks for me."

Sighing, a look of relief briefly crossed Frank's face, only to quickly be replaced by a look of concern.

"Listen closely, Remy. Jordan, no Michael, since yes, that is the name I know him by, is no one to mess around with. He was, maybe still is, an enforcer for a mob family. The head of the family is still in jail. Probably will be for the rest of his life. I can't fathom why Michael got out early, or even how he managed to weasel his way into owning a club here. But if he's asking about me, he already knows you're my daughter, and he thinks you know something about what we were involved in. He'll do anything he has to in order to get his hands on the missing items. Including getting you involved in something you don't want to be, just to hold it over your head as leverage."

Hanging her head, she heaved a deep breath. "Yeah, well, that's already happened."

"What do you mean that's already happened? What did you do?" Frank demanded.

"It wasn't much, really. I and another girl, who I thought was a friend, but now I'm finding she's probably in on this with him too, were a distraction at a bank. Two other guys he has working for him were the ones to actually hold up the tellers. But yes, he's holding that over my head."

"I see. So, despite your being a part of it, if the cops were to come after you, you could say you were a witness then. Unless he has something more concrete involving you in the actual planning of it too."

"No, he doesn't have anything like that. So maybe I could weasel my way out. I've got a friend who's a cop, who knows I was a witness of sorts."

"The guy from the Blue Pelican?"

"Yeah. He's a decent guy. I had him run a background check on Jordan too, so that's how I found out about his other name. I've only been back from Indian Springs for a couple of days and no, before you ask, I don't think Jordan knows that's where I went. He thought I was away with Mom for a doctor's appointment. But Neil was nice enough to join me, and he's aware of what's going on too."

Nodding his head, Frank sat for a minute, taking in everything she had shared.

"Good. I'm glad you got Neil to help out. I guess I should reach out to him too. I'm sure he has plenty of questions for me."

"You think?"

For the first time since they sat down, Frank laughed, a smile crossing his face. Seeing him like this settled Remy's nerves a little, until she asked, "So what's next then?"

"Next is we may still have some time and even some leverage," Frank replied.

"What do you mean, leverage? What do I have that is possibly leverage? Or are you holding something else back that could get me out of this mess that I never wanted to be mixed up in in the first place?"

"Listen to me carefully. You have leverage because, one, you know who he really is. He doesn't know you know. My guess is he thinks you only know him as Jordan, even though he and I have a connection from my days in Las Vegas. He probably doesn't think you are aware of his ties to the Costa family either. He assumes you have knowledge of where the diamonds are only because of your relationship to me. Or even if you don't know about them specifically, you may know of a safe deposit box I kept. I'm betting that's his next play. He's either going to ask you to go to the box, or even go so far as to take him along with you. He won't trust this to anyone else. Not after all these years."

"But - " she interrupted as Frank continued talking over her.

"Here's what you are going to do. Go back to work like nothing's changed. When he starts demanding answers, try to stall as best you can. Even if it's for a day or two. Don't try to put him off any longer. He'll figure out for sure that you're hiding something then. As much as I hate for you to use your mom as a pawn, you can tell him you're not aware of any bank box, but that there might be something at your mom's house. But because she's so sick, you have to take precautions before going over, and doctors' orders are that she's not to have guests. That will at least keep him from trying to go with you. He's callous, but I don't think he'd be foolish enough to jeopardize her health any more than it already is. Because if something were to happen to her, and he got caught, there's a chance it could turn into a murder or manslaughter charge. On top of whatever he gets pinched for, and his past crimes, he'd be looking at the rest of his life behind bars. Which is where he should be anyway."

"And then what do I do? Once I've stalled him or have to pretend to go to momma's, that is."

"I'll take it from there."

"How? Won't he recognize you if you randomly show up after all this time? And speaking of, how did you manage to get into the Carrington for the masquerade party? I'm surprised you weren't spotted."

"Promises of big commissions on accounts that won't actually exist will open a lot of doors. I feel bad for the broker who's gonna get stuck explaining to your former stepfather and others what happened. But he should have done his due diligence too. And hiding behind a mask helped out at the club. I avoided talking to him or pretty much anyone else working that night. Once I didn't see you there, I didn't stick around long."

"Oh. The poor guy. There was a group in last night who were partying on your dime. Or at least on the commissions they thought would be coming their way. Guess someone's going to get stuck with a huge bill to pay." Remy giggled, a little tension leaving her body. "But you didn't answer my question. What will you do?"

"Whatever I have to do to keep you safe," Frank said, his tone deadly serious.

Chapter Thirty-Five

Returning to work Sunday night, Remy was surprised to not find Jordan there. When she asked Marcus about it, he replied Jordan was going to be out of town, with some other business dealings to take care of. Thinking to herself this would give her a little more time and breathing room, she settled in for what turned out to be a few uneventful nights at work.

Keeping her guard up, even with him gone, Remy showed up for work and did her job. Not wanting to bring any attention to herself, she left behind some of her flashier costume jewelry she would typically wear. No sense in giving anyone any ideas about missing diamond necklaces or wearing any other pieces which might be mistaken for more than they were.

It wasn't until the following Wednesday when she walked into work and Jordan was sitting at the bar, back from wherever he had been. He acknowledged her with a brief tip of the head as she walked back to the staff room.

Upon returning to the bar to check in for the evening, she found him and Marcus deep in conversation.

Once they finished, Jordan turned to her, brusquely saying, "Office. Now." Sensing something was wrong, she quickly followed him down the hall, not asking any questions.

"Close the door," he demanded.

Doing as he asked, she returned, standing in front of his desk, while he settled down into his chair. Trying to hide her apprehension, she held her hands in front of her, waiting for him to start the conversation

"Now that you've had a little time to think it over, what do you have to tell me?" he questioned with no lead in to the subject at hand.

"I'm not sure I know what you're talking about," Remy meekly replied.

"You know damn well what I'm talking about. Your father. Missing diamonds. Where are they?" Jordan's voice rising to a shout, she thought the entire club would hear.

Remy could tell something definitely had agitated him while he had been away. In all her past conversations with him, she had never seen him escalate so quickly. Trying to conceal a deep, steadying breath, she insisted. "I don't know."

"I don't believe you."

"Believe what you want, but it's the truth. As far as I'm aware, my dad is missing. Or dead. And no one I've ever talked to has ever said anything about the theft of these diamonds you claim he was supposedly involved with."

Jordan stood up from his desk, shoving his chair back against the wall. "You're lying. I can see it on your face. Is this really how you want to play this? You know all it takes is one call from me to the police and you're spending months, if not years, in jail."

Taking a step back, Remy looked at him. Seeing a vein bulging in his neck, she wondered if maybe he'd just have a heart attack. That certainly would solve everything.

"I know about your conversations with Lily. I know your dad is still alive. And if I had to guess, he's here in town. I wouldn't be surprised if you've been in touch with him and are planning something. You think you have the upper hand here, but I'm telling you, you don't," Jordan growled.

"You want to know the truth about daddy dearest. Fine, here it is. During his time in Las Vegas, he worked for the mob. He did what he was told. Mostly, they were simple thefts. Stealing from the guests often went unnoticed as they would chalk it up to a terrible night at the tables and a wicked hangover the next morning. On more than one occasion, he'd have to rough someone up for one reason or another. And yes, he did also have to pull the trigger once. But once was all it took. My boss held that information close. Didn't share it with anyone for the longest time. I only found out after I got out of jail and came here. He figured I could use it to my advantage when I tracked down your dad."

"But you haven't found him, have you?" Remy asked.

"No. I found something better. His daughter. He always did have a soft spot for you. And now, once he gets wind of the trouble you're about to find yourself in, I'm sure he'll come out from wherever it is he's hiding, and to your rescue. What he won't expect to find is me."

Biting her tongue in an effort not to give anything away, Remy stared at him. "So who are you really then? I'm guessing your name isn't Jordan Dubois."

"Oh, I think you already know who I am. But just to put your pretty little mind at ease, you're right. My name isn't Jordan Dubois. It's Michael Leon. And thanks to your dad and his girlfriend at the time, I spent the last eighteen years in jail. It took me a little while to get my feet back under me and get established here. But now that I have, I'm the darling of the town. Heck, I'm on the police chief and district attorney's Christmas card lists. In such a seedy town as this, they were more than happy to see an upstanding businessman come in and take over this place."

Remy let out an unintended scoff as he continued to stare her down before asking. "So now you know the truth, what do you have to say for yourself?"

"I think you're delusional," Remy said, suddenly finding her courage to confront him. "The fact that you think you're an upstanding part of this community is a load of shit. You're just what we call here in the South, a *Damn Yankee*. Someone who's come to town and tries to insert himself into our culture, our history, our belonging. No, you'll never be a genuine part of this city. Maybe you get Christmas cards from city officials, but guess what, we all do. It's a part of community relations. Make the people feel special so they don't really see the wool getting pulled over their eyes the rest of the year. As for my father, believe what you will. But like I said, I have no idea where he is or where the supposed diamonds are either. So go ahead. Do what you will. Call the cops. I don't think you'll find me behind bars for long."

Remy turned and stormed out of the office, stopping only long enough to grab her coat and purse, before walking out the door. She heard Marcus calling out, asking where she was going. As soon as she was outside, she turned the corner and leaned against the building. Hands and knees shaking uncontrollably, she couldn't believe she had just done and said what she did. What was she thinking? And better yet, what was she going to do now? She was sure Michael, eh, Jordan, whatever name he wanted to call himself, would set whatever plans he had for her in motion.

Feeling betrayed by Lily, she held back a scream, not wanting to draw any attention to herself. She thought they were working on getting out of this together. She should have never trusted her in the first place. And telling her about her dad being alive was a mistake she hoped she wouldn't wind up regretting more than she currently did. She was going to have to find Frank now and fill him in on what happened. This had the potential to upend whatever he had planned.

Chapter Thirty-Six

After walking back to her car, she sat for a few minutes trying to regain her composure before deciding to drive to her mother's house. It was still early enough; she knew her mom should be awake. About to pull up to the house, she was surprised to find an unfamiliar car parked out front. Maybe it was someone visiting a neighbor, she thought. The nurses who normally came would park in the back if they drove. Not wanting to block them in if they were still there, she parked in front of the mystery guests' car.

Walking up onto the porch, she heard voices, laughter even, coming from inside. Now she was really confused. Her mom rarely had anyone over because of health concerns. The few friends who would come by, scheduled their visits and always during the day when they could sit outside. Hearing a man's voice, muffled, as though he were farther away in another room, she pushed open the front door, calling out to her mother.

"Momma? Are you here?"

"Remy, cher. Come in. I'm in the living room."

Walking into the room, she saw two glasses on the table, along with a tray of fruit, cheese and bread. Her mom, spotting her, waved at a chair. "What are you doing here? I thought you were working this evening?"

Shaking her head, trying to figure out what was going on, Remy replied, "I was, but. I'm sorry. I didn't mean to intrude. I didn't realize you had a guest."

Laughing, "oh he's no guest. It's -" as Remy looked over her shoulder and saw Frank walking towards her, glass in hand.

"I think you could probably use this," he said, handing her a drink.

Looking between the two of them, Remy sat bewildered. Her mom, sensing something more was troubling her, asked, "What's going on? You look like your world is about to crash down around your ears, darling."

"Where to start? I wasn't expecting this," she said, waving her hand between the two of them, both now seated on the couch next to one another.

"I think I can explain," Frank interjected before her mom said anything. "After our conversation the other day, I felt it only right to come see Vanessa and tell her what was going on. When you told me she thought I was dead, it hurt deeply. I never meant for either of you to think that. I realized I should have reached out and let someone, at least her, know I was okay. But I thought I was protecting you both. And Neil. And well, yeah. Again, I'm sorry."

Vanessa reached over and took Frank's hand in hers.

"It's okay. Really. You did what you thought best. Remy and I have been fine. Sad, yes. But otherwise, we've had each other to lean on. You're back now, though, and that's what counts."

"I don't think I'd say fine, Momma," Remy snipped at her. "After what the doctor just told us the other day, you are the furthest thing from fine."

Frank glared at Remy. "That's no way to talk to your mother. I may not have been around all these years, but you are still my daughter, and you will show your mother some respect."

"You're right. You haven't been around. And now that you're back, my world has turned upside down," she practically shouted. "Do you have any idea what I just went through?"

Both Frank and Vanessa sat quietly, waiting for her to continue.

"Fine. You want to know why I'm not at work tonight. Well, I'll tell you. I was threatened by my boss. Turns out he is Michael. He admitted as much to me. Also told me you were involved in some pretty shade stuff, daddy dear. More than stealing a necklace. Something about pulling a trigger, amongst other unsavory behaviors."

"Now, just a minute," Frank interrupted.

"No. You are going to let me finish. Then you can make your excuses or tell your tales of what you think we want to hear. I can't say I believe everything he said. But because I now have the diamonds, and your confession, that answers the questions about your involvement."

Seeing the look of bewilderment on her mother's face,

she continued. "Oh, yes, Momma. Frank here was involved in the theft of Marilyn Monroe's diamond necklace all those years ago. And now some of those diamonds are sitting in a box, right here in this house."

"Frank, what is she talking about?" Vanessa asked, shifting away from him.

"Vanessa, I. Please, let me explain," Frank implored as Remy stood up and walked out of the room.

Returning with the box she brought in from her car, Remy set it down hard on the coffee table. Lifting the lid, she pushed some letters aside and pulled out a small black bag. Placing it on her mother's lap, she glared at Frank as she said, "here Momma. Ask him about these."

As her mother opened the drawstring, her eyes widened upon seeing the contents. Quickly closing it and shoving it back in the box, she glared at Frank.

"Explain," she spat at him.

Taking a deep breath, and then a gulp of his drink, he stalled for time. Seeing the looks on both Vanessa and Remy's faces, he knew he had to confess everything he had kept hidden from them.

"Alright. Yes. I was involved in the theft of the necklace. What is in that bag is what remains of the stones I took from it. Your cousin Neil has a few. Or at least he did. I'm sure after all these years he's found them. Though what he's done with them, I have no idea. Back then, I knew the large stones would be too recognizable to try to sell outright, so they were cut and reset into other pieces. The last I saw of them was when I gave them to Nick Costa. My guess is they wound up in police evidence and are probably still collecting dust. Or maybe they made their way back to the jeweler. That's not my concern." Looking between the two, he saw no sympathy, so he continued.

"No one got hurt during the heist. And yes, I'm ashamed to admit now, there were some other thefts I was involved in while I worked for the Costa family. Nothing so big as that one. But that was my last one. I swear. Right after I got back from Los Angeles with Neil was when I staged the car accident. That's also when the others I was working with got picked up by the cops and went to jail. As for Michael telling you I pulled the trigger and I guess supposedly killed someone. No, that never happened. I know you have no reason to believe me. But Vanessa, please. You've known me all these years. You know I would never hurt anyone. Not like that anyway."

Staring at Frank, Vanessa shook her head, while Remy continued to shoot daggers at him.

Sighing, Vanessa leaned back in her seat and closed her eyes. Opening them again, she looked at Frank and asked, "Why now then? What's changed or happened that suddenly this has become a threat to Remy and now you too?"

"Michael Leon. Remy's boss, who apparently people here know as Jordan Dubois. I had heard he was released from jail a while back, but had no idea he was here or living under an assumed name. I guess he's still working for Nick Costa, the guy who was in charge of everything at the Crossroads. I really thought I had convinced them all I was dead."

Turning his attention to Remy, he continued.

"Remy. I can't tell you enough how sorry I am. I regret

not being around more and not coming back sooner. I had no idea you were mixed up in all of this. I don't know how Michael found out about you. If I could go back and fix it, I would. But now, we are going to have to find a way through. But you can't keep the diamonds here. I thought you told me they were in another safe deposit box. Keeping them like this is not safe for either of you. And if something were to happen, I couldn't live with myself."

"Little consolation now, don't you think dad," Remy said, poking him. "What do you suggest I do then?"

Thinking for a moment, Frank's eyes lit up with an idea. "Your mom has another appointment with the doctor in Baton Rouge soon, yes?"

Remy nodded as he continued. "Okay. Take her to the office as usual. Unless there is a reason for you to stay, you leave and go find a bank where no one will recognize you. Use an assumed name. I'm guessing you have at least one you haven't used in a while and some ID you can use too?"

"But what good will that do? Michael knows I go up there all the time for mom's appointments. Won't he think to look for something up there if he can't find anything here?" Remy asked.

"Maybe. I don't know. But if it's under a name he doesn't associate with you, then it will make it that much harder to find. Just be sure when you go you're not followed. Don't tell anyone, not your mother, not me, no one, where the bank is. Don't leave any paperwork here or at your place either. And hide the key. The last thing you want to do is keep that on you. I'm more than familiar with Michael's tactics when it comes to asking questions. I don't want you being on the receiving end of any of those."

"Frank, are you sure this is such a good idea?" Vanessa asked. "Maybe we should just give him the diamonds and be done with it all."

"No. Even if we did, he wouldn't stop. He's determined to settle a score with me, and he's going to do it in the most hurtful way possible. The diamonds would only be a trophy for him. I don't think he even really cares about them at this point."

"And what are you going to do during all this? It seems like I'm the one taking all the risk," Remy demanded.

"I'm going to find a way to take care of Michael once and for all," Frank said nonchalantly. Seeing the look of fear on both their faces, he resumed. "No, not like that. I told you, I don't hurt people in that way. No, it's going to be legal and aboveboard. I've dealt with law enforcement before and managed to stay out of jail. I'm hoping I can do it again."

"Are you sure, Frank? I mean, aren't your past crimes going to come into play?" Vanessa asked worriedly.

"I don't know. But what I am going to do is protect both of you. Again, I'm more sorry than I can say for all the years I wasn't around and the hurt and pain I've caused both of you. I will do whatever I have to in order to set things right. If that means I have to go to jail now, then so be it."

Softening her expression, Remy looked back and forth between her parents. Knowing she had been too hard on him, she apologized. "I'm sorry, Dad. I shouldn't have jumped to all the conclusions I did. I know you were only doing what you thought was best. You might want to give Neil a call too while you're at it. He's been pretty worried about you too."

After a few tears and hugs and assurances from her dad, Remy left the two alone as she went to put the box away. Knowing she'd have to take yet another day off of work, she contemplated what she was going to come up with to give to Jordan in order not to raise any more suspicions.

Chapter Thirty-Seven

Much to her surprise, when Remy asked for the following Tuesday off to take care of her mom, Jordan just waved a hand at her and said, "Fine." It was as though he couldn't be bothered with her now. Maybe something had happened that she was unaware of to put him in such a mood. But whatever it was, she wasn't going to question her good fortune.

Back out on the floor, she was making her rounds when Marcus approached her. Pulling her off to the side, he reminded her of the big gala coming up that weekend. "I want to make sure you're going to be here for this. You were missed at the masquerade party. This is an all hands available event. Unless you are on your deathbed, you need to be here."

"Of course. I didn't plan on not being here."

"Good. I heard you saying something about needing to go back to Baton Rouge again," he said, head tipping to one side in question.

"My mom has another appointment with the doctors.

But that's Tuesday, and I should only be gone for the day. I promise I'll be here for the gala. Dressed in my party finest," she smiled.

After letting her go back to work, Marcus made his way back down the hall toward the offices. Seeing Lily watching from across the room, Remy made her way to the bar to restock her tray as though nothing had happened. Her mind kept racing with thoughts of everything she had learned over the past few days, and she wondered how well she was hiding her apprehension. When she heard a throat clear next to her, she turned to come face to face with Matt.

"Matt. My goodness. You scared me. What are you doing here? I thought you'd never set foot in here again," she said, trying to play off her excitement at seeing him.

"I'm here with a client. Turns out he's a member here and wanted to stop in for a drink. He's trying to convince me to come to a gala being hosted here this weekend. Thought I'd check in with you to see what you thought."

"I, well, um. Sure, I guess. I mean, I don't see a reason why you wouldn't want to come. Practically all of New Orleans is going to be here. I think the mayor is even supposed to put in an appearance."

"Huh. Guess it's going to be pretty swanky then," he laughed.

"Sure. That's one way to describe it. Me, I'm hoping for them all to be big tippers. But more times than not these parties, they wind up being pretty stingy. Not sure why? I guess they think they're being generous just by being here or something," Remy said bitingly.

"Is that a little sarcasm I hear in your voice?"

"No," Remy drawled. "Whatever would make you say that?"

Matt laughed. "Sorry, you're right. I guess we are kind of deserving of that dig. I hope I was never like that."

"No. You can be assured, you were always one of the good ones," she said, patting his arm. "But we're starting to attract attention, and I don't think it would be good for either of us right now," she continued as she inclined her head in Lily's direction.

"Sure. Well, it was good to see you. I guess I'll see you Friday night then. Unless of course you're taking care of our table tonight?" Matt winked.

"I'll see what I can do," Remy smiled as he walked back to the group he came in with. Picking up her tray, she made her rounds of her other tables when she saw Lily approaching the table where Matt and his group were seated. 'Guess that answers that question,' she thought.

As she returned to the bar, Lily walked up and stood next to her. "Remy. Hey. We haven't had much of a chance to talk lately."

"Yeah. Life's been kind of crazy these past few days."

"Oh. Sorry. Everything okay with your mom?" Lily asked, feigning concern.

"About the same. She's got another appointment coming up I need to take her to," Remy offered, not giving any other details.

Nodding, Lily suddenly changed the subject. "So, it looks like Matt is back, huh?"

"Yeah, I guess so. Some client or something is trying to wine and dine him, I guess."

"It's a shame things didn't work out between you two. He seems like a really great guy."

"He is. I'm surprised he actually came in. As you know, it didn't end well, and the last I heard from him, he was pretty clear about never wanting to see me again."

"You two seemed friendly enough a few minutes ago," Lily smirked.

"He's a gentleman through and through. He was asking about my mom. They both developed a soft spot for each other."

"Sure. I get that. Glad you two are able to get along now," Lily said, picking up her tray. "Well, these drinks aren't going to deliver themselves."

As Lily walked away, Remy took a minute to consider their interaction. It had felt strained to her, but maybe it was because of her being on edge. Was Lily trying to dig for more information? Remy didn't feel like she could trust her or Theo, or anyone else here for that matter now. How she longed for simpler days. The days before she wound up embroiled in the mess she now found herself in.

Clearing her head, she resumed her duties, circulating throughout the club, keeping an eye on her tables as well as any other movements that seemed out of the ordinary. Matt and his group stayed only for a couple of hours, long enough to finish their drinks and meal. He simply nodded at her when they left, not making a show of it or drawing any other notice.

Thankfully, Jordan and Marcus were still locked away in the back, doing whatever it was they were up to. She was surprised neither of them had come out at any point during the night. And the more she thought about it, the more concerned she became.

Sitting down at the bar at the end of the night, Kenny mixed her a drink as she counted out her tips. "Good night?" he asked as he set down her gin and tonic, and two more glasses next to hers. Turning her head, she saw Lily and Theo sit down as well.

"Not bad. I'm really hoping the gala on Friday will be the big night for tips this week. Momma's bills are piling up again."

"I'm sorry to hear that, Remy," Theo interjected. "Is there anything Lily or I can do?"

"Thanks, but no. Not unless you have some miracle cure or voodoo to make it all go away," Remy said, picking up her drink and swirling it around in the glass before setting it back down again.

"Why don't you let us take you out for an early dinner tomorrow before work? Get your mind off of things for a couple of hours," Theo suggested, with Lily nodding in agreement.

"That's sweet of you, really, but I - " Remy said but was abruptly cut off by Marcus joining the group.

"I think that's a grand idea. In fact, maybe I should join you guys. We can make it a foursome. Drinks, dinner, some laughs. What do you say?" he suggested, one eyebrow raised as if to say they had no other option but to say yes.

"Uh, yeah, sure. Why not?" Remy acquiesced. "That is if it's okay with you two?" she said, turning to Theo and Lily.

"Hey, why not. The more the merrier, right?" Theo stammered.

Watching the looks passing between Lily and Theo,

Remy wondered if maybe Lily was telling the truth after all. Maybe they really wanted to get out from under Jordan's influence. It was hard to tell, as now everyone was acting a little uncomfortable.

"Okay. Well someone let me know where we're meeting, and I guess I'll see you all tomorrow then," Remy said as she picked up her things, leaving her drink untouched on the bar.

Hearing Lily call after her, she didn't wait around and instead made a quick exit, practically running to her car. Arriving home, she double locked her door, then walked through the apartment checking the windows to make sure they were secure as she pulled all of her blinds and curtains closed. Stopping in front of the French doors leading to the balcony, she noticed the truck she had seen before was once again parked across the street. Knowing now it wasn't a coincidence, she stepped back from the doors and retreated into her bedroom.

Chapter Thirty-Eight

After a fitful night's sleep, Remy rolled out of bed late the next morning. She was not looking forward to dinner tonight. Especially now that Marcus has inserted himself into the plans. She was sure Jordan was behind that and was still unsure about where Lily and Theo's loyalties lay. Maybe they had been putting on an act last night too. Trying to make her think they were unwilling, when in reality they were in on whatever was going on too.

Or maybe she was just being paranoid now. Conjuring ideas in her head that would never come to pass. Maybe she should call her dad and see what he suggested. After all, he had said he would take care of Jordan, Michael, whoever he was. This was getting so confusing. She was thinking of them as two different people when in reality they were one and the same. And regardless of the name he went by, she knew he was dangerous.

With the gala coming up on Friday, she was wondering if she could get through the night and then be done. Done with the Carrington Club, done with her supposed friends there, heck, even done with the diamonds.

"Maybe I should just give them to Frank and let him handle it from here," she said to herself. "After all, they belonged to him to begin with. And I'm sure it would only bring more attention to me if I suddenly had all the money to take care of Momma." She mused.

Wandering aimlessly around her apartment, a loud knock on her door startled her. Looking through the peephole, she saw Frank standing outside as if she had wished him onto her doorstep. Opening the door, she waved him inside, quickly closing and relocking the door behind him.

"What are you doing here?" she demanded.

"Nice to see you too," he said.

"I'm sorry. But do you really think it's a good idea for you to be coming here? Don't you think someone might see you? Put two and two together," she stopped, rushing to the window as she was reminded of the truck that was out there last night.

"What are you looking for?"

"A truck. It was out there last night. I first saw it a couple of months ago, and then a few weeks ago too. I've seen it multiple times now. I never saw who was in it, but I know someone was."

"What are you talking about, Remy? And why didn't you tell me about this before?" Frank demanded.

"When dad? When was I supposed to tell you about this? It's not like you've been around all my life," she snapped.

Holding his hands up in defeat, he agreed. "You're

right. I'm sorry. I'm worried about you and your mom right now."

"Honestly, should I be mad at you or grateful that you're here?" Remy asked, sinking down into a chair.

Seeing the look of distress on her face, Frank sat down across from her. "What's going on? Did something happen at work? Is Michael making more trouble for you?"

Looking up at the ceiling and then back at Frank, Remy sighed. "This entire situation is making trouble for me. I wish I had never found those letters or gone to Indian Springs. I really wish I had never found those damn diamonds."

Frank sat looking at Remy with concern on his face. "How many times can I say I'm sorry? I have no more words to make you believe it. Those diamonds were supposed to be a safety net for you. Never in my wildest dreams did I think your mom would get sick like this, or that any of the Costa family members would get out of jail. Or that you'd wind up working for one of them. You have to believe, when I gave my statement to the feds, they should have had enough evidence to keep everyone locked up for not just years, but lifetimes." Shaking his head, he continued. "What do you want me to do? How can I fix this?"

"Take the diamonds back," Remy scoffed. "If I don't have them, then no one can come after me."

"Oh, trust me. They'll still come after you. Because whether you want to accept it or not, they think you know where they are. Even if you don't have them, you are still my daughter and, by default, you're involved."

Furious at Frank for everything he had done wrong in

her life, Remy shouted at him. "So what am I supposed to do now? It's not like I can just pick up and leave. I have a life here."

"I know. I'm just trying to make you aware that no matter what you do, you're involved in this now. And there's not going to be an easy way out. For now, what you need to do is keep going on with your life as though everything is normal." Seeing the look she was giving him, he shrugged.

"So you think I should go to dinner tonight then with Marcus, Lily, and Theo?" she questioned.

"Wait, what dinner? Okay, I think there are some more things you need to explain. First off, tell me more about the truck, and then about this dinner."

Remy explained about the truck she had been seeing. It had been mostly around her apartment, but there had been a couple of times she thought she saw it when she left work at the Blue Pelican. Of course, she wasn't sure because, to her, all trucks looked alike, and she never got a look at the license plate.

"As for the dinner, it started off with Lily, Theo, and me talking about grabbing a bite before work. Then, Marcus came out while we were figuring out where to go and basically invited himself. And now I don't know what to think. Can I trust Lily anymore? Or have she and Theo been in on this from the beginning? If so, then they are both really good actors and should get some kind of award for what they've managed to pull off."

"Listen to me. No one is that good. While I wouldn't say to trust her or even Theo, I think she's probably trying to find a way out. As for Marcus, keep him at arm's length, but also you can't do anything about him joining your group tonight. If he's working with Michael, then he's not one to mess around with either. Watch what you say, do, eat, and drink. Do not under any circumstances leave him alone with anything or anyone."

"You really think he would try something?"

"I wouldn't put anything past him at this point. But if I had to guess, tonight is a fishing expedition. He's probably coming along to see what information he can get out of you. Be careful. And if it comes to it, and you really don't feel safe, call me. Immediately. In fact, where are you going?"

"Pascal Manale's. But you can't show up. Surely you'd be recognized."

"No. But I can send a friend to keep an eye out. And I'll be close by. Like I said, if for some reason you don't feel safe, call this number and leave a message. It will notify my pager, and I'll be on my way immediately. I'm not going to leave you hanging. And no, before you ask, I'm not going to tell you who it is either. The less you know at this point, the better I'll feel."

Feeling more apprehensive about her upcoming dinner, Remy took little solace in the idea of someone she didn't know would be keeping an eye on her. Between the strange truck and now this, she felt like she was living her life under a microscope.

"Fine. I guess. I just really want to be done with all of this. I want to live a simple, quiet life," Remy lamented.

"Trust me. This will all be over soon. We just need to get through this next week. I suspect the upcoming party Michael has planned will be his downfall." Frank intoned.

Chapter Thirty-Nine

The first to arrive for dinner, Remy was shown to the table reserved for them. Set back in a corner, she chose the seat facing the rest of the room. She wanted to be able to see what was going on around her at all times. It was another piece of advice her dad had given her before he left earlier that day. Ordering a soda, she requested it in a highball glass in order to make it look like she had a drink already.

It did not surprise her when Marcus was the next to arrive. He marched across the room as though he owned the place, bypassing the hostess and telling a passing server what he wanted to drink and to bring another for the lady already at the table. Remy knew he was going to try to exert control over the evening, and as such there went all of her thoughts maybe this was going to be a normal dinner with no agendas.

"Remy, you're early," Marcus smiled, the pleasure he was trying to convey not reaching his eyes.

"As are you, Marcus," she replied, giving him no hint of emotion.

Starting off at a stalemate and with no additional conversation, he toasted her when the drinks came. "Sorry, I didn't realize you already had a drink. Here, let me take that extra one off your hands," he said, reaching for her glass.

Grabbing it and taking a sip before he found out it was only a soda, she said, "No, really. It's fine. I was thirsty when I got here, so I'm sure I'll finish both of them."

Sitting back in his chair, he looked around the dining room as though he were scoping out the place.

"Looking for someone?" Remy asked innocently.

Turning his attention back to her, he shrugged. "No. Just never been here before. I was admiring the decor. So what's good here?"

Handing him a menu to peruse, Remy picked up her own in an attempt to hide behind it and gather her thoughts. Something was definitely going on with him already. Did he have someone else here keeping an eye on them? Someone who was certainly connected to him and Jordan? Just as she was about to offer a suggestion of what to order, Lily and Theo arrived at the table, completing the foursome.

"Sorry we're late," Lily said. "It was all my fault. I broke a strap on my shoe, and well, that set off an entire chain of events."

"Oh, it's fine," Marcus said. "Remy and I were discussing what's good. I've never been here before, despite having heard about it ever since I moved to the city."

"Where did you move from, Marcus?" Remy inquired.

Clearing his throat, he started, "Here and there. I never seem to stay in one place very long. In fact, it's been almost two years I've been here. I think that's the longest I've been in any one place since childhood." Waving down the server, he ordered another round of drinks for everyone. The server, looking at Remy in question, nodded when she tipped her glass. It was their agreed upon signal she said she would give to keep serving her in the decoy glass. So far no one had caught on, and she meant to keep it that way.

"That sounds awful," Remy replied. "I can't imagine moving so often."

Lily added, "Moving is no fun. I'm hoping Theo and I can stay here for a long while. We've both really come to like New Orleans. Weather and all."

"I imagine coming from the desert it was definitely a change for you both," Remy said, turning her attention to the two of them. "How long were you living in Las Vegas?"

"Um, about a year, or so. We weren't there long. It was more of a fluke we even stayed as long as we did. But we're here now and have no intention of leaving," Theo said, looking pointedly at Marcus.

"Good to hear. I'm sure Jordan will be pleased too. He's really been happy with all three of you and your performance lately. I'm sure he'd hate to lose any of you. For any reason."

The undercurrent in Marcus's voice silenced the table, only to be interrupted by the server asking if they were ready to order. Once appetizers and entrees were chosen, he departed, and the table returned to a deafening silence.

Eventually Marcus broke the silence. "So."

Remy, Lily, and Theo all turned to face him, waiting for him to continue. Seeing no one was going to respond or offer to continue the conversation, he went on.

"Right. I guess you all are wondering why I invited myself to your dinner this evening."

"You could say that," Remy responded acerbically.

"Now there's no reason to get testy, Remy. I just felt like it was the right thing to do. We've all been working together for a while now, but I don't feel like we've really gotten to know each other. You know what I mean?"

"No. Not really. It's not exactly typical for a manager to go out with his subordinates outside of work. Especially not when we work in a place like the Carrington," Remy said. "In fact, I don't think I've ever worked at a place where I've been out to dinner with coworkers, unless it was for business purposes. And this doesn't feel like club business to me."

"And just what does it feel like then?" Marcus asked, turning his full attention to her.

"Honestly, it feels like you're trying to insert yourself into our lives. Like you are here trying to get information from us. Is that what you're doing, Marcus? Here because Jordan wants you to find out what we're up to?"

Theo objected, but Lily placed a hand on his as a sign not to say anything.

"Remy. Lily. Theo," Marcus started, looking at each one of them. "Is that really what you think? You think Jordan sent me here with orders to spy on you? Why on earth would you even think something like that?"

"Oh, gee. Maybe because he's holding our involvement with the bank over our heads. Maybe because he thinks we're plotting something against him. Like we'd discuss it in front of you if we were."

She scoffed, hoping this act she was putting on would convince him the three drinks she supposedly consumed had gone to her head.

"Remy, darling," Marcus said, trying to take her hand in his.

As she pulled her hand back into her lap, she glared at him. "I am not your darling, and you don't get to call me that."

"Right. Okay, sorry. I was out of line. I'm only trying to put you at ease. All of you. Trust me. This dinner is nothing more than the four of us getting better acquainted. I'm sorry if you think I had any ulterior motives. Cross my heart, I don't," Marcus smiled. Again, the emotion not reaching the rest of his face.

'He really needs to work on his tells,' Remy thought to herself as she straightened up in her seat. "Sure. Apology accepted. For now, anyway. Lily, Theo, are you okay with this?"

The two nodded, looking back and forth between Remy and Marcus.

"Fantastic," Marcus said. "So, one quick piece of business and then we can enjoy the rest of the meal. Yeah?"

Seeing no one was going to respond, he resumed. "The upcoming gala Friday night. It's going to be a big deal. I know Jordan has already gone over this with you all. But I need to reiterate it too. We've got some seriously influential folks coming that night. There's going to be a lot of money changing hands. The games set up in the private rooms are going to be very high stakes, more so than usual. The guests who will be allowed into those rooms will be highly controlled as well. If you see anyone who doesn't belong, let me or one of the other security staff know. Right away. Also, it's possible an uninvited guest may try to gain entry."

"Who might that be?" Theo asked.

"I'm not at liberty to say who exactly. What I can tell you is it might be someone Jordan used to work with and isn't welcome," he said, pointedly looking at Remy.

"So how will we know who this guest is?" she asked.

"Oh, I'm sure you'll recognize him," Marcus said, picking up his drink and tipping it in her direction.

Feeling the hair on the back of her neck stand at attention, Remy shifted ever so slightly in her seat, picked up her glass and tipped it at him in acknowledgment. Sensing Lily staring at her, she did her best to control any expression which might give away any suspicions she might have.

Interrupted by the delivery of their meal, Remy took the brief respite to consider what Marcus was implying. 'Did they think Frank would try to make an appearance at the gala? Or were they worried about someone else, another player in this game she was unaware of.' Knowing she would need to get in touch with Frank, sooner rather than later, she had to get through the meal and leave as soon as she could. Still unsure of who else was watching them in the restaurant, she glanced around, hoping maybe whoever Frank had stationed there, overheard at least a part of the conversation.

Not seeing anyone getting up to leave or even head to the phone, Remy's heart started pounding. Could she excuse herself from the table long enough to make a call without raising any flags? She was going to have to try. Frank needed to know what was going on before he made another move.

"Excuse me for a minute, won't you?" she said, rising from her seat.

"Everything alright?" Marcus questioned.

"Fine. I need to go to the ladies' room if it's any of your business," she wisecracked as she stepped away from the table.

Sensing she was being watched, she headed straight back to the where the restrooms were located. Once in the hall, where she saw she was out of the line of sight of at least Marcus, she diverted to the phone mounted on the wall. As she was placing the call to Frank, Lily startled her by tapping her on the shoulder.

"What are you doing, Remy? I thought you had to use the ladies?" Lily demanded.

"Excuse me, but what business is it of yours?" she said, as she heard Frank's voice coming through the handset pressed to her ear. Not wanting to give away the fact he had answered, she continued berating Lily. "I'm starting to think you are siding with Marcus and Jordan and their plans for the gala next Friday? Is that it? Is that why you're following me back here? Are you meant to be keeping an eye on me?"

Taking a step back, Lily gave Remy a look which only confirmed her suspicions. Shrugging and admitting she was caught, she laughed. "You're right. Theo and I are working for Jordan. We have been since the beginning. I guess you were just so desperate for a friend, you didn't take the time to consider you might be the one getting conned. Thought you were better than that. After all, you learned from one of the best. Your father."

Staring at her incredulously, Remy continued to grip the phone as Lily resumed her invective.

"So yeah. Jordan has a pretty good idea that your dad will probably try to show up at the party Friday night. No masks to hide behind this time either. Yup, based on the look on your face, I'm guessing you didn't know we figured out he had been there. Of course you weren't working that night, so you didn't get to see it all. No, you were conveniently absent. Off to take care of your mother, right? Or perhaps you were actually in the Las Vegas area. Retrieving something that never belonged to you in the first place? Whatever. I don't really care what you were doing. What I do care about is that I, well we, get our cut of the proceeds. Once that's done, Theo and I are off to some island somewhere. A new life awaits us. Again."

Hearing Frank in her ear trying to get her attention, Remy instead turned to face Lily. "That's some tale you've woven there. I'm not sure where you're getting your information from. But I don't have to justify myself to you. In fact, I don't have to answer to any of you."

Hanging up the phone, she turned and walked back down the hall to the table. Picking up her purse without a word, she wove through the tables towards the exit of the restaurant. She heard Marcus calling after her, but she kept her face forward and didn't give him the satisfaction of a response.

Chapter Forty

Returning home, she walked in to a phone ringing off the hook. Before picking it up, she guessed it would be Frank, only to be surprised to hear Neil's voice on the other end.

"Remy. Hey, it's Neil. Are you okay?"

"Neil. Hey, yeah, I'm fine. To what do I owe the call?"

"I just got off the phone with, uh, you know. He was worried about you, but couldn't call. So, I'm checking in to see how things are going. Make sure you're okay."

"Oh. Sure. No, everything is fine. I just got home from a dinner that ended a little abruptly. Which was too bad, because I didn't get to actually eat my meal and I was really looking forward to it."

"Well, that's a drag. Maybe we should meet for lunch tomorrow. I'm sure it won't be the same, but at least it will give us a chance to catch up."

Unsure of why Neil was being vague, Remy played along. "I didn't realize you were in town. Sure. Lunch sounds great. Where should we meet?"

"I'm in town for a meeting that got scheduled with some executive who's here. But why don't you come by the hotel and we can figure out where to go from there. I'm staying at the Royal Sonesta."

"Oh, swanky. You really must be doing okay for yourself," she laughed.

"Ha ha. It's on the record company's dime. Though I'm sure somehow, I'm paying for it. But I admit, it's pretty nice being right in the middle of everything. So, see you tomorrow then?"

"You got it. See you then," she said, setting the receiver down.

Sitting down on her couch, she kicked off her shoes, pulling her legs up underneath herself. She was happy and relieved at the idea of Neil being here. Though what help he could be remained to be seen. Maybe using the cover of his hotel room would be enough. She guessed Frank would show up as well, and this would give her the chance to fill him in on everything she learned.

Arriving at the Royal Sonesta the following morning, she walked to the reception desk and asked what room Neil Evans was in. Being directed to a suite on the third floor, Neil opened the door as she walked up, revealing it to be one of the rooms facing out over Bourbon Street. Walking in, she hugged Neil and took her time looking around, admiring the surroundings.

"Looks like you've done okay for yourself there, cousin. Need a personal assistant on this journey of yours?" she joked.

"Well, actually..." he started to say.

"I'm kidding. Well, sort of. I mean, if this is the kind of

place you're staying in every city, maybe I do need to rethink my idea of staying in New Orleans."

Hearing a deep laugh coming from the balcony, she spotted Frank leaning against the wrought-iron railing, a cup of coffee in hand.

As she and Neil walked out to join him, she noticed the spread of food already laid out. "Guess it's lunch in then?" she asked.

"I thought it might be better, away from prying eyes and ears," Frank said, pulling out a chair for her.

Remy nodded as she sat looking at both her dad and her cousin.

"If you'll excuse me, I have a call I need to make," Neil said as he walked back inside the suite, partially closing the French doors.

Turning her attention back to Frank, Remy waited for him to start the conversation.

"Please help yourself to whatever you'd like," he offered as he poured her a cup of coffee.

Picking up an empty plate, Remy chose half a muffuletta sandwich, some fresh oysters, and a small shrimp cocktail before returning to her seat.

"So I guess last night didn't go all that well," Frank quizzed as he sat across from her with his food.

"An understatement if ever there was one," Remy replied sardonically.

"Tell me what details I'm missing, then."

"I'm not sure what you know and what you don't, but I can tell you they knew you were at the masquerade party. And they are guessing that you're planning to be at the party Friday night too."

Seeing the look of surprise on Frank's face, she continued.

"Somehow they found out about my trip to Las Vegas. As I'm sure you overheard on the phone, Lily confronted me about that. But what I can't figure out is how. How did they know I went out there? I thought I fed her a plausible story about Neil discovering the house out there."

"I'm guessing you were followed. I'd also guess they've been listening to your phone calls for a while now too. Were you away from home for any period of time, aside from working, when someone got in and bugged your phone?"

"I suppose it could have happened back when I was traveling with Matt." Seeing the look of confusion in Frank's eyes, she explained who he was and the con she had attempted to pull on him.

As he sat taking it all in, she finished explaining, took a bite of her sandwich and ate the oysters, while waiting for his next question.

"Okay. That makes sense. You had Lily bring in your mail, so it would have been the perfect cover to let someone else in. While this adds another wrinkle to our plan, it's not something we can't overcome."

"How? How do you expect to overcome any of this? They are assuming you are going to show up Friday night. In fact, I think they want you to show up. Are you telling me that you are just going to walk in with this hanging over your head? You're signing your death warrant!" Remy exclaimed.

"Remy, please. You may not think it right now, but I do know what I'm doing. Honestly, I'm surprised it's taken this long for my past to catch up to me."

"But,"

"No. No buts. Do I regret not spending more time with you and your mom over these past years? A resounding yes. Do I have my doubts about how things will turn out Friday night? Also, yes. But I've had this hanging over my head for so long now, it's time for me to settle this score. Once and for all. If all goes according to plan, then by the end of the party Friday night, Michael will be hauled back off to jail, the rest of his little gang should be joining him in adjoining cells, and you should be in the clear."

"You still haven't told me how you're going to do this, though."

"You're right. And I'm not going to. The less you know, the better. You need to go into work that evening like any other night. Michael is not going to confront you then. He's got too much riding on this event. If I had to guess, he'll wait until the night is over to make his next move on you."

"So, should I still go up to Baton Rouge then? I mean, if all of this will be over soon, does it make sense to hide the diamonds again?"

"Yes, go and rent the box, keep them safe. Along with any other paperwork, letters, anything else you deem important. Those are your insurance policy Remy. You need to guard all of it with your life."

"Dad, I, I'm scared. What's going to happen? To you? Me? Momma? Heck, even Neil. I guess he's been involved in this since the beginning."

"No, he hasn't. He knew nothing of it back then. At least not when it happened. After the fact is when he found out. Just like you. And I owe him an apology too. I put the kid through a lot after life had already dealt him a rough hand.

And while I understand you're scared, and it sounds like just words that I'm saying, please hear me when I tell you, everything will be okay. You and your mom will be safe and taken care of. I've made sure of it."

"So you're really not going to tell me anything else then, are you?"

"No, it's for your own good. This week has to appear as normal as possible. Go about your job as you ordinarily would. Take your mom with you to Baton Rouge. Have a nice lunch while you're up there. Enjoy the day. Before you know it, Friday night will be here, and you'll be so busy charming all the guests, you won't have time to think or notice anything else going on. If all goes according to plan, let's all meet for a family meal on Sunday at the old house. I'm sure Victor's family would love to see you again."

Realizing she wouldn't get any further in changing her dad's mind, she let the subject drop. Neil came out and joined them for the remainder of the lunch, regaling them with tales of life on the road.

Chapter Forty-One

The rest of the week passed, sometimes slowly, other times with alarming speed. Remy and her mother drove to Baton Rouge as planned, making it appear as though they went to the doctor's office. After parking in the lot, they entered the building, only for Remy to sneak out the back and walk three blocks to the bank. Unsure if she was being followed or not, she did everything possible to hide her identity.

After successfully setting up her account and storing everything she brought with her, she returned to the medical offices, walking back out with her mother. They lunched and even did a little shopping. Remy decided a new dress was in order for Friday night, and she wanted to be able to say she bought this one on her own without any strings attached. Too much of what she had been wearing these past months at work came with reminders and memories of events she'd rather soon forget.

On the drive back into New Orleans, she spotted the

same pickup truck she had seen so many times before. Certain now that whoever was behind the wheel was connected to Jordan somehow, she hoped they hadn't been following her all day. She should have been paying more attention to her surroundings, but was so wrapped up in everything else going on, she let that one detail slip.

After dropping her mom off at her home, Remy drove over to the Garden District, where she found a parking spot not too far from the Batiste family home. Walking down the street, she paused when she got to the front gate. It looked a little smaller now that she was grown. The house loomed so large in her memory when she was a child. It was still a grand home, well maintained all these years. Memories of sitting on the porch swing, drinking sweet tea and watching the Mardi Gras parades flooded her mind. How nice it would have been to have a normal childhood in a house like this. Instead of the tumultuous life she had lived. Moving on quickly before anyone came out to inquire what she was doing, she continued on down the block. Finding a small local bar, she stopped in for a quiet drink to help settle her nerves before returning home.

For the next two nights, she kept to herself at work, doing her job, while keeping her interactions with everyone else to a minimum. Most everyone else was too busy with party preparations, except Lily. She confronted Remy Thursday night at the end of their shift.

"Remy. We need to talk," she said.

"No Lily. I don't think we do," Remy tartly replied as she tried to push past her.

"Yes, we do," Lily said, grabbing hold of Remy's arm. "Not here. Meet me at The Abbey in half an hour. Alone."

Resigning herself to the meeting only because she was curious what Lily had to say to her now, she muttered under her breath, "Fine."

Putting on her coat, she hastily made her way out of the club before anyone else stopped her. Taking her time, she walked to The Abbey and took a seat at the far end of the bar, ordering a club soda. Waiting for Lily to arrive, she wondered what was so important they had to meet this late and here of all places. As the bartender set down her drink, Lily walked in the door, making her way straight to the seat next to Remy, and began talking.

"You need to watch your back tomorrow night. Jordan is mighty pissed right now, and he's determined to find out where you've got the diamonds. Yeah, yeah. I know about it all now. He filled Theo and me in on everything. Remy, you thought we were friends. Why didn't you tell me?"

"Friends?" Remy practically shouted. "I realize now that ever thinking we were friends was a huge mistake on my part. And you have the audacity to wonder why I didn't tell you? Even if I didn't know that you would have just gone and blabbed to Jordan, that's not really something you randomly share with anyone. And it's not his or anyone's business. You are all trouble. With a capital T. And after tomorrow night, I never want to see any of you ever again. Seriously, why am I even here now?"

Reaching for her purse, she rose from her seat when Lily shot her a look.

"Sit down and listen to me," Lily implored. "I'd say I'm sorry, but you wouldn't believe me. And I know it's too little too late now, but I wanted to give you this warning to be on your guard tomorrow night. At some point in the evening, Jordan is going to assign you to one of the private rooms. He apparently has some associates in attendance who will be waiting for you. I don't know specifically what he has planned for them to do to you, but I know it's not going to be good and certainly not what you deserve. That's all I wanted to tell you. Do with that what you will. If I were you, I probably would not even come to work tomorrow night. Skip town now. If you do have the diamonds, take them and run. Start a life somewhere else. Somewhere new."

Lily hung her head in defeat as Remy stared at her.

"Why are you telling me this? You've obviously been a part of this since the beginning. What do you get out of my leaving now? Won't he figure out that you told me, and then he'll turn on you too?"

"Theo and I had a long conversation last night. And just because we're in over our heads, doesn't mean that any of this was fair to you. We were simply doing what we were told because we didn't have a choice. I'm sure we're going to face the consequences of what we've done. Jordan already alluded to as much in our last conversation. Since neither of us has a way out, I guess I just thought, what the hell. The least I could do was try to throw you a lifeline. You don't deserve to be hurt like that."

Considering her options, Remy took a sip of her soda, then set it down on the bar. "Thanks for the warning. But I need to see this through. I can't go through life always having to look over my shoulder. So I guess I'll see you at work tomorrow."

Grabbing her belongings, she threw a tip down on the

bar and walked back out into the night with visions of what she would be stepping into tomorrow night racing through her head.

Chapter Forty-Two

Friday morning started off stormy, as if Mother Nature knew what was on the horizon for that night and was trying to send a warning to the entire city. Thunder rolled on throughout the day, the skies threatening to open at any moment and rain down their wrath in an attempt to cleanse the city. Remy watched from her window as she prepared for what was to come.

Leaving her apartment, she opted to drive, not wanting to leave anything to chance. Tossing her shoes and purse on the seat next to her, she arranged her dress in order not to wrinkle it as little as possible, at least. Arriving at the club, she found a parking spot relatively close, seeing as how most of the regular parking was reserved for the VIPs, and made her way inside. Just as she closed the door behind her, the skies opened, rain and wind blowing down the streets, the old lanterns lighting up in response to the sudden darkness. Not waiting to see what would transpire next, she made her way up the stairs and prepared to face whatever was going to come her way.

Walking in, she found most of the staff busy bustling around, putting the last minute touches to the flourishes that decorated every area of the club. Not wasting any time, she quickly changed her shoes, grabbed a tray, and joined in. Avoiding Jordan as much as possible, she bumped into Marcus, who barely grunted in greeting. Tensions were definitely running high as the first guests arrived.

Women in gowns, dripping in diamonds and other fine jewels, and men dressed in their finest black-tie poured in through the doors as peals of thunder rumbled in the background, ushering them inside. The strains of the jazz band playing, along with the clinking of glasses, and conversations filling the room soon replaced the sounds of the storm if not the tension.

Remy made her rounds, making sure no guest was empty-handed. Some were immediately directed to private rooms upon their arrival, as the others made their way to the open tables in the main room, set up either to enjoy a meal or a friendly game of poker, blackjack, or gin rummy. The money being raised at this event was supposedly for charity, and while some would go to worthy causes, most would find its way through the business coffers and eventually into Jordan's personal accounts. Though Remy had no tangible proof of this, based on everything her father had told her, she wouldn't be surprised if it were true. Perhaps that would just be one of many charges in a long list to be brought against him once this night was over.

Making her way to a table to deliver another bottle of champagne, Marcus stopped her. "Your presence is requested in one of the private rooms." He insisted.

"Uh, sure," Remy stammered. "Let me finish taking care

of the tables I have currently, and I'll be back as soon as I can."

Raising an eyebrow in question, Marcus glanced around the room. About to turn back to her, he stopped when the front door opened and he saw Frank boldly walk in. "Yeah, uh, never mind. I'll have Lily go take care of them instead. You can stay out here on the floor for now. I've got to go take care of something." He said, moving quickly towards the back hall to Jordan's office.

'Guess the storm is about to pick up in intensity,' she thought to herself, seeing Frank making his way to the bar. Delivering the bottle to the table, she turned to drop off the remaining drinks for the next group, when she noticed Matt had joined them.

"Oh, I'm sorry, sir," she apologized, not revealing that she recognized him. "I didn't get your drink order before. Can I get you something?"

Playing along, Matt smiled, "Yes, please. I'd like a glass of your best bourbon, straight, please. Uh, I'm sorry, I didn't get your name."

"Of course. Remy, sir. Nice to meet you. Let me get you that bourbon right away," she replied, hastily making her way to the bar.

His presence here now added another layer to an already complex night. Especially since she hadn't been able to find a chance to fill him in on everything that had taken place since they last spoke.

Returning with his drink, she asked, "Is there anything else I can get for you right now?"

"Not at the moment, thank you. But I'm sure we'll be

ready to order some food soon, if you wouldn't mind checking back shortly."

Nodding in agreement, she turned as he slipped a piece a cocktail napkin into her hand. Tucking it under her notebook, she glanced around to make sure no one else noticed. Seeing Frank watching their interaction, she wondered if he had a connection to Matt too. Add it to the list of questions she had. At this point now, nothing would surprise her.

Returning to her station at the bar, she slid the napkin out and held it below the bar where no one else could see it. All he had written on it was, "I'm here when you need me".

While it was nice of him, she couldn't quite decipher what he meant by that cryptic message. Was he meaning tonight? Or in general? Before she could figure it out, Frank leaned over and said in a voice barely above a whisper, "When it's time to go, find Matt," before turning his attention back to the couple on his right.

Okay, so Matt and Frank had met before, she decided. How long that had been going on barely crossed her mind as Kenny set down the next round of drinks to deliver. "Earth to Remy. You in there? No time to be flaking out on us, girl," he said.

"Sorry. Just a momentary lapse. I've hardly had time to breathe since coming in. Looks like it's going to be nonstop all night."

Stepping away from the bar, she wove through the crowd, trying not to spill any of what was on her tray. Rounding a corner, she caught sight of Jordan coming out of one of the VIP rooms, a deadly look in his eyes. She ducked behind a group of guests, watching as he made his way to the bar where Frank was now standing alone. She saw him slide up next to him, stand still, and wait.

Trying to keep her composure, she quickly delivered the drinks and made her way back towards the bar. When she heard Kenny ask if he wanted anything, she saw Jordan shooing him away before turning to face Frank straight on. "Frank Barnes, as I live and breathe. Or have you gone back to Batiste since you're back home now?"

Frank turned to face the voice coming from behind him, giving nothing away when he saw Jordan, or rather Michael as he knew him. "Michael Leon. Oh, I'm sorry. I should say, Jordan Dubois. Since that's the name everyone here knows you by. I didn't think I'd ever see the day we'd come face to face again. Last I heard, you were still somewhere out west, I believe."

Frank was being coy, not wanting to draw any unwanted attention to himself, while letting Jordan make the next move. As the band launched into a rendition of Professor Longhair's "Big Chief" the crowd got up on their feet and began to march around the room. Jordan took this opportunity and waved at a table off to the side. "Let's have a chat over there, away from some of this noise. What do you say? We've got a lot of catching up to do."

Frank followed, carrying his drink in one hand, the other tucked into his pocket. Walking towards the table, he caught Remy's eye, holding up the glass as if to indicate he would like another one. Wondering if it was a good idea, she shrugged, turning to the bar and requesting another drink for him and one for Jordan as well.

Approaching the table, she caught only snippets of their conversation over the music. It was sounding mundane enough, Jordan explaining how he came to be in New Orleans and owning the Carrington club. Frank nodded, as though he were riveted to the information being shared.

When she heard Jordan explain how he was released from jail, she felt a chill run down her spine. So it was all true. He had been involved with the Costa family and everything else her dad had told her. Once again, she found herself mixed up in something she didn't want to be. She really should have listened to the voice in her head all those months ago when it told her to get out of here.

As she set down the drinks, Jordan turned to her. "Remy, glad you could join us," he taunted.

"Can I get you gentlemen anything else right now?" she asked, trying to maintain her composure.

"Yes, you can have a seat. Better yet, let's take this conversation somewhere more private. Go tell Kenny you need someone to cover your tables. You'll be off the floor for an undetermined amount of time."

Seeing she had no choice in the matter, she simply replied, "Of course."

As Jordan stood, extending his arm in a gesture for Frank to go first. "Down the hall, last door on the right. Go ahead. Have a seat, and I'll join you in a moment."

Remy made her way to the bar, setting down her tray and giving instructions to Kenny to pass along to whoever picked up her tables. Before he asked any further questions, she headed down the hall, finding the door open, Frank already in one of the chairs in front of the desk. Drink in hand, he appeared nonchalant, looking around as though he were taking in the overall design of the office.

"Frank?" she questioned.

"Not now," he quipped as Jordan walked in and closed the door behind him. It grew deathly quiet, the band hardly a murmur in the background. This was the first time Remy had noticed how soundproof the room was. Why didn't she pick up on that detail before? Just another mistake to add to her ever-growing list of blunders.

"This is a touching little family reunion, isn't it?" Jordan asked, looking between the two of them. "It really has been too long, I'd say. At least for us, Frank. What it's been twenty years now?"

"Something like that. Though I thought it would have been longer based on what I had last heard of you and, well, everyone else," Frank replied, as Remy sat dumbfounded by how casual the two were being.

"Everyone except Redd, of course. Don't know if you heard, but he turned state's evidence too. Guess just cause he married into the family didn't mean that he had the balls to do what needed to be done."

Frank nodded, waiting for Jordan to continue. When he didn't, Frank asked, "So what is it you're planning to do here, Michael?" Seeing Jordan's reaction to being called by his old name, Frank made a mental note of how much it irritated him.

"It's Jordan now, if you don't mind," he snapped.

"Of course. My mistake. But you haven't answered my question. What are your plans? After all, you have a room full of the city's highest officials here. I don't think you'd be able to get away with much with all that security present."

"No, you're right about that. Though I will admit, a lot of that security is on my payroll. I learned some valuable lessons working with you and Mr. Costa. No, this evening you both will walk out of here of your own accord. That is after you tell me where the diamonds are."

"Did you really think it would be that easy, Michael? Really, you say you learned so much, but I don't think you did."

Noticing Jordan seething now, Frank continued. "No, you're going to let Remy and me leave. After you pay her out what she's owed, and throw in a substantial tip, seeing as how you've pulled her away from her tables for the evening. And then you are going to forget either of us even exists. As for the diamonds, um, no. No clue where they are anymore. And I'm sure Remy has no idea what you're talking about either. Seeing as how she was only a small child when all of that happened."

"I don't believe you. And if you think for a moment it's going to be that easy to walk away, you have got to be delusional."

"Have it your way then," Frank said. Giving no indication of what he meant by that. He stood, extended his hand to Remy, and led her out back into the club. "Grab your things and meet me outside. I've got a car waiting."

Chapter Forty-Three

Just as Remy was walking out the front door, she ran into Matt, who was walking back in. Seeing her leaving, he stopped, sending Ella and a couple of other employees of his on ahead. Ella shot a questioning look, which he shook his head in response to. "Everything is fine. Go on. Have a good time this evening. I'll see you all at the office on Monday."

Turning back to Remy, he asked, "Is everything okay? I'm surprised to see you leaving already."

"No, everything is not okay. But I can't talk about it here. Not right now. My dad has a car waiting," she said, nodding her head in the direction of a black sedan.

Ever the gentleman, Matt escorted her to the car, opening the back door for her. Seeing Frank sitting inside already, he paused. "Are you sure you're alright?"

"Yes, I'll be fine. I really have to go," she said as she climbed into the empty seat.

As he started to close the door, he heard Frank's voice, "Matt. Why don't you join us? I think this might be something you would be interested in as well." Hearing it not so much as a suggestion, but a strong request he couldn't refuse, he opened the front passenger door and settled into the seat as they pulled away from the curb.

"Matt Hanson, nice to meet you in person. I'm Frank Batiste. Remy's father," Frank said as he extended his hand across the back of the seat.

"Nice to meet you, sir," Matt said, shaking his hand and looking at Remy, who had unasked questions written across her face. Noticing they were headed towards the Garden District, he turned his attention forward, not asking any more questions until he had a better idea of what he had stepped into.

The tension in the car was heavy, no one saying anything, until they stopped in front of the Batiste family home. "Pull around back, if you wouldn't mind," Frank instructed the driver.

Once safely around the backside of the house, Frank exited the car, opening both Remy and Matt's doors, before leading them to the carriage house. Unlocking the door, he let them enter before closing and relocking the door once again. Turning on a few lights, Remy saw the place had been lived in recently.

"Dad, is there were you've been staying since you got back?"

"Yes, Victor's kids have been kind enough to keep it up for me while I was gone and, well, have pretty much let me have the run of this space since I've been back. I thought I would have seen you over here sooner. But I guess you haven't really kept in touch with your cousins much, have you?"

"Uh, no. Not really. Well, other than Neil. As you know, even that was recent too. But a family reunion is not what we're here for, now is it?"

Seeing the look of confusion on Matt's face, she was wondering herself why her dad would have brought them here. Wouldn't this be one of the first places Jordan came to look?

"Right. I owe you both an explanation. Matt, I'm sure you have way more questions than we have time to answer right now. Let me give you the pertinent details. If you decide to leave after that, I will have my driver take you back to the Carrington, and you can go on with your life. However, I must warn you. If you stay, you're going to find yourself involved in some things which could impact your life in not so pleasant ways." Seeing Matt nod in agreement, he briefly explained his time spent living in Las Vegas, being involved in the diamond theft, and who Jordan really is and his history.

Once finished with his explanation, he got up to get everyone something to drink, giving Matt time to digest all he heard. Frank overheard Matt asking Remy questions about her involvement, and her answers were vague at best. Frank had put her in a tough spot, he knew, and as much as he wanted to protect her, she was going to have to come clean with Matt about her involvement as well.

Handing them their glasses, he sat down across from Remy and looked pointedly at her. "You need to tell him everything. He deserves to know the truth."

"Are you sure? I mean, even I don't know what to believe anymore."

Seeing him nod, she turned to Matt and began detailing

what had transpired earlier in the week, how she found out about Lily and Theo deceiving her the entire time as well, ending with telling him about the diamonds hidden away in Baton Rouge.

"So, everything you thought you knew was completely upended then. And the information I found out about Jordan and his business dealings - information I haven't been able to share with you yet - proves he's not been legal in those areas either. Not that I can say I'm surprised now."

"No. But now with you having that information, it's another proverbial nail in his coffin. But I don't want to see you get hurt too. I've already put you through too much as it is. You need to leave now. Go live your life. Settle down with someone like Ella, who's not going to bring danger to your door."

Sitting back in his chair, Matt took a sip of his drink before setting it down and picking up one of Remy's hands.

"No. I don't think I'm going to do that. I appreciate the concern both of you have shown me. But I'm able to take care of myself. Plus, I think I may have some resources you don't, which might be of some help to get you out from under this once and for all."

"What do you mean? What kind of resources?" Remy asked as Frank sat stoically, taking it all in.

"First off, I have a safe where, if you want, you can set the combination and store whatever you need to. I know you've already taken them to Baton Rouge, but if you'd feel better having them close by, then my offer stands. Second, I have friends in law enforcement that I can say with certainty are not connected to Jordan in any way. I'm pretty sure they would be more than happy to hear what you have to say and to do whatever is necessary to take him down. I will make sure you both have immunity too. No sense in going through all this just to have to go to jail too. And lastly, well not last, but for now, know this. I forgave you already. I've put the hurt behind me. Because when I think about most of the time we spent together, Remy, you touched me in a way that no one else has. You didn't expect anything from me. In fact, it felt as though you were quite uncomfortable taking any of the presents I gave you. Which tells me you weren't really interested in conning me like you were supposed to do. So, if you are ready to give up that life and turn over a new leaf, let me help you. However I can."

Frank leaned in, focusing his attention on Matt. "Are you sure about this? You get mixed up further into this quagmire, and there's no turning back."

"I'm sure. I don't know why, but I believe both of you. That you want to put this all behind you and live a normal life for a change." Turning to Remy, he implored. "Please let me help. Both of you, and your mom too."

After much discussion about the next steps and setting plans in place for what everyone had to do next, Frank called for his driver to take Remy and Matt home.

"I'll be in touch once I've had a chance to make some calls," Matt said, shaking Frank's hand.

Leading them out to the driveway, Frank opened the car door, letting Matt and Remy get settled before leaning in with one last word of advice.

"Remy, for your safety, I'd suggest you go stay somewhere else tonight. I'm sure Michael has someone keeping an eye on your place. Stop by home if you absolutely must.

But if you do, try to make it look like you're in for the night before you try to sneak out again. If he's following his old ways, once he thinks you're in, he'll call off whoever is keeping watch and send someone else early in the morning. It was always one of his faults back in the day, and if I had to guess, he's still cocky enough to think the same ruse will still work."

"Hmm...," Remy mused.

"What?" Frank asked.

"It would explain the truck randomly parked across the street from my apartment. There's been no rhyme or reason to it, but whoever it is always does a really bad job of parking. That's the only reason I ever noticed."

Rolling his eyes, Frank replied, "Stupid man. I can't tell you how many times Nick and I both got onto him about that. But yeah, that's yet another tactic of his. It's like he wants to give himself away. So if you see it again when you get home, keep an eye on it. Once it leaves, you should be clear to go."

"Sir, I will take responsibility for Remy's safety tonight. And for however long it may take after tonight as well." Matt stated.

Frank closed the door and patted the roof as a sign to say it was clear for the driver to pull away. He was thankful Matt was stepping up, even after the way Remy had treated him. Maybe life would turn out differently for her after all.

Chapter Forty-Four

So as not to be seen with Matt, Remy asked the driver to drop him off first. If someone was watching her apartment, she didn't want to give them any more information to take back to Jordan. Once the truck was gone, if it was indeed back again tonight, she would call Matt and he would send a cab for her. He had told her to bring only what was necessary. Anything else she needed, he would happily get for her.

Not wanting to take advantage of him or the situation, she packed a few days' worth of clothes and the safe deposit box key. Knowing all the other letters and papers were back at her mom's house, she didn't worry about someone breaking in here, since they wouldn't find anything. Of course, she had the nagging thought someone might try to get into her mom's place too. That would be something she would ask Matt to look into. Some sort of security, whether it was an alarm or an actual bodyguard for her mother. She'd be devastated should any harm come to her.

Shutting off the lights, she crept around her apartment, trying to make it appear as though she was going to bed. Pushing a curtain aside ever so slightly, she saw the same pickup truck still parked outside. Had her dad been wrong this time? Would it remain parked, watching all night? Going back to her bedroom, she shut off the light, and lay down on top of her made bed. With all the thoughts running rampant through her head, she tried calming herself down, but jumped at every little noise she heard.

Half an hour later she heard the rumble of an engine starting, followed by the sound of a vehicle driving away. Without getting up to look, she couldn't be sure it had been the truck. Yet she felt as though she were pinned in place, unable to move due to fear. Lying still for another ten minutes, she took the time to calm herself until it was safe to get up and look outside. Tiptoeing across the floor, even though she knew the apartment below hers was unoccupied at the time, she walked to her balcony doors. Seeing her reflection in the glass, she slid off to the side, hoping no one was watching and saw her moving around. Thinking quick, she made her way to the kitchen to make it appear as though she was getting a glass of water. Her view of the street was mostly obstructed by an old oak tree, but thanks to the earlier storm and the leaves that had blown off, she saw the truck was no longer parked where it had been. That didn't mean it hadn't moved somewhere else where she couldn't see. But she had to take the chance. Whoever had been there, was now gone.

Calling Matt, she wasn't surprised when he answered before the first ring even finished. "I was getting worried," he said breathlessly.

"Me too," she sighed. "But it looks like the coast should be clear now. I don't think it's a good idea for the cab to pick me up out front, though. Just in case someone else is out there too. I'll go out through the courtyard, which leads to the alley behind the building. It will put me out close to Bienville, and I can hail a cab over there. I'm sure there will be enough tourists and others still out and about giving me enough cover to go unnoticed."

"Are you sure that's such a good idea?"

"I think it's better this way. I don't want some poor cabbie trying to find me. I feel like that would just draw more attention than is needed right now. If I don't arrive in forty-five minutes, then call my dad. Not that I have any idea what he'd be able to do. Otherwise, I'll see you soon." Remy hung up before Matt could protest. She was certain she didn't want to see anyone else get hurt, and this was her best course of action.

Grabbing her duffel bag, she exited her apartment, walking down the two flights of stairs to the lobby. Turning towards the back of the building, she made her way out into the courtyard, pausing for a moment. This was the feature that sold her on renting in this building. Little hidden spots like this where you found an escape from the hustle and bustle, while still being in the city. Realizing she was only delaying herself, she picked up her pace again, exiting out into the alley, and turning towards Bienville. Finding it still busy with locals and tourists alike, she blended in with the crowd, moving down another block before attempting to hail a taxi.

After three cabs passed her by, she wondered if this was the best idea. Maybe she should turn around and head back to her apartment and let Matt send one for her. In one last attempt to try, she flung her arm out to wave down the approaching taxi, when a hand grabbed her arm, a voice grating in her ear. "Don't say a word. Don't yell for help or fight me. Or your mom won't like what happens to her next."

Hearing the intensity of Marcus's voice, she dropped her arm and turned to face him. "Leave my mother out of this. She's sick and has nothing to do with anything."

"Not my call to make. Now, are you coming with me or not?"

Knowing she had no choice in the matter, she let out a long breath and fell into step beside him. Walking half a block down, she saw the same pickup truck that had been parked outside her place earlier. Marcus opened the door for her, took her bag and threw it in the bed of the truck, telling her, "You won't be needing that right now."

Settling into the seat, she was glad she had hidden the key in her shoe. At least when they searched the bag, they wouldn't find anything more than her clothes and toiletries. Though she was sure it wouldn't be long before they'd search her too.

Driving for what she guessed to be fifteen minutes, Marcus took the last corner too tight and hit the curb, causing Remy to slide in her seat and knock her head against the window. Feeling slightly disoriented, she tried to regain her focus on where they were going when he pulled up in front of what looked like an old abandoned building.

Exiting the truck, he barked, "Follow me." Not bothering to grab her bag or even open her door. For a moment she considered bolting, but knew she wouldn't get far on foot.

Following a few paces behind, she kept glancing around, looking for any discernible landmarks. Seeing a street sign for Jourdan Road, she thought it ironic but easy enough to commit to memory. She'd be able to give that information to either her dad or, better yet, the police if she found her way out of here. She was sure Matt would be worried even more now. Hopefully, he did what she asked and called her father. Frank would know what to do, if not where to look.

Walking into a warehouse, Remy smelled the remnants of whatever business had been here before. From the odor assaulting her nose, she assumed it had been a seafood processing plant, which meant they were close to the river. Easy dumping grounds for bodies was another one of the reasons for being here, she guessed. Approaching a door to an office, she stopped when she found Jordan pacing back and forth, obviously agitated and in no mood for anything other than straight answers.

Marcus pushed her further in, then left, closing the door behind him. Regaining her footing, she stood still, waiting for Jordan to say something. Anything. Instead, he continued his stomping, back and forth, each step heavier than the last. When he turned to face her, she saw the fury in his eyes.

"So this is what it's come to. You are going to pick up that phone and place a call to your father. He is going to come down here with the diamonds."

"And?" she questioned when he stopped mid sentence.

Glaring at her, he stomped away and back again.

"And then, you'll either become food for the alligators or food for the fish. I'll leave that choice up to you."

"Gee, that's a tough decision to make," she replied sarcastically. Knowing her attitude would aggravate him more, and it was the only power she had available to her at the moment. In an effort to stall as long as possible, she opened her mouth to ask Jordan a question. Before she was even able to get a word out, he shoved the phone into her chest. "Call," he demanded.

Dialing the old rotary phone as slowly as she could get away with, she first dialed her number and listened as it rang until her answering machine picked up. Seeing him seething at her stall, she hung up and dialed Frank's number this time, again letting it ring. When no one answered, she placed the receiver back on the cradle. She cocked her head to the side and smiled. "No one's home."

Jordan's face bloomed red in response. Grabbing the phone from her hands, he started as if to throw it across the room, then thought better.

"Fine. I guess we'll just have to make ourselves comfortable while we wait then. Oh no, instead I think I'll go make myself comfortable. You, on the other hand, can go wait over there," he said, gesturing to the adjoining room.

Marching her into the even smaller area, she winced when her foot squished what she guessed were the remains of dead fish and shrimp. How long they had been festering, she didn't even want to hazard a guess.

"Sorry, don't have a chair for you to sit down on. But I'm sure you'll find someway to keep yourself entertained while you're waiting," he said as he slammed the door closed behind her.

Stepping over piles and trying not to lose her footing, she tried in vain to find a small area not covered in unknown goo. Eventually winding up in the middle of a wall, she found a spot to at least lean back and try to regain some semblance of thought. Looking at her watch, she noticed it had been well over an hour since she last spoke to Matt. Surely he and Frank would be doing all they could to find her now. But would they know to look here? And how would this all end?

Chapter Forty-Five

When Remy didn't arrive by the time she was supposed to, Matt became more frantic. His hands shook as he dialed Frank's number. When Frank answered after the third ring, Matt began verbally vomiting his worst fears about what he thought was happening to Remy.

"Matt, slow down. Start from the beginning. I can hardly understand what you're trying to say." Frank replied, trying to get a hold of both his and Matt's thoughts.

"Sorry. Yeah. So, Remy was supposed to be here by now. After she dropped me off, she went home to get a few things and then, once it was clear, she was going to come back here for a few days. We figured it would be the safest place for her. Last I heard from her, she was going to get a cab on Bienville. But she never showed up. All I can guess is that she got grabbed by Jordan, or one of his guys."

"I wish I could say I was surprised, but I'm not. He really doesn't have any new plays in his book. Alright. Here's what's going to happen. I'm going to come by and pick you up. We'll head to her place first and see what we can find. If I know Michael like I do, he will have taken her somewhere relatively close, but deserted at this time of night. Somewhere I'm sure he controls too."

"I may have an idea of where that might be," Matt interrupted. "Remy had me doing some background digging on him. Seems not only does he own the Carrington, but he's also bought an old warehouse, down by the Industrial Canal."

"That's it. That's where he'll have her then. This guy really has no imagination. It's no wonder he got caught and sent to jail." Frank grumbled. "I'll be there shortly. Be ready."

Hanging up the phone, Matt grabbed the address of the warehouse, along with a gun he had stashed in his desk. While he didn't enjoy having it in the house, he knew he was always a target because of some of his past business dealings, and felt better having it at hand. Never did he think he'd have to use it. And he hoped he wouldn't have to tonight either.

Closing the door behind him, he walked down to the sidewalk, looking around for any unfamiliar cars or people. Living in a quiet neighborhood, he easily recognized anything out of the ordinary. Most of the residents here were older, having lived here since they first came to the city. It was one of the many things he liked most about this area. Life moved at a slightly slower pace, more gentle. It always relaxed him when he came home, especially after stressful days at the office.

Seeing Frank pull up, he jumped into the car and gave Frank the address of the warehouse. The drive over was fraught with emotion, Frank trying to come up with a plan that would get Remy and themselves out alive.

"What about the diamonds? Surely Jordan, Michael, whoever this guy is, he's wanting those more than anything else. Can't we use those as a bargaining chip?" Matt asked.

"Maybe. Of course, the problem is Remy has them locked away at a bank in Baton Rouge. So it's not like we can easily go and get them now, in the middle of the night, and certainly not during regular business hours without her. And I don't think he's going to just let her walk out either. I'm sure he thinks she's his leverage against me. Which she is, but I can't give him the satisfaction of knowing that either."

"So what's our way through this then? If Jordan won't let her go, but he's demanding the diamonds, we're spinning our wheels here."

Pulling up half a block from the warehouse, Frank shut off his lights and killed the engine, not wanting to give any advanced warning of their arrival. Letting his eyes adjust to the darkness, he took his time canvassing the area to see what security was posted outside. Surprised by the fact that only one car was parked outside the door, he wondered if Michael was even there.

Motioning for Matt to stand behind him, he tried the door, finding it unlocked. This was either fortuitous for them or stupid on the part of whoever was inside. Or perhaps it was a part of the plan by whoever was inside, expecting him to show up. Putting his finger to his lips to silence any comment Matt was thinking of making, he slowly opened the door, revealing a dark, cavernous space, with light spilling from a back corner. Stepping inside, he closed the door as soon as Matt was through, and gestured for them both to stay alongside the wall. Not wanting to give away their position by making any more noise than necessary, both men slid down the length of the wall slowly.

Knowing their element of surprise would be gone as soon as they opened the door, Frank turned to Matt and whispered, "Go see if you can find any other rooms or offices. The fact that this one is the only one lit tells me it's a trap. No sense in both of us getting caught up in it."

"Are you sure? I mean, wouldn't he keep Remy close?"

"Exactly. But he's also not stupid enough to make it this easy. Now, go."

Watching Matt move on towards another door, Frank decided this was the now or never moment. Flinging open the door, he shouted when he saw he faced an empty room. "Damnit. Michael, I know you're here. Why don't you show your face, like a man?"

Hearing a chuckle coming from behind him, he spun around, coming face to face with Michael and a gun pointing at his head.

"I really should have done this years ago," Michael said. "Maybe things would have turned out differently. I'm pretty sure I wouldn't have spent all those years in jail if I had."

Frank eyed Michael while listening for any other noise he could detect to tell him Matt was making progress in his search for Remy. "You wouldn't have succeeded back then either," he replied as he swiftly kicked Michael in the groin, knocking the gun away in the process. "You always were a little bit slow in your reflexes."

Grunting in pain, Michael gasped, "You son of a bitch. You think you're going to save your daughter now? When I get done with the two of you..."

As they both lunged for the gun now lying a few feet away, Frank laughed at him. "You'll what? You have no leverage left." Pointing his gun at Michael, he continued, "I'll give you credit for trying. You were always good at that. But man, your planning and execution skills still leave a lot to be desired. As long as someone else did that, you could be relied on to be the muscle. I guess that's why Nick kept you around as long as he did."

In the split second that followed, Michael managed to scoop up the gun before Frank got it. Now as each of them had a gun pointing at the other, he threw his last Hail Mary, and shouted. "Remy, where are you?" just as Michael's fist came in contact with his jaw.

Hearing her call out from a darkened corner, he shifted, side-stepping another punch aimed at his gut this time. He also heard Matt's footsteps running towards where he was assuming she was being held. Not wanting to give away who was with him, he continued to engage Michael, throwing a few punches of his own, in hopes it would be enough of a distraction to give Matt the time he needed.

When Michael reacted to the sound of a door crashing open, it was just enough of a distraction to give Frank the opportunity to pull the trigger and shoot Michael in the stomach.

"Dad!" Remy screamed.

"I'm alright," he shouted back as Michael got off a shot of his own, hitting Frank in the upper arm. He barely noticed the pain of the wound as adrenaline coursed through him now. Barreling towards Michael, he knocked him back down to the ground. Trying to keep him pinned long enough to wrestle away the gun, he was relieved when Matt and Remy came running over.

Matt landed a right hook to Michael's ribs, knocking the breath out of him. As Frank grabbed the piece of rope he had stuffed in his back pocket, Remy picked up the gun. Flipping Michael over, he tied his hands behind his back, leaving him face down on the putrid floor.

Remy, shaking, reached out to touch Frank's arm when she saw it bleeding. "You need a hospital. Now," she cried.

"I'll be fine," he said to her while looking around as the lights came on when Matt found an electrical control panel. "Is there a phone in this place?"

"Yeah, in the office. I was trying to call you, but didn't get any answer. Guess you were already on your way then."

"Go call the cops. Tell them where you are and someone has been shot. He'll live, but needs an ambulance. I can't be here when they arrive. But I think you and Matt will be able to handle it from here. That fella of yours is pretty good in a fight, it seems."

Remy looked at Matt and smiled before turning back to Frank. "Where are you going?" she demanded.

"I'll be around. I just can't be here when the cops show up. Go on now, make the call and I'll be in touch in the next day or two." Frank replied as Matt came walking back. "Take care of my girl."

"Yes, sir," Matt said, first looking at Remy, then turning his attention to Michael, still face down on the ground. Placing a foot on his back, he gave her the exact address of where they were and a second number to call once she finished with the police.

"Who is that?" she asked.

"The district attorney. His home number. I'm sure he won't appreciate being woken up, but once you tell him who we have here, I'm pretty confident he'll be paying attention."

While Matt and Remy were distracted, Frank began his escape. Wrapping a handkerchief around his arm, he made sure he wasn't leaving a trail of blood behind and quickly left the building. Hearing Matt say he had a relationship with the district attorney set Frank's mind a little more at ease. With friends like that, the two of them would be cleared of anything in this matter, and surely Michael would be returning to jail for many years to come. Unsure how long he would have to stay out of sight, he would keep his word and would get in touch with his daughter as soon as he deemed it safe.

Chapter Forty-Six

Matt had been right. The district attorney gave Remy his full attention as soon as she gave him a basic rundown of what had taken place. Having attended the gala earlier in the evening, he was very familiar with everyone involved. He said he would send officers to pick up Marcus, Theo, and Lily right away. For a brief moment, Remy considered sparing Lily and Theo but knew in the end they would have to face whatever consequences came their way too.

After spending the rest of the night and most of the following morning at the police station, Matt was finally able to take Remy home. Since her bag had been in the truck it was being kept in police custody as evidence. Having no clean clothes or toiletries with her now she desperately wanted to wash off the smell and memories of the last night. She convinced Matt to make a stop at her apartment, where he insisted he would stay while she showered and changed.

"I'll wait out here until you're ready. Then we'll go get

something to eat. I don't know about you, but fights and gun battles always make me hungry," he joked.

Shaking her head, she looked at him. "I am so sorry. Truly. I never meant to get you involved in any of this. And if something had happened to you, I don't think I would have forgiven myself."

"Hey now. Nothing did happen though. So don't even think about that. Everything is going to be fine. You're in the clear. Jordan, or whoever he is, is going back to jail for a long time. And the others, well they'll face whatever comes their way too."

"You're right. I just kind of feel bad for Lily and Theo. I mean, they brought it on themselves, but still. And what about my dad? He got shot after all. Is he alright? I've had no messages or anything from him." She said, looking over at her answering machine again as if the message indicator light would start blinking only because she willed it to.

"He's fine. I'm sure of it. We would have heard otherwise."

Seeing she wasn't convinced, he continued. "He promised you he would be in touch in a few days, and from what little I know of him, I think he's a man of his word. While we didn't have a lot of time to dig into each other's psyches or relationships, he genuinely cares about you and was terrified of what was happening. Despite what you've told me about your rocky past, I think he really wants to make amends with you now."

"How can you be so sure? Like you said, you barely know him."

"I'm a pretty good judge of character and people. I saw

how much he loves you in everything we did trying to find and save you."

"You weren't such a great judge when it came to me," she replied.

"You're wrong. I saw your character, and it was good even then. Your intentions may not have been in the right place as you were following someone else's orders. But underneath it all, you were always who you truly are." Placing a kiss on her cheek, he continued, "Now, go take a long hot shower. Wash it all down the drain and think about where you want to go for lunch."

As Remy pulled off her shoes, the key she had hidden fell out, onto the floor. Picking it up, she considered it for a moment, trying to decide what to do with it now. Despite Matt knowing about the diamonds and the safe deposit box, she thought it best to hide it again, at least until she heard from her dad. Another pang of guilt hit her for hiding something else from him, especially when he had shown such confidence in who she was. As she slid the key between her mattress and box spring, she told herself she really wanted to be the person he said he saw in her. Maybe the diamonds and the proceeds from the sale of the house would be the way for her to leave her old life behind, and make a new start once and for all. Or maybe she should give the key to her dad and let him deal with the contents of the box. After all, it was his problem to begin with.

Stepping out of the shower, she heard Matt humming in the living room. For a minute, life sounded so mundane, so normal. Who was she kidding, thinking she could ever aspire to something like that? Even her parents couldn't sustain a relationship. What model did she have to learn from? Getting dressed, she fished the key back out from where she had hidden it, tucked it into the pocket of her jeans, and slipped on her shoes. Coming out, she saw Matt setting something down on the table on the balcony.

"Hey, I thought you said we were going out for lunch? I didn't think I had all that in my fridge," she laughed, in an attempt to hide the tumult of feelings she was now having seeing him being so domesticated.

"As soon as I heard the water start, I ran out and picked up a few things. Nothing fancy. But after all the chaos of last night, I thought this might be better. No rushing through a meal in a crowded restaurant. And we can have a leisurely conversation or none at all. Whatever you prefer." he said, gesturing towards the chair he had pulled out from the table. "Have a seat, and I'll be back out with the rest."

Sitting down, she saw iced tea in the glasses, a bowl of salad with the dressing on the side just as she preferred. When he walked back out with Po Boy sandwiches, she knew how much he had remembered from their short time together.

Looking over at him, she smiled. "You remembered. All of it."

"Yup. And I figured what better way to redeem the day than with some comfort food. I even have a bread pudding keeping warm for dessert," he said, placing a sandwich down in front of her.

As they ate, the conversation was mostly small talk about what had been going on around town, each of them avoiding the elephant in the room.

When Remy couldn't find anything else inconsequential

to talk about, she cleared her throat. "Um, Matt. I, well, I have something I need to ask you."

"Go ahead." he said, with a moment of hesitation betraying the self assured attitude he had been portraying.

"How do you think this is all going to end?"

"What do you mean? All the bad guys go to jail. The good guys walk off into the sunset," he joked.

"Yeah, I don't think that's really how it's all going to go in reality. I mean, there is still the fact I've got these stolen diamonds stashed away."

"There is that. Frank and I had some time to talk on the drive to find you. Despite my having the address to the warehouse, he had to make sure you hadn't come back here or gone to your mom's place first. I was worried, of course, that if we took too long, something bad might happen. But he assured me he knew Jordan well enough to know he wouldn't do anything until either you told him where the diamonds were or Frank showed up. He also gave me more details of his time in Las Vegas and of his involvement with the Costa family."

Letting out the breath she was holding, she sank down into her chair. "Oh. Wow. Okay. I guess that wasn't the answer I was expecting, but then again, I'm glad he shared that with you."

"It also doesn't change how I feel about you either. If that's what you're asking."

"I'm not sure what I'm asking. To be honest, I'm finding myself at a bit of a crossroads here. I'm sure Jordan is going to try to point fingers back at me and my dad, trying to cut himself a deal. I mean, I keep coming back to how do I explain the fact that I have these missing diamonds no one has seen in over twenty years?"

"Remy, listen to me. Jordan doesn't have a leg to stand on. I had a long talk with my friend, the district attorney, this morning while you were busy talking to the detectives. He's got enough else to send this idiot back to jail for the rest of his life. It seems he's been dragging a lot of others down with him since he's come to town. And not just you, Lily, and Theo. Add to that the fact he kidnapped you, tried to kill us both. He doesn't stand a chance. If he tries to say anything about your dad or the diamonds, it's just going to sound like he's making up stories to deflect from himself. As far as anyone is concerned, it's an old cold case and remains in the hands of the feds."

"Huh. Okay. That's not what I was expecting at all. So in other words, I'm now sitting on a small fortune and a house out in the middle of the desert which may or may not be contaminated by nuclear fallout?"

"Yup, pretty much." Matt laughed as he sat back in his chair. "Though I think maybe selling the house would be something you should consider. I don't think it would be good for you or your mom's health."

"In all seriousness though, what am I supposed to do with these diamonds then?"

"I think that's something you and your dad are going to need to work out. For now, my offer still stands. Keep them in the bank in Baton Rouge or move them to the safe at my house. It's your call."

Chapter Forty-Seven

Signing the papers to sell the house in Indian Springs was the last item on Remy's checklist of things to do. Having retrieved the diamonds and other papers from the recently opened safe deposit box, she closed that account as well. After she filed away most of the papers, along with the old letters that had started her on this crazy journey, she was now left with the diamonds. Which were currently stored in a safe at Matt's house. Since she hadn't been able to get in touch with her dad in the week following Jordan and his crew's arrest, she didn't know what else to do with them.

As promised, Matt set it up so only she knew the combination to the safe. She had shared it with her mother, just in case something were to happen to her. Even with Jordan still in police custody, she could only assume he still had friends on the outside who would do whatever he asked. It was a story she had heard from Frank too. Despite cutting off the head of a corrupt organization, there were always those left behind who would either follow orders or take it upon themselves to finish what their boss had started.

Matt had also provided security for both her and her mom. He was really going above and beyond what a normal friend would do. Okay, maybe he wasn't a normal friend any longer. She was well aware of how he felt about her, and she had pretty strong feelings for him too. But with all the uncertainty remaining in her life, she couldn't shake the feeling of waiting for the other shoe to drop. And she didn't want to get him mixed up in anything which may harm, or worse, kill him. Despite his assurances that he would be fine, she still felt like she needed to keep her distance from anyone she cared about.

She heard from the police that Lily had been released and wouldn't face any charges. At least not here in New Orleans. Theo was too tied up in everything taking place behind the scenes at the Carrington and would face charges of tax evasion and other financial crimes. While he wouldn't spend the rest of his life in Angola, he was facing a sentence at a minimum security prison. Marcus, having been involved with just about everything illegal that took place, was facing a long list of crimes and punishment unless he gave some sort of testimony against Jordan and the others. He would face at least the next twenty-five years of his life behind bars. Jordan, who had been exposed as Michael Leon, was back to facing the remainder of his life in jail. It seemed his release from prison resulted from an elaborate ruse on the part of one of his Las Vegas lawyers, who also helped him successfully change his name and evade capture until now. Between those old charges and everything he had orchestrated here, there was no chance of him ever setting foot outside the walls of a maximum security prison ever again.

Remy knew she would be called on to testify and was certain the defense would try to paint her as an unreliable witness. After all, she had been conning people long before she got involved with everyone at the Carrington. But the district attorney assured her he would do what he could to redeem her reputation. The rest would be up to her.

Which brought her to the decision she was now facing. In the next room was her entire family. Her mom, Neil, the entire Batiste clan with aunts, uncles, and cousins she hadn't seen or spoken to in years. Matt was even there too. The only person missing was Frank. No one had heard from him. The carriage house had been empty all week. The phone at the house in Indian Springs went unanswered. When asked, nobody had any idea of where he might be. If he excelled at one thing, it was disappearing. Remy worried that one of Jordan's crew had caught up to him, and maybe he had been lost in a remote swamp, but a feeling in her gut told her that wasn't true. No, she just had to trust he would return when the time was right.

Walking into the parlor of the house in the Garden District, the emotion of being surrounded by those who supported her unconditionally overwhelmed her. Everyone was smiling, laughing, and having a good time. The doors leading to the wrap-around porch were open wide, letting in the scents that always defined the city for her. Magnolias in bloom, the lingering scent of jasmine and fresh cut grass mingling as well. As she passed through the room, making her way towards the porch, she stopped to greet some of the guests, promising others she would return to them shortly. She needed one more moment, a chance to take in a deep breath and steady her nerves, before announcing her intentions.

Stepping out onto the porch, she turned the corner, looking out towards where the carriage house stood, when she heard footsteps behind her. Thinking it was Matt or her mom checking on her, she jumped when she heard Frank's voice say, "I'm so proud of you."

Turning to face her father, she looked at him, truly seeing him for the first time. "Dad, I…"

"No, let me first. Please. I owe you an apology, an explanation, and a lot of time I don't know how I'll ever make up for. It was never my intention to get you caught up in this mess."

"Dad, stop," Remy interrupted. "You didn't get me mixed up in this. I walked into it all on my own. Granted, I had no idea about the missing diamonds and that Jordan would turn out to be someone from your past life in Las Vegas. But every decision I made was mine alone. Right now, I want us to move forward. What that looks like, I don't exactly know. But I've already made some choices and decisions about what I hope life will look like as I go ahead. And I'd like you to be around and be a part of my life. If that's what you want."

"More than you will ever know," Frank said, smiling.

Remy smiled back at him, reached out for his hand, and replied, "Good. Then let's go inside and make some new memories. There are a lot of people in there who would like to see you too."

Walking back into the room, she caught her mother's eye watching them, Vanessa's face lighting up when she saw the two of them together. 'This is what it should be like,' Remy thought to herself.

Picking up a glass of champagne, Remy cleared her throat and raised her voice to get everyone's attention. "Thank you all for being here today. I want to propose a toast. To family, friends, love, forgiveness, and new beginnings. May today be the first day of a new life for all of us."

Acknowledgments

The 1980s were quite the decade. For those of us who experienced it firsthand, we definitely have some stories we could share. Probably best not to. Or if you do, make sure to change the names, places, etc., to protect the innocent and not so innocent.

Some people I knew from back then may or may not be the inspiration for some characters in this book. Though none of them were con artists or jewel thieves. At least not to my knowledge.

In no particular order, I want to shout out Jack, Sonia, Bea, Lori, Kelly, Billy, Dena… and I know if I keep going and try to list everyone, you'd be reading a city phone book and I'd be sure to forget someone. To all the bands I saw back in the day, the staff I worked with at various bars and restaurants. You all made those times fun and memorable.

To my writer friends and community, you all are incredible. The stories you write, the support you give, the memes we all share. Thank you all.

As always, thank you to you, my readers. For investing the time to read this book, that for so long only lived inside my head. If you've read all three books now, I'm sure you've recognized some characters and places along the way. Thank you for coming along on their journey of discovery. I do hope you enjoyed reading it as much as I did writing it. And if you would be so kind, drop a review wherever you purchased it, so others can find it too. If you are new to my books, be sure to check out the first two, Between The Beats and Gambling On A Dream. Available at your favorite book retailer.

About the Author

M.E. Cooper has been making up stories since childhood.

Her stories transport readers through time and across continents. Drawing inspiration from her extensive travels, she brings vivid settings and rich cultural textures to each novel. Her work spans decades, seamlessly blending historical authenticity with deeply personal character journeys. Whether set in mid-century Las Vegas or the jazz-infused streets of 1920s New Orleans, M.E. Cooper's novels delve into the inner lives of her characters, exploring identity, memory, redemption, and the human spirit. When she's not writing, she can be found wandering through hidden alleyways in unfamiliar cities, always chasing the next story.

Where To Find Me

Drop by and visit her author site at http://me-cooper.net

There you can buy books direct, sign up for her e-mail newsletter, read short stories and get all the news on upcoming books and more.

www.ingramcontent.com/pod-product-compliance
Lightning Source LLC
LaVergne TN
LVHW091714070526
838199LV00050B/2402